# *The* House on
# Blackberry Hill

# *The* House on Blackberry Hill

### DONNA ALWARD

St. Martin's Paperbacks

THE HOUSE ON BLACKBERRY HILL

Copyright © 2014 by by Donna Alward.

For information address St. Martin's Press, 175 Fifth Avenue, New York, NY 10010.

ISBN: 978-1-250-04516-4

Printed in the United States of America

St. Martin's Paperbacks edition / May 2014

St. Martin's Paperbacks are published by St. Martin's Press, 175 Fifth Avenue, New York, NY 10010.

10  9  8  7  6  5  4  3  2  1

*Jewell Cove—and* The House on Blackberry Hill—
*would never have come to be without some wonderful
people nudging me forward from the sidelines.*

*Many thanks to Margrete and the staff at Prescott House
for being lovely, for inviting me to visit so often, and for
making me fall in love with the library.*

*For Julie Cohen, who inspired me by going before, and
for being a wise writer and wonderful cheerleader.*

*To Barb Wallace and Fiona Harper, my bestest peeps
who were with me every agonizing, self-doubt-soaked
step of the way, and to Jenna Bayley-Burke, who has the
pleasure of saying "I told you so."*

*To Jenn Schober, for being my guru of Zen and positivity.*

*And especially to Darrell, for being so very patient for
so very long.*

# CHAPTER 1

Abby Foster didn't want to like the town of Jewell Cove. It was just her bad luck, then, that the place appeared annoyingly cheerful and quaint; a postcard-perfect sea town on the Maine coast dotted with colorful buildings nestled above the pristine inlet of Penobscot Bay. In response to her irritation, she cranked up the radio and rolled down the window. The breeze blew her hair back from her face, and she gave her head a toss as she continued into the town, tapping her fingers on the steering wheel along with the music. She had to be here. She didn't have to like it.

But she couldn't put the trip off any longer. Something had to be done with the house. The estate was paying the taxes on the damned place but her aunt Marian's lawyer kept pestering her about the condition of the property and what she was going to do about it. The constant correspondence made it impossible to pretend the house didn't exist. So she finally put in for a deferred leave from her job as an elementary school teacher and decided to deal with the family mess once and for all.

Family, heh. Abby gave a short laugh to herself. Up until a year ago, she hadn't realized she actually *had* any family. And if it weren't for Ian Martin, Marian's pesky lawyer, she'd happily ignore the connection altogether. It was easy to resent a family she'd never known—a family who could have reached out to her at any time over the last twenty-five years and hadn't. Ever since she'd received the so-called happy news that she was practically an heiress, she'd refused to use her inheritance from her great-aunt Marian for anything. She considered it somehow tainted, like guilt money sent too late to make amends for past transgressions. Not that she knew what those transgressions were other than years of silence. Abby's Gram had staunchly refused to talk about her childhood, and Marian certainly hadn't reached out. All that Abby knew was that Gram had been raised by her grandparents, who'd died right before she'd gotten pregnant with Abby's father. In many ways, it was like Gram's life hadn't existed before the Prescotts took her in.

Abby frowned and picked up the slip of paper with directions scrawled on it. Now that she was here they didn't exactly seem to make sense. She couldn't tell if she was facing south or east, the way the road twisted around. Why hadn't she bought a GPS or even printed the directions out from Google?

Seeing a gas station up ahead, Abby made a sharp turn and pulled into the broken paved lot. Situated at the edge of town, the old-fashioned gas pumps and faded sign definitely had a "vintage" feel to them—if you considered rundown to be vintage. She needed to fill up with gas anyway, and she could ask for directions to Foster Lane. She blew out a breath. For Pete's sake, there was even a road named after the family . . . a side of the family, she reminded herself bitterly, who'd apparently been as rich as Croesus and left the rest of them to be poor as church mice.

A grizzled man in a navy shirt came out of the shop,

wiping his hands on a rag as she pulled up to the gas pump. "Afternoon," he called out, and when he smiled, she saw he was missing a few teeth. Great.

"Hi, there," she answered back pleasantly, determined to be friendly. Gram had always said you could catch more flies with honey than vinegar, and the smoother this went the faster she'd be out of here, leaving nothing more than a vapor trail. "Fill it up, please."

"Sure thing," he replied. He went to the pump and opened her gas cap. "Nova Scotia plate. On vacation?"

"Um . . . sort of." She pasted on her biggest smile. "I was wondering, can you tell me how to get to Foster Lane? The directions I have aren't very clear."

The old man's head snapped up. "Foster Lane? Only thing up there is the house on Blackberry Hill."

A little zing of excitement that she didn't expect coursed through her. "The House on Blackberry Hill" sounded positively poetic, and much more evocative than plain old Foster House. "Yes, that's it. The Foster mansion, right?"

The pump clicked off and the man put the gas cap back on and came to her window. "No one's lived in the Foster place for years. Not since Marian got sick and had to go to the home." He pushed his cap back on his head. "Heard some distant family member inherited it, but we've never heard a whisper from him. It's a wicked mess up there after being left so long."

Unease settled on her again, erasing the tingle of anticipation she'd felt. How much of a mess was she walking into? Maybe this grand mansion was nothing but a derelict disaster after all. The joke would be on her, wouldn't it, if she had inherited a rundown money pit. "Could you give me directions to it anyway?"

He peered at her keenly. "Hey, *you* ain't that relative, are ya? The one she left everything to?"

Abigail held in a sigh and tried to relax her shoulders.

"That would be me. I'm Abigail Foster. Marian was my great-aunt." It felt strange just saying the words.

He tilted his head and squinted at her. "You Iris's blood, then? No one from Iris's side's set foot here since '45."

Her smile faltered at the reminder. She had to be here to do something about the house, but as she sat in her car, Abby realized that perfect strangers knew more about her family past than she did. It wasn't exactly a comfortable feeling.

"The directions, please?"

He stepped back at her sharpish tone. "Sure, sure, right enough. Follow this road through town, then go another few miles and you'll find Blackberry Hill Road off to your right, starting up the mountain. Foster Lane's about half-way up, to the left."

"Thank you so much." She took some cash out of her wallet to pay for the gas and started her engine. But before she could drive away, the man—Bill, his shirt said—leaned his elbows on the window.

"You're gonna want someone to have a look at the place, Ms. Foster. It's going to need repairs for sure. I can give you some names . . ."

Abby forced a smile. "Maybe some other time, once I've had a chance to look around. But thanks for the directions, Bill. You've been a real help."

He got the message and stood back, his lips pursed at the polite but clear indication that she wanted to be on her way. Abby lifted a hand in farewell as she pulled away from the pumps, knowing that she couldn't hide forever. Sooner or later—probably sooner, once Bill started the proverbial ball rolling—the people of Jewell Cove would know that the Foster mansion and the bags of money that went with it all belonged to her. And if Abby knew anything about small towns, they'd all want to know what she planned to do with it; they'd all have suggestions and want their piece of the pie, wouldn't they?

She rested her elbow along the open window as she slowed coming into town limits. She'd driven through fog until somewhere around the New Brunswick border, but now there was nothing but blue skies overhead as she crawled down Main Street.

Her first impression of the town had been that it reminded her of the seaside villages on Nova Scotia's South Shore—a cheerful kaleidoscope of colorful homes and businesses above a small but vibrant harbor. That was fairly accurate, she realized, as fishing and pleasure boats bobbed on the surface of the cove. She slowed to watch a restored schooner slide effortlessly into the harbor to dock. The water glittered in the summer sun and the tangy scent of the sea filled her nostrils.

She paused at the one and only traffic light. The town looked like something off a brochure—complete with patriotic flags along storefronts and pots of cheerful geraniums, white petunias, and trailing lobelia. She snorted. Nothing was ever as perfect as it seemed on the outside. Especially innocent-looking, quaint towns with well-tended flower beds and wreaths on the doors and little girls in pigtails walking down the sidewalk eating cones of ice cream. Abby couldn't help but think these little towns were painted so cheerfully as a form of defiance against the tragedy that always seemed to surround them. Fishermen lost at sea, that sort of thing. Resilience in the face of adversity. She'd seen enough of that growing up, moving from small town to small town.

Bill's directions had been to follow Main Street to the end and turn on to Blackberry Hill Road, and from there up the mountain to Foster Lane. The only problem was Main Street didn't end until it met the coastal highway again. She'd have to guess at how far a "couple of miles" was and hope she didn't miss it.

She lifted her chin and let out a breath of relief as the sign for Blackberry Hill appeared. If she had her way, the house was going on the market and the sooner the better. She'd be free of this mess and could go back to Halifax with a clear conscience. No more nagging lawyer invading her e-mail and voice mail every few weeks.

She flicked on her blinker and made the turn.

Tom Arseneault put down the phone and sat back in his chair, his brow wrinkled in what was, lately, a constant state of worry.

Everyone said the economy was rebounding. He'd yet to see the proof. That was the second job he'd bid on that had gone under. A man needed to make a living and people simply weren't spending. As it was, he was nearly finished with a basement reno project and the only thing on the immediate schedule was Jess Collins's back deck at her shop. Seeing as Jess was family, Tom didn't stand to make a lot of profit from that deal.

When the phone rang again he almost didn't answer it. It seemed the only time it rang lately was to give him bad news. But on the third ring he couldn't stand hearing the incessant chime of Beethoven's Fifth—his assistant Cassidy's attempt at office humor. The assistant who, at the moment, was taking yet another sick day. He picked up.

"Arseneault Contracting," he said.

"Tom. It's Meggie."

His aunt. He relaxed in his chair and crossed an ankle over his knee. "Hey, Aunt Meggie. What can I do for you?"

Meggie didn't waste time on pleasantries. "I have some news about Josh."

His stomach clenched. His cousin Josh was still living

in Hartford, but Tom wasn't sure how long that was going to last. Josh's wife, Erin, had been killed in action overseas on her last tour as an army medic. There wasn't a lot of reason for Josh to stay in Hartford anymore.

The last time Tom and Josh had been in the same room together, Tom had come out of it with a split lip and Josh had sported a few bruised ribs.

"Is Josh okay?" Despite the bad blood between them, his heart squeezed a little at the thought of anything happening to his cousin. They had too much history.

"He's coming home, Tom. To stay."

The air went out of Tom's lungs. He'd known this day would eventually come. Jewell Cove was Josh's home. His family was here. He'd never belonged in Hartford, going into practice with Erin's father. Josh, like the rest of the Collins family, was a small-town boy who needed to be close to the water. Not a city dweller.

And yet knowing Josh was coming home made the dull ache of Tom's grief threaten to swell up again and he swallowed thickly. Josh was a constant reminder of all the things Tom didn't like about himself, and despite how much he loved his cousin he couldn't stand to look at him.

Tom had been in love with his cousin's—with his best friend's—wife. And he still felt like shit about it.

"Tom?"

Aunt Meggie's voice came gently over the line, cutting him with its understanding. He took a breath and closed his eyes. "I'm still here. Sorry, Aunt Meggie."

"No need to apologize. I thought you should hear it from me. It's not like Josh is going to call with the happy news, is he?"

Tom chuckled at the wry tone in Meggie's voice. Despite being Josh's mother and naturally biased, she'd always been fair. Meggie and the girls had never despised Tom the way Josh did.

"When's he coming?"

"Soon. He's going to take over Phil Nye's practice. He's sharing the space with Dr. Yang until Phil retires in July."

It was a done deal, then. In a way Tom was relieved. Things had been unsettled too long. If Josh came home they could at least sort out how they meant to go on. Hopefully resolve it without fists. More likely it would be with stonewalling silence. Josh was really good at keeping his true feelings hidden.

"That's good, Meggie. You must be real happy. He doesn't belong in Hartford."

"I'm glad you agree, Tom. And I'm calling for another reason, too."

He should have known there would be a hitch.

"We're having a barbecue on the long weekend. I expect you to be there. Your parents and Bryce and Mary have already said they're coming. It's time to let bygones be bygones. For both of you. There's nothing left to fight over."

Tom ran his free hand over his face. No one seemed to understand that there was more to the situation than two cousins fighting over the same woman.

"I'm not sure that's a good idea. The last time . . ." He paused, unsure of how much to say. It wasn't the fight he couldn't let go of, it was the grief. She was his cousin's wife, yet Josh wasn't the only one mourning. He had been grieving too, only he had never been able to show it. He hadn't felt entitled to his grief.

"The last time you both were stupid. You're cousins. You have to start somewhere. And if either one of you starts any trouble, I'll kick your asses. You know I can do it."

Aunt Meggie had tanned his backside enough when he and Josh had been boys that he knew she meant it. The same way his mom would say the exact same thing to

Josh. The two sisters had raised their boys with tough but loving hands.

He respected her far too much to let her down now. "I'll be there. On my best behavior, promise."

"You could always bring your hot wings as a peace offering."

He laughed. "You're pushing it, Aunt Meggie."

"I know." The line went quiet for a minute, as if she were deciding on her next words. "He needs you, Tom. He needs all of us right now."

Tom's heart thumped. He wanted to ask, *What about me? What about what I need*? But he had no right. Erin hadn't been his wife. And through the bitterness was another tangle of emotion. He and Bryce and Josh—they'd all been like brothers. He'd missed his cousin, too. Yet he knew it would never be the same between them again.

"Hot wings it is."

"Good. I'll let you go now. Hope I didn't keep you from anything important."

"Another canceled job is all. Looks like Jess's decking will be getting my full attention."

"Oh! That reminds me. I was down at the grocery store this afternoon. Gloria told me that Bill at the service station said that the new owner's finally showed up at the Foster place. Marian's heir, and with Nova Scotia license plates."

Tom sat up straighter in his chair. The Foster mansion. For as long as he could remember, he'd wanted to get inside and get another good look at the old monstrosity. It was well over a hundred and fifty years old, and he'd bet any money it was gorgeous. They just didn't build them like that anymore. But it had been closed up since Marian had taken ill. Now that it was in new hands . . .

He recognized an opportunity when it hit him in the face. He enjoyed his work as a contractor, but the idea of restoring an old place like that . . . it wasn't work. It was a privilege.

"Thanks for letting me know," he said casually, trying to hide the excitement in his voice. "I'll have to pop in one of these days." One of these days, hell. He'd be up there within the hour.

"See you at the barbecue, Tom," Meggie answered. "Bye."

He hung up the phone and stared at it for a minute. Josh, home. Family gathering. Recipe for disaster. But the house up on Blackberry Hill?

He pushed his chair back and grabbed his keys. This was his dream project. First thing he had to do was meet the new owner and get inside. Word would spread fast and he didn't want another contractor swooping in and stealing the chance away from him. There was no one else in the area as qualified for the job as he was.

It was just the thing he needed to keep his mind occupied. Idle hands meant an idle mind.

And with Josh coming home, he needed to find a way to forget about Erin. For good. For all their sakes.

# CHAPTER 2

Whatever Abby had expected, it was not the massive Georgian-style home that greeted her at the end of the lane. White and imposing, it was both majestic and intimidating. With the unpruned shrubs around the yard and a tangle of ivy grown over several of the windows, Abby couldn't shake the idea that the house looked a bit, well, eerie.

Slamming her car door behind her, Abby started up the uneven pathway to the front porch. As she got closer she could see the chipped paint on the trim and rungs missing in the railing that ran between the two scarred pillars of the veranda.

It really had been neglected. For a moment she felt almost sorry for the old home. It was a shame that something that had once been so grand and beautiful had fallen into such a state.

The boards of the stairs creaked wearily beneath her feet as she climbed the three steps to the covered porch and took a key from her purse. Walking carefully, Abby silently prayed that the floor was termite-free and structurally sound before fitting the key into the lock and pushing the solid wood door open with the groan of long-unused hinges. Hesitantly Abby stepped inside, searching along the wall for a switch in the dim light. She found it and flipped it on. Thank goodness the arrangements to have the power switched on before her arrival had been a success.

The place was strangely silent and her shoes made hollow sounds on the hardwood floors as she went farther inside. She shivered. With the house shut up and all the curtains closed, it reminded her of a tomb.

The first thing she needed to do was get some natural light into the dreary rooms. The dim glow of the wall sconces barely penetrated the dust and stale air. She entered the room on her right—what appeared to be a formal dining room—and went directly to the window, spreading the heavy brocade curtains wide and tying them back with silky tassels. Sunlight spilled in through the gap and she went to the next window, and the next, until the room was flooded with warmth even through the dusty windows.

Turning around to finally get a good look at the room, Abby gasped. The antique dining table and chairs, which she'd only seen in outline, were now clearly visible and utterly magnificent, ornately carved, and even under the layer of dust she could see they had to be real mahogany. The table could easily seat a dozen. A set like this would have cost a fortune. Worth even more now if it was as old as she suspected.

Who on earth were the Fosters? And why had this all been kept a secret from her side of the family? At times her grandmother had barely made ends meet.

A fireplace with a white mantel graced one end of the room, but the mantel was empty except for a single, framed portrait. Abby went closer, her fingers gliding over the silver frame as she examined the face behind the glass. The woman was beautiful, perhaps in her twenties, with long dark hair and full lips. Her dress appeared to be chiffon, cut in a vee at her throat, a necklace of oval stones at her neck. Even in the black-and-white photograph her skin seemed to glow as she sat in a wing chair with a baby dressed in unending ruffles cradled in her arms.

Abby turned the frame over and slid the old photo out, careful to keep her fingers on the edge of the paper. There was nothing written on the back, no indication of who the woman was or when it was taken. Disappointed, she put the picture back inside and placed it precisely in its spot on the mantel. Was this Marian? Perhaps Marian's mother, Edith? Abby frowned, feeling a brief surge of anger at being left in the dark about her own family. She and her grandmother had been very, very close. How could Gram have failed to mention something as big as a family mansion to her only granddaughter?

Shaking off her melancholy, Abby turned her attention to the rest of the room. A gilt-edged mirror hung above the fireplace and it reflected an unlit chandelier over the table. For a brief moment she imagined the clinking sounds of silver on china and crystal. She'd figured out that the Fosters had been well off when she'd seen the value of the estate. But this . . . this was living on a grand scale.

Eager to explore now, she made her way back to the wide hall. There was another chandelier here, prettier than the last. It would be gorgeous all lit up, but on closer examination she saw that the lights within were oil and that it hadn't been wired for electricity. It seemed a shame to waste its beauty simply because it was stuck in the past.

Across the wide hall she found what could only be called a drawing room. She opened the curtains in this room too, feeling an irrepressible need to let light into all the dark corners. There seemed to be an odd feeling about the house. Something heavy and dark, like a terrible secret.

It was just her overactive imagination, she chided herself. She turned her attention to the fireplace, identical to the one in the dining room, idly wondering if each room had one and if they still worked. It probably wouldn't be safe to light a fire anyway. Birds or bats or something likely lived in the chimneys, she thought, shivering. She hated bats.

Abby returned her attention to the space around her. It was too formal for a parlor or mere sitting room, and the warm yellow walls were in dire need of a fresh coat of paint. The furniture was old and frayed around the edges but she could tell it had been opulent in its day. An upright piano was pushed against one wall and she went over and lifted the cover, her fingers pushing a few keys as she played an arpeggio. A tinny, twangy sound erupted from the instrument, in need of a good tuning. She shut the cover again with a shudder as the dissonant notes echoed uncomfortably through the air.

According to the records, Marian had put in central heating in the sixties, and the house had been completely rewired only twenty years ago. As Abby's gaze took in the scarred floors and dingy rugs, not to mention the faded and chipped paint, she was at least thankful for that. Maybe the mansion had been grand in its day, but right now it looked as if it had been forgotten. Discarded. It would take a lot of work and a lot of Marian's money, she thought with dismay, to get it into marketable shape. It was worse than she'd feared. It didn't just need tidying up. It needed fixing.

Abby went back to the main hall. Past a small powder room was a kitchen with modern appliances—modern compared to the rest of the house, at least. There was a four-burner stove and a refrigerator that sat quietly. The fridge and stove were the only concessions to modernity. There was no microwave, no dishwasher. The tile floor was faded and the walls were painted a very dated—and dowdy—avocado green.

Uck. Aunt Marian had apparently been old-school.

Next to the kitchen was a door leading to what Abby could only surmise was the basement. Abby put her hand on the latch but then drew it back as a cold feeling skittered down her spine. She'd leave exploring for another time. She had visions of the basement in Gram's old house—stone walls, damp and cold, and the dreaded spiders. She hated them with a passion, even more than she hated bats. When she was a child, going down in the basement for a simple jar of jelly had felt like a penance.

The uneasy feeling she'd had touching the door was even stronger as she crossed the hall, pausing to look up the grand staircase. She shivered, cold again, as her gaze settled on the upper landing. Abby knew she was being ridiculous, but something about the staircase unnerved her and made the little hairs on the back of her neck rise with apprehension. She shook her head and tried to laugh, the sound mocking in the silence. This was foolish. There was nothing there. Maybe the queer sensation was simply because the house was so huge and, well, quiet. Everything echoed, even the sound of her breathing. It wasn't the sort of house meant for one person. It was meant for parties and socializing, with men in dashing suits and women in long dresses. For the popping of champagne bottles and maids in white aprons serving canapés off silver platters.

Shaking off the heavy feeling, she entered the room beside the stairs, her uneasiness evaporating as her mouth dropped open in wonderment and delight.

Tattered or not, the old room was gorgeous. There were solid mahogany cases on each wall crammed full of old books, their spines faded and dusty. Their dark width was broken only by the dirt-smudged windows looking out over the vast gardens and peeking into what had to be an added-on sun porch at the back of the house. The drapes were faded and dirty but had once been a marvelous wine-and-tan-striped brocade.

She stepped into the center of the room, completely enchanted. In addition to the bookcases there was a gorgeous rolltop desk and a sewing table next to a pair of stuffed armchairs. And yes, another fireplace, backing on the same wall as the one in the drawing room. The walls that were visible were goldeny yellow, like burnt sugar. The color set off wide white trim and wainscot. The dark cherry hardwood floor was utterly stunning—or had been. It was quite scarred after years of use. But in its heyday . . .

It was the first room she'd visited that felt anything like a home. She could imagine herself curled up in one of those chairs with a Jane Austen novel and a pot of tea, a fire blazing in the fireplace . . .

She turned herself around in a circle, gave a huge, contented sigh, and choked on a puff of dust stirred up by her movement.

The romanticism of the moment was shattered by the harsh sound of her coughing as she doubled over, effectively raising an even bigger cloud. She was a fool to let herself be seduced, even for a moment.

The coughing fit eased and she gasped for air, holding herself very, very still to keep from disturbing more dust. She wasn't sure how long this place had been locked up, but Marian's lawyer had mentioned something about a few years. Considering the grime and neglect she'd witnessed just on the first floor, she'd guess it was closer to "several" rather than "a few."

But despite the dirt and grime, the library was glorious. She could almost smell the redolent tang of cigar smoke, the bite of brandy mingled with the scent of leather and paper and ink. She closed her eyes, imagining for a moment what it must have been like during the glory days. Another time and place.

She opened her eyes, watched a mouse scurry into the corner and raised an eyebrow. Rodents and God knew what else were not romantic. The mouse disappeared behind a wing chair and she sighed. In reality she knew that this was just a room. What she needed to do was stop daydreaming and find the name of the nearest pest control company. So much for being in and out of Jewell Cove within a few days. Her first order of business was going to be looking into contractors. And to do that she was going to need either the yellow pages or an Internet connection—neither of which could be found at her current location.

A crash followed by the sound of muffled yet spectacular swearing from the front of the house propelled Abby out of her thoughts and sent her rushing to the front door with her heart pounding. Judging by the frustrated, not pained, language—which she had to admit was really quite inventive—coming from the porch she figured whatever was happening outside wasn't an emergency, and at a particularly creative curse couldn't help but choke back a giggle. Still chuckling, she threw open the door.

The man on her veranda was big and he was burly, with blazing black eyes and matching hair a touch too long as it curled around his collar. He looked like a lumberjack, if that lumberjack happened to be on the cover of *Sexy Outdoorsman* magazine. His jeans were faded but clean, and he wore a white button-down shirt rolled up over tanned and muscled forearms. His very civilized attire seemed slightly out of place against his rugged good looks. Abby wasn't much into facial hair, but a day's growth of stubble framed his jaw and the total package was so completely masculine and sexy that something hot and forbidden wound its way through her abdomen. She scrambled to put together a coherent thought but couldn't seem to make the connection between her brain and her tongue.

"Are you Miss Foster?"

She nodded her head quickly in response to his sharp demand. And realized one of his feet had gone through the floorboards of the veranda and now the splintered fragments settled around his boot like jagged teeth.

"You broke my veranda." *Brilliant, Abby,* she chastised herself. She crossed her arms in an old habit and bit down on her lip. *The most gorgeous example of masculinity you've ever seen shows up on your doorstep and that's what you come up with? You broke my veranda?*

"Me? The damned thing is rotten through. You're lucky I didn't break my neck."

Abby wasn't sure how to respond. A part of her felt the need to be polite and apologize—after all, he was standing ankle-deep in splintered wood. At the same time, he was a stranger, uninvited, and he'd already damaged the property she'd only been in possession of for a scant hour. She was tired and his abrasive tone seemed to ride on her last nerve.

"I beg your pardon, but it appears *you're* trespassing. I don't know you and I certainly didn't invite you here, Mr. . . ."

"Arseneault," he answered. He gave his boot a good yank and pulled it from the hole. He planted both feet on the floor after testing the strength of the boards and then looked up at her with a grin that melted the edges off her annoyance. "Tom Arseneault. And from the looks of this place, you're going to be seeing a lot of me."

Tom looked down into Miss Foster's astonished face as he issued his declaration. She was a pretty little thing, if you took away the coating of dirt that seemed to cover her from head to toe. Her mouth was a little too wide for the daintiness of her nose, and her hair was mousy brown, coated with dust, and fell limply to her shoulders. But she had good eyes—a nice clear blue, kind of like Penobscot Bay on a clear summer's day. She wore faded, ripped jeans that seemed perfectly shaped to her figure and a plain cotton T-shirt that emphasized a nice pair of breasts. She was the kind of woman he probably would have given a glance to on the street—but not a second look. Tom's first impression was of a sweet rather than a second-look kind of woman.

Until he saw her feet. She wore silly little flip-flops—the strappy bit that ran across the top of her foot crusted with sparkly stuff—and her toenails were painted hot pink. Ultrafeminine and sexy as hell.

Shaking off his sudden foot fetish, Tom tried to gather his thoughts. So the dusty little mouse had pretty feet. So what? She certainly didn't embody what he imagined Marian's heir to look like. He'd expected a man, actually, and older than the snippet of a girl before him. More regal, perhaps, in keeping with the family name and fortune. He frowned, not liking the feeling of being off balance. Miss Foster looked like she'd fit in at his cousin Jess's craft shop stringing beads on hemp bracelets rather than having a head for business.

First thing he had to do was make her see how much she needed him. And he wouldn't do that by glowering at her. It wasn't her fault the floor was rotted through, and it wasn't her fault she had sexy feet. He took a breath, slapped his best trust-me smile back on, and prepared to make nice. But her uptight little voice cut him off before he could begin to argue his case.

"I have never heard of you, Mr. Arseneault," she replied, as if oblivious to his smile. The pert nose lifted a little higher into the air. "But you can take your big boots and your bigger attitude and leave the way you came."

Had he really just thought she wasn't regal? The proclamation was delivered in such a dismissive tone that he laughed. He couldn't help it. She was going toe-to-toe with him like she was the Queen of England. Maybe there was a good dose of Foster blood in her after all. She looked so serious it was very nearly adorable.

"Honey," he said smoothly, "we started off on the wrong foot." He chuckled, looking down at his foot recently freed from the porch. "Why don't we just talk and—"

Her cheeks colored. "I'm not your honey, my name is Abigail. I asked you to leave, and I am not afraid to call the police."

"You don't want to do that," he replied, his smile sliding away. All he needed was for Bryce to answer the phone. There'd be no end to the teasing. God knew Bryce didn't need any more ammunition. It was already too easy for Jewell Cove's chief of police to get beneath Tom's skin.

"Oh?" Her gaze brightened as if she sensed a victory in her grasp. "And why not?"

"Trust me, I'm doing you a favor. You'll look stupid."

She pursed her lips. "Do I seem like the kind of woman who worries about looking stupid?"

She raised an imperious eyebrow. Impressive, he thought, with a glimmer of respect. Abigail Foster had a glint of challenge in her blue gaze that intrigued him. He was willing to call her bluff just to see how it would all work out. "Go ahead," he prompted. "Ask for Bryce Arseneault. That'd be my brother, by the way."

She looked like she wanted to stomp her foot and he marveled at how cute she appeared just then. Immensely satisfied, he hooked his thumbs in his jeans pockets. The sooner this mess of an introduction got over with, the sooner they could get down to business.

A sound of frustration escaped her lips. She went inside and surprised him by slamming the door in his face. He checked his watch. One minute. He'd give her one minute before knocking. He was pretty sure she'd come back out. And when she did, he'd make a better case for himself. He'd gone about it the wrong way, trying charm and humor. It didn't usually fail him.

Twenty seconds. Ten.

The door opened, precluding the need for him to knock and make nice. She stood in the gap, clicking her cell phone off. "Right. Bryce says hello and that Mary expects you for dinner at five-thirty."

He could rub it in her face but decided not to. The blush tainting her cheeks right now was satisfaction enough. He looked around the sagging veranda, caught sight of the crumbling chimney, the cracked paint around the windows. "You're lucky it was me who put their foot through just now. Someone else might have been right angry. Maybe would have sued. It's a litigious world we live in."

Her lips puckered like a drawstring bag. "I feel *so* fortunate," she replied, and the sarcasm washed over him. He liked it. It seemed to level the playing field somehow. She might be tiny, but he guessed that she'd make a worthy opponent if given the opportunity.

Despite her quirky toes and ripped jeans, he just bet Abigail Foster liked to dot all her i's and cross all her t's, the complete opposite of his more laid-back approach to business. And looking at those pursed lips and the challenging glint in her eyes, he felt a shiver of anticipation that had nothing to do with the house and everything to do with the client.

Abigail might be the Type A organizer, but things just weren't done that way in Jewell Cove. They were normally settled over a pint at the Rusty Fern followed by a hand-shake. If she stayed, she'd soon learn how things were done. And how they weren't.

Besides, Jewell Cove could use some new blood to stir things up. It had been awfully dull lately. The gossip mill needed a new topic of conversation. Why not Abigail Foster and the Foster mansion? It was a damned sight better than ruminating over Josh's return and reviving long memories.

She tucked the phone into her back pocket. "Remind me who you are again?"

He smiled, determined to get it right this time. "The best contractor on the mid-coast. And the answer to all your troubles."

# CHAPTER 3

Abby couldn't stop the peal of laughter that bubbled up from her chest and out her mouth. The situation was so surreal. She looked at Tom Arseneault's expression—puzzled and then annoyed—and laughed some more. It felt good. Tom Arseneault had pushed her buttons with his scowl and God's-gift attitude and it was liberating to push right back.

This really took the cake. Hadn't she just been thinking she needed to find a contractor and poof! Here he was. She hadn't rubbed a genie's lamp but he'd appeared just like Aladdin, and didn't he look like just the kind of man who could make her every wish come true?

It was like God had suddenly plopped everything in her lap, including a gorgeous man, and then sat back, rubbing his hands, to watch the show as she decided what to do with it all. God, she decided, had a warped sense of humor. But she was willing to play along. To a point.

"I don't need a handyman for this place," she joked, catching her breath. "I need a demolition crew!"

He looked so horrified at the idea that she giggled all over again.

"That's not remotely funny," he said shortly. He took a step forward and she felt a little thrill as she looked up into his rugged face. He was over six feet tall and from the looks of his arms, he was solid muscle. She swallowed. Lumberjack man was very . . . virile. She caught her breath as he towered over her. Funny how she didn't feel as threatened as she should by his size and proximity.

"The condition of this place *is* a travesty," he admitted. "But it's also town history and needs to be preserved, not knocked down. What are you planning to do with it, then? Don't tell me you're seriously going to tear it down. Because I'll have something to say about that."

He was dead serious and looked genuinely upset. It was just a house, albeit a magnificent one. She thought back for a minute to the walls of books in the library. Well, maybe not *just* a house, but why on earth would Tom Arseneault take it so personally?

"What's it to you? Last I checked it was my name on the deed. And I don't recall my lawyer mentioning any Arseneault having a claim to the property."

"Are you serious? Have you been inside yet?" His eyebrows lifted so that they nearly touched the black curl of hair that dropped over his forehead. "In its heyday, this house was the center gem of this town. The old gossips still talk about the Roaring Twenties parties that were held here before they were ever born. Jed Foster imported most of the furniture from his journeys around the globe."

The sheer volume of antiques would fetch a pretty penny at an estate auction, wouldn't they? But she didn't think it wise to say that out loud right now. This Mr. Arseneault seemed to take the house quite to heart.

"I haven't had time to examine everything properly."

He took another step forward, encroaching on her space. "There are even rumors about it being haunted since the war, at least if the old-timers down at Breezes Café are to be believed. The mansion is a town icon."

She took a step back, alarmed by his assertion of it being haunted, especially after her strange sensations at the cellar door and stairs. "If it's such a gem, then why did it ever fall into such disrepair?"

He shrugged. "Marian Foster turned it into a home for unwed mothers, and then she lived in it alone for years. Rumor has it she spent a fortune maintaining it before closing it up when she could no longer care for herself."

"How long ago?"

"Ten years, easy. It's stayed vacant since then as Marian insisted that it remain untouched. Some say she was a little . . ." He paused, searching for the right word. "Dementia, probably," he said, quieter now. "Not crazy. Just not in the same reality, you know?"

"And now she's left it to me."

"Seems that way." The tone of his voice made it sound like the fact only confirmed her aunt's precarious state of mind.

She met his gaze honestly. "Believe me, I'm just as confused as you are. I never met the woman. In fact, my grandmother Iris, Marian's sister, never even mentioned having a sister. The Fosters never saw fit to give her a red cent when she was alive, so leaving it to me now is confusing to say the least. I didn't even know Gram came from money. God knows we could have used a bit of it from time to time."

"You could be the one to come in and restore the house. Bring her back to her former glory. I'm pretty sure her bones are sound. She just needs sprucing up . . ."

"With your help, of course." She injected a fair dose of sarcasm into the words. It didn't escape her notice that he referred to the house as "her." Good grief.

"Come here," he commanded. Tom reached out and

gripped her wrist, tugging her through the still open door and into the foyer.

She shook his hand off. "What are you doing?" She put her fingers on the skin he'd touched. His hands were so big his fingers had dwarfed her tiny wrist. What was worse, she'd found it exciting, being tugged along in his wake. She hadn't exactly felt threatened. She'd felt . . . exhilarated. That was more surprising than anything else that had happened today, and that was saying a lot.

Their gazes clashed and she felt the strange swirling again. There was something in the dark depths of his eyes, some sort of awareness that made her breath catch in her throat. Finally he stepped forward, picking up her hand in a gentle way that sent her heart knocking against her ribs. "Trust me, okay?"

She watched, fascinated, as Tom's lips formed a sexy half-smile that did nothing to remove the heat in his gaze. With her hand cradled in his, Abby had the sensation of being enveloped—completely and utterly. It wasn't just his size, but the sense of the muscled physique beneath the cotton shirt and his control over it. All that manual labor had honed him into a strong specimen of manhood, but there was something honest about him as well. And standing there in the foyer of her newly inherited home, Abby suddenly realized that she did trust him . . . to a point. She may not know Tom Arseneault but she knew he wouldn't harm her.

"We really did get off on the wrong foot," he continued, as the moment stretched out.

"Pun intended?" she asked, softening when his smile grew. Their gazes met for a few seconds more while things between them seemed to settle. "All right," she granted softly, removing her hand from his and looking around the room. "Now, if you'd care to explain what you mean without hauling me from pillar to post, I'll listen."

"I haven't heard that particular tone since I was in fifth grade and was caught running through the school library by Miss Haines."

"Apparently the lesson bore repeating. What did you want to show me?"

Something—amusement, respect, perhaps a combination of the two—gleamed in his eyes. "All right. For starters, look at this." He reached behind her and ran his fingers over the dark wood of a grandfather clock. "This clock is over a hundred and fifty years old."

Abby dutifully looked and tried to ignore the way his long, capable fingers caressed the dusty wood. Instead she focused on the clock face. She wondered what had been happening at the house at the time that the hands had stopped moving. They sat precisely at 3:26. "It doesn't work."

"Maybe it can be fixed. Even if it never keeps time again, the actual construction is in fantastic shape." He gestured to the right, to the dining room. "And this room. It's full of antiques. Look at the mantels on the fireplaces— all the wood trim is original to the house. The dining table and chairs were shipped from South America to Captain Foster himself, made from mahogany out of the Amazon."

"How do you know that?"

"Everyone knows that." He regarded her curiously. "You really don't know anything about the house, do you?"

Tom did, apparently. Her annoyance at her own ignorance warred with a very real curiosity to listen to what he knew.

"Did you think I was lying?"

"Well, no, but . . ."

"Scout's honor." She lifted two fingers. "I never knew anything about this side of the family. Nothing about the house, nothing about the money, nothing about Marian. My grandmother never spoke of it."

Silence filled the hall. "Seriously?"

"Seriously. It appears the two sides of the family were completely estranged."

"Why?"

She shrugged. "I wish I knew. I'd like to find out, though. It makes no sense that there's a whole history I never knew about. A whole family." And it hurt that the person she'd trusted most hadn't trusted her in return.

He paused. "I don't know what to tell you. There might be a few old-timers left who could help, if you really want to know. No guarantees, but it's worth a shot."

She looked up at him. "Do you think?"

He shrugged. "It's possible. But for now, I can give you a basic history of the house if you'd like."

"That would be nice."

He smiled. "Right. Well, let's go back to the beginning. Captain Jedediah Foster built this house in the late nineteenth century. His father, George, was one of the founders of Jewell Cove, along with Edward Jewell and Charles Arseneault. The Fosters made their fortune on the seas. Jed built himself a mansion for his growing family. Both his sons were killed in World War One, so his grandson, Elijah, took it over when he married Edith Prescott. Marian and Iris were their daughters."

He walked farther into the foyer, gesturing above them. "This chandelier was brought over from France by Elijah Foster before the start of World War Two. While Jed had been a captain, the family fortune was really built on shipping, until Elijah sold the company in the late fifties. He died within two years of selling the business, leaving everything to Marian."

And nothing to Iris. Abby didn't like Elijah already.

"Is the chandelier electric?" she asked, changing the subject.

"No, that'd be whale oil. It's much older," he explained.

"You can actually raise and lower it so it is closer to the table for dinner lighting."

"Dinner? In the hall?"

"Haven't you noticed how wide it is?" He turned back to the hall and they both looked up at the light hanging from the ceiling. "The Fosters were rumored to be great hosts. The dining room seats twelve. Out here you could easily seat fifty. Then when dinner is over, up go the lights, out go the tables, and you have a space large enough for dancing."

"How do you know all this stuff? Were you here a lot?"

He shook his head. "Not since I was a little kid, and Marian hosted some picnic or something. But the house on Blackberry Hill is the stuff of legend in this town. You'll find everyone knows something about it. The construction is in my wheelhouse, so to speak."

It was the second time that day someone had called it that. It gave Abby a little thrill and a jolt of apprehension. She was the outsider here. And while she was the owner of this . . . mausoleum, she was fully aware that not "everyone," as Tom put it, might appreciate a stranger coming in and taking over. She was just a name on the deed. She understood that in some way, the house belonged to the town, too. Certainly it was part of the town identity and history.

"So, what you're saying is, don't be surprised if someone decides to barge in, boss me around, and then proceed to share his rather forceful opinion about what I can and cannot do with my property?" Abby asked with a pointed stare.

Tom chuckled, understanding her completely. "Exactly. If that happens, you should also definitely listen to him. He sounds like he knows what he's talking about. Now, have you explored yet?"

She angled him a wry look. "I just got here. There

hasn't been time to see anything besides dirt." She indicated her now dusty outfit to prove her point.

Tom gave her clothing a slow perusal and she felt her cheeks heat beneath his scrutiny. Not only was the house a mess, but Abby knew that after her earlier exploration, she was as well.

Lifting her chin, she treated him to the same overt examination—looked at his boots, up the long length of his faded jeans, past every button on his cotton shirt, and into his darkly handsome face. She nearly shivered with pleasure. If she looked in the dictionary for "rugged, sexy, and capable," it would have a picture of Tom Arseneault. What a dumb idea it had been to give him the slow once-over. All it did was highlight his yumminess while she felt drab and dowdy in comparison.

He put his hands on his hips, the movement emphasizing the impossible breadth of his chest and shoulders, and grinned, displaying a mouth full of perfectly white teeth. Abby was suddenly unsure if she was standing in front of the woodsman or the big bad wolf. That grin was *lethal*. It was the charming grin of a man used to getting his own way. She might not be a pushover, but she discovered she wasn't quite as immune to that smile as she should be.

Abby sighed. "I take it Jewell Cove is like any other small town? No privacy whatsoever?"

His dark gaze settled on hers. "None whatsoever," he echoed. "Listen, Miss Foster . . . you know as well as I do that you can't sell it the way it is."

"Who said anything about selling?" she challenged.

"You're going to stay here? Live in it? By yourself?"

He sounded so surprised he wanted to say yes just to enjoy his reaction. But she couldn't, not when she wasn't planning on staying a moment longer than was necessary. She knew he wanted the job of fixing this place up and he wanted her to hire him on the spot. Well, despite her earlier whimsical moment in the library, her good sense hadn't totally abandoned her.

"I didn't say that, either. I realize it needs work, whether I stay or I put it on the market. But I've been here . . ." She made a show of checking her watch. "Less than two hours. I'd be foolish to make any decisions in such a short amount of time. Rest assured, if I require your services I'll look you up." She was rather proud of the tone that came from her mouth. She might look disorganized but she wasn't incompetent.

Tom raised his eyebrows. "Wow. You've got the cool-dismissal bit down cold."

She took it as a fine compliment and sighed dramatically. "And yet here you still are."

His lips twitched at her obvious set-down. "You're somethin', Miss Foster."

She felt slightly guilty at her sharp tone—after all, he'd been quite friendly once he'd begun showing her the inside of the house, and he'd given her information about her relatives. Still, she couldn't let a cheeky smile and a pair of bedroom eyes distract her. "I assure you, Mr. Arseneault, when I want help, I will ask for it."

"No need to be so prickly," he commented, backing away and putting his hands in his pockets. He withdrew a business card and held it out, waited until she took it before he spoke again. "Give it some thought. No matter what you do with this house, it needs work. I promise you I'm the best contractor for the job."

"And why is that, exactly?"

"Because I'll take the time and care to preserve the very best of it, and keep as much of the original workmanship as I can. Not everyone would, you know. And because there's no one on the mid-coast with a better hand for finish work. Ask around."

Tom gave her one more long look before he nodded.

"Now I'll show myself out. I can see I've taken up too much of your time."

She heard his boots clomp back down the hall and the predictable squeak and groan as the door opened. Then another crack and a loud curse. Abby stifled a laugh in the silence that followed.

Then he was gone and she was left alone once more with the dirt and the mice, and the house seemed strangely quiet again.

Waiting. She just wished she knew for what.

# CHAPTER 4

Tom endured dinner as best he could. His older brother, Bryce, had married four years earlier and he and Mary had an adorable baby girl who was just beginning to crawl. Their whole life was a contrast to Tom's. Simply put, it was full of love and family, while Tom's life centered around his cottage out past Fiddler's Rock and his workshop. Dinners with Bryce and his perfect family always highlighted what Tom didn't have.

Nights like tonight, watching his brother gaze into his wife's eyes with such affection, or seeing Mary touch baby Alice with unconscious, ever-present love, made him long for things he'd given up hope of ever having for himself.

"Best blueberry buckle in town," he said, leaning back in his chair and rubbing his full belly, trying to chase away the maudlin thoughts. "Thanks for dinner, Mary."

"Figured you needed something more than a grilled burger now and then." She put her hand on his shoulder and squeezed while Bryce got up to get mugs for coffee.

Mary was a natural mother, and whether she realized it or not, she tried to mother him, too. He let her because she had made his miserable brother happy and because she was the best damned cook this side of Portland. She knew him well enough to know that his dietary staple was burgers on the barbecue, chicken wings, and bacon and eggs. Occasionally he mixed it up with a box of mac and cheese or a sandwich. But he was no cook, and most of his meals came from the café in town, right here at Bryce and Mary's table, or Sunday dinners with his parents.

Bryce came back to the table and put the coffee in front of Tom. "So you met the new Foster woman. What'd you do to piss her off? She sounded mad as a wet hen when she called the office today."

Tom's pulse gave a little thump as he remembered the way her blue eyes had widened when she'd opened the door. "She doesn't appreciate the workmanship in that house." He scowled into his coffee cup, looking up when Bryce laughed. "What?"

"You're going to tell me your foul mood has to do with workmanship?"

He'd gone to the house on Blackberry Hill with one goal in mind and he'd left without achieving it. At times he'd nearly had the upper hand. But she'd been stubborn. Sassier than he expected. "What else would it be?" he asked innocently.

Bryce blew on his coffee as he raised a skeptical eyebrow. "Nothing. But Tom, that house is a mess and you know it."

"Doesn't mean it's not worth fixing."

"I'm guessing you told her that in no uncertain terms."

"Hell, yes, I did. Can you think of anyone who would do a better job than me?"

Mary was at the sink with her back to them but Tom heard the light snort and saw the movement of her shoulders. Bryce was grinning like a fool. Tom knew how cocky his words sounded just as he knew his brother was having fun winding him up. So predictable . . .

"Of course you'd do a great job," Bryce replied. "And it would keep your mind off . . . other things."

Tom didn't miss the not-so-subtle reference and he gritted his teeth. "You know, it would be much easier to move on if people quit bringing Erin up all the time. I'm *fine*."

"Right."

Okay, so he wasn't totally fine. He was still carrying around a fair bit of guilt about the way things had gone down. It had been hell falling in love with Erin, watching her marry someone else, and then losing her on some distant battlefield. That was perhaps the hardest part— knowing she'd been alone and so far away. At least when Erin had been alive he'd told himself he was satisfied with the knowledge that she was happy—or so he thought, until just before her last deployment.

It was just his bad luck that Tom had spent the evening in the Rusty Fern when Josh and Erin had announced their engagement and he'd been a little too vocal expressing how she was marrying the wrong man. Nobody ever forgot anything in a small town. Everyone knew by the next day at noon how he'd professed his undying love over one too many pints of beer. It had nearly been a relief when Josh had been deployed as an army doctor, and then when he'd gotten out of the forces he and Erin had stayed in Hartford, close to Erin's family. Jewell Cove was small and seemed even smaller when you couldn't look a man in the eye. Tom had got to her first, but Josh was the one who'd put a ring on her finger. That was all that counted.

Tom looked into Bryce's face. He knew his brother cared, but moving on was something he had to do on his own time and in his own way. "I promise you, I'm fine."

Mary's soft gaze tore into him. "Honey, when did you last go on a date?"

He looked back at her evenly. "Small town. Slim pickings. Especially since my brother got the only woman worth having in the county."

A pretty flush glowed on her cheeks. "Go on with you."

"So what about this Foster woman?" Bryce sipped his coffee and leaned back in his chair. "Maybe you should ask her out. I heard she's the right age and has all her teeth and everything." He grinned wickedly.

"Abigail? Huh. She's a mouse with a sharp tongue. Kind of plain, actually." A hint of a smile cracked his lips. He'd gotten a peek at a fine bottom tucked into those snug, ripped jeans, not to mention her blinged-up feet.

"Plain, huh?" Mary questioned, a note of disappointment in her voice.

Abigail Foster was far from plain no matter what he said, but he wasn't about to encourage Mary or Bryce. "Not my type. Look, all I want from her is the chance to work on that house. There's not another to match it on the coast. Jed Foster built it with the best and built it to last. If she's planning on selling it, she'll get a better price if it's restored properly first."

Bryce shrugged. "If you're so hot for the house, why don't you buy it yourself? You could get it for a lower price now and either keep it or turn it over for a nice profit. Then her lack of appreciation wouldn't matter and you could do it how you wanted." He made air quotes around the words "lack of appreciation."

The idea was a good one, and Tom had some money put by he could use as a down payment and for renovation materials. He tried to imagine flipping it for a profit after putting all the work into it. How could he invest all the time and energy just to hand it to someone else? But then he tried to imagine living there. What would he ever do with a house that big? Wander around in it and become a recluse. He was close to becoming a hermit now and he knew it. Besides, maybe he could scramble to put together a down payment, but the mortgage and taxes would bankrupt him. Flipping it was his only option.

Still, the idea was tempting. And if he bought it, at least it would be restored the way it should be. Who knew what atrocities some outsider might inflict upon it? Maybe Miss Foster would cover those gorgeous floors with carpet and rip out the fireplaces, cover everything with floral chintz or something. Unthinkable.

"I'll think about it. It would be a lot more challenging than my current job."

"Which is?"

"A new deck and pergola outside Jess's store. She has some new idea of displaying windsocks or something outside this summer." Their cousin Jessica Collins owned Treasures up on Lilac Lane. Josh had always said she got the creative genes in the family, but none of them had guessed at how well she could apply her business sense to that creativity. In the summer, at the height of tourist traffic, Treasures would be jam-packed with people. Generally Tom tried to avoid it, especially in the evenings when Jess held classes above the store. Too many women. Too much chatter. Cluck-cluck.

"A big project might be just what you need," Mary said, putting a casserole dish in a low cupboard. Her smile flickered for a second as she gripped the edge of the counter for support.

"Okay?" Bryce asked. Tom had gone cold seeing how Mary had swayed on her feet, but Bryce was cool as a cucumber. He hadn't even shifted in his chair. What was wrong with the man?

"It's gone now. Just a head rush." She looked at Tom and grinned. "Happened the last time, too. All the time."

"The last time . . ." His gaze dropped to her belly and back up to her wide smile. "Alice isn't even a year old!"

She shrugged. "We always said we wanted them close together."

An emptiness opened up inside him and he refused to fill it with jealousy. He was happy for them, of course he was. He got up from the table and gave his sister-in-law a gentle hug. "Well, congrats again," he said, then backed up, giving Bryce a thump on the shoulder. "Another one past the goalie, huh?"

He didn't waste time over long good-byes, but alone in his truck on the way back into town, he let the feelings in. Maybe they were right. Maybe a big project was what he needed, because having too much time on his hands gave him too much time to think. And the truth was, seeing his brother so happy made him realize how empty his life had become.

The washer and dryer at the house hadn't been used in so long that everything had calcified or rusted, and Abby had the persistent, icky thought that mice might have built nests in the dryer ducts. There were no clean linens on any of the beds; the gorgeous four-posters had mattresses but nothing else. A search of a linen closet revealed two sets of sheets coated with the ever-present layer of dust, but no blankets or comforters.

Realizing there was no way she could stay here in the house's present condition, she bundled up the sheets, got in her car, and started back into town to check into a motel for the night. Tomorrow she'd wash the sheets at a Laundromat and stop by the grocery store to stock up on cleaning supplies.

Abby slowed as she got closer to the town limits. There was more than enough dirt at the house to keep her busy for at least the next few weeks. For a few moments she fantasized about using some of Aunt Marian's money to hire cleaners to come in and do the work for her. And yet, despite her dislike for dusting and scrubbing, she knew she didn't want anyone else going through the contents of the house. If nothing else, she owed it to her grandmother to find out what she could about this side of the family. Who knew what she might discover beneath the grit and grime?

And once that was done she'd decide what needed to be fixed and contact a Realtor. She hadn't planned on staying in Jewell Cove very long but plans changed. It wasn't like there was a pressing need to be on any schedule. Or anyone waiting for her to return. She could afford a few weeks to take care of personal business. That's all this was. Business.

She didn't want the intimacy of a bed-and-breakfast—too many curious questions—so she turned into a small roadside motel just past the waterfront and the commercial area surrounding it. The room came with a porch that boasted a stunning view of the main drag. Since she had no desire to sit in the camp chair and watch traffic, she checked out the view from the back window. The harbor spread out below her, boats tied to the docks and bobbing on the smooth water in the mellow late-afternoon light. She watched as a fishing vessel chugged its way into the far end of the dock, its grayish-white prow breaking the gentle waves.

A long, low growl sounded in the silence and Abby pressed a hand to her stomach. When had she last eaten? Not for hours. There was no on-site restaurant at the motel, only vending machines in the office, so she had a quick shower to wash off the dust before looking for some dinner. Revived, dressed in clean navy trousers and a soft pink top with ruffles along the hem, she set out to explore Main Street and see what might tempt her. Since she hadn't eaten since before crossing the border, she didn't expect it would prove too difficult to find something appealing.

She passed Memorial Square with its well-kept gardens, a gazebo, and upon close examination, a statue of Edward Jewell, the town's founder. Right next to the dock there was a fish-and-chips place—more like a canteen, really—with the smell of fresh fish and hot oil clinging to the air. Farther along she saw Breezes Café, a promising-looking diner, right next door to an Italian place called Gino's that filled the air with the pungent smell of garlic, tomatoes, and fresh bread. Deciding to keep looking, Abby walked down the sidewalk next to the water admiring the view of the boats coming to dock, when a door opened farther down the street and country music erupted through the breach like a siren's call.

It had been a long day, and Tom Arseneault's sudden appearance was the icing on her already overwhelming cake. The reassuring twang of a recent country hit mingled with the delicious scent of grilled beef toppled her over the edge. What she needed was some red meat and a stiff drink. She kept going until she reached the brick-red building at the end of the block that looked more like a barn than a restaurant, a faded wooden sign outside announcing THE RUSTY FERN. She pulled open the door and stepped inside.

Was there anything more universal than a local watering hole? Abby let out a breath as the familiarity of it soaked into her tired mind. Neon signs boasting beer slogans hung above the solid wood bar. Thick tables and chairs filled the open space, with one end of the room spared for two pool tables and a dart board, where one lone man was throwing darts with varying accuracy, pausing to take a drink from his glass after each shot. Easy chatter blended with the country music, the long Maine accent thick in the air after a few drinks. But best of all was the smell coming from the kitchen—garlic and beef and grease. Abby's mouth watered just thinking about it, and she found a small table for two close to a window overlooking the wharf. It was perfect.

A waitress approached. "Something to drink, darlin'?"

The *r* was soft, reminding Abby of the childhood trips she'd made to Lunenburg and Bridgewater with her parents. She smiled. "Spiced rum and ginger, please."

"You got it. Do you want a menu?"

Abby looked up at the woman's face and smiled. "If somewhere on it says a steak sandwich, that'll do."

The woman nodded in approval. "Sure does. How do you want your steak?"

"Medium, and a salad instead of fries, please."

"Sure thing. I'll be right back."

Her drink was brought straightaway and Abby savored the spicy, fizzy taste of ginger ale and Captain Morgan on her tongue. The window provided a view of the wharf and a smattering of small shops on its edge, each one with a different colored siding. Reds, blues, yellows—there was even one green with pink trim around the windows. It should have been garish but somehow it worked.

Despite the bad start to the day, she had to admit Jewell Cove was a pretty little town with lots of character. Main Street was vibrant with shops and businesses ranging from the quaint to the cute, the foot traffic steady even in the off-season. From what she could tell, there wasn't even a Starbucks or McDonald's in Jewell Cove. The place was delightfully free of chain stores and fast-food outlets.

All in all she could have landed in worse places.

"Fancy meeting you here."

Her head snapped back to see Tom standing by her table looking down at her. She felt smaller than ever, seated as he towered above her. The fact that his deep voice sent something shimmering along her nerve endings was a nonissue. He was aggravating on a lot of levels.

"My, my, it is a small world, isn't it?" She hoped her cheeks weren't giving her away as she picked up her drink and took a sip. Blushing would give him the wrong idea entirely.

"Isn't it just?"

There was a long pause as he waited, standing by her table, and she finally sighed with irritation. "Is there something I can do for you, Mr. Arseneault?"

"Aren't you going to ask me to sit down?"

She swallowed, but made a point of lifting her chin and doing her best impression of disdain. "I wasn't, no."

"Tsk-tsk, Miss Foster." He began to smile, popping a ridiculous dimple. She would not be charmed. *She would not.* His dark eyes sparkled at her. "How very rude."

The blush she hoped wouldn't appear heated her cheeks and she looked away, tempted to smile. "Oh, sit then. You're going to anyway, and looking up at you is putting a crick in my neck."

He pulled out the chair and sat, putting his elbows on the table and leaning forward until she could smell his clean, spicy scent. "Where are those Canadian manners we keep hearing so much about, *eh*?"

He was baiting her and she was terribly close to giving in. All she wanted was to have a decent meal in peace. Instead she was face-to-face with Mr. Sexy Lumberjack—again.

"I'm half American," she stated, as if that explained it all, and he laughed.

"Well played, Miss Foster."

She merely sipped her drink. The glass was only half empty and she was starting to feel the alcohol tingle through her legs and fingers. One drink would definitely be enough.

"I was born in Maine, you know. In Houlton," she explained. "That's where my gram lived, and where she had my dad."

"So what prompted the move to Nova Scotia?"

"How did you know that's where I'm from?" Good heavens, was nothing sacred around here?

He had the grace to look slightly sheepish. "It might have been mentioned that you had Nova Scotia license plates. Besides, I saw your car at the house."

Abby couldn't stop the smile that curved her lips as she thought, "Small towns." "Of course. Good old Bill at the gas station, right? Anyway, my mom was from Nova Scotia, and we moved there when I was young." There was more to the story, but Abby wasn't about to get into her long, screwed-up family history with Tom. No one wanted to hear a sob story about how her mother was more interested in being a party girl than a mother or her childhood spent traveling from one trailer to another. There was a difference between presenting basic facts and airing dirty family laundry. Especially to someone who was practically a stranger.

"So you have dual citizenship."

"Comes in handy sometimes." Her stomach rumbled and she wondered how much longer the food was going to take. "I just came to have some dinner," she said, turning her glass around on the cocktail napkin. "If there's something you wanted, now'd be a good time. I'm hungry."

His face lost all trace of teasing. "All right, I'll get right to my point. I want to buy your house."

She nearly dropped her glass, the condensation slipping down her fingers as she stared at him. "What?"

"You don't want it, right? And you're going to sell it anyway. So sell it to me."

Abby hadn't seen the offer coming, but she could tell he was dead serious. "I thought you were a contractor."

"I am."

"And I didn't say I was selling it." The words came out, even though she knew them to be a lie.

He sat back in his chair. "So you're keeping it? Staying here?"

"I didn't say that, either." She folded her hands. "You were right about one thing. I can't sell it as it is. It needs work, but I'm still trying to get a full picture. It would be irresponsible to sell to you right now. After all, I doubt I'd get market value. You'll do the renovations and then flip it for a tidy profit."

"So? I'd be saving you a lot of headache," he persisted.

"The house hasn't exactly been the source of my headache today," she pointed out.

The waitress came and served Abby's meal. The smell was enough to make her nearly wilt with pleasure. With a smile the woman turned to Tom. "You want a pint of the usual, Tom? Something to eat?"

"I ate at Bryce's, thanks, Tanya. But a pint would be good."

So much for getting rid of him, then.

Abby poured a little of her dressing over her salad and speared a circle of cucumber. "I hope you don't mind if I eat. I'm starving."

"Feel free."

She was self-conscious eating in front of him, wondering if he could hear every chew and swallow, but refused to let him take away her enjoyment of the food.

She washed down the cucumber with her rum and ginger and put down her fork. "Tom . . . may I call you Tom?" At his short nod she continued. "I'm not going to unload the house on an impulse or because someone pressures me." Tanya came back and served his beer and slipped away again. Abby cleared her throat. "I'm spending the next few weeks evaluating, and that's all. I'll be talking to my lawyer and looking at my options, which may include contractors. I'm sure you're not the only game in town, and I intend to cover all my bases." She looked squarely into his eyes. "I feel like you've ambushed me twice today. It's not exactly doing you any favors."

He took a long drink of his beer and put it down on the table. "Since we're moving to a first-name basis . . . Abigail." He sighed. "Look, maybe I seem a little pushy—"

"A little?" She raised her eyebrows, challenging. "You barged into my house an hour after I arrived and now you've interrupted my dinner."

His lips curved. "Okay, a lot pushy. The truth is, I have a thing for old houses and the one you've inherited is a doozy. It was and still is a landmark and just needs some TLC. It's no more complicated than that. The idea of restoring a house like that is a dream come true for a guy like me."

He was being completely honest. She could read it in his gaze and the passion in his voice. Why couldn't he have said that earlier? Knowing he had a personal stake in it rather than simply seeing dollar signs softened her a bit.

"All right. I'll consider your offer. After looking into all my options, of course."

He turned his glass in a circle on the tabletop, leaving a wet ring. "Thank you," he conceded. "It's just that the house is a real treasure. It deserves to finally be looked after. If you don't want to do it, I'd like to. There's so much history there, it would be a shame for it to disappear or be covered up."

"If it's got such historical significance, maybe it should be a museum."

His eyes widened. "The town tried to convince Marian to sell it to them for years. She always said no. Said it was supposed to stay in the family." He looked away. "Or so the story goes."

The last sip of her drink soured in her mouth. "In the family? That's odd, considering we never met when she was alive. Family couldn't have been too important." She felt tension build at the base of her neck. So the town had pestered Marian. They'd probably approach her, too. She should be prepared for that.

"Maybe she wanted to make up for that by leaving you the estate."

"It's not like I can exactly ask her, can I?" Abby replied bitterly. There'd been ample time for Marian to connect with Iris or even Abby, but she never had. Not once. The idea of selling it outright and being well shot of it had a certain allure. "Look, as I said, I'll consider your offer. I can't promise more than that."

"That's all I ask." He sat back in his chair and she examined his face once again. Did he really have to be so good-looking? It wasn't fair. Maybe it made her shallow but it was harder to say no to a man like Tom than it would be if he were short, fat, and balding.

But it was more than just good looks with Tom. He was so sure of himself, so confident in his abilities. She envied him his self-assurance. It came naturally to him, while she had to work at it every day.

She cut into the rest of her sandwich with vigor, Tom be damned. She was hungry and she was tired and she was starting to come around to his way of thinking and didn't want to. If she hired him—and it was a big if—he would be at the house all the time. She would see him on a regular basis. She would be tied to him for *weeks*. And while the idea of being tied to someone like him was attractive, in reality it would be trouble. He was interested in her house and that was all.

And wasn't that a laugh. Someone was interested in her for her money when all her life she'd barely had two pennies to rub together. It was why she had to keep a clear and logical head about this whole thing.

"What do you do, Abby? For a job, I mean?"

She finished the last crumb of French bread and pushed her plate aside, feeling ridiculously giddy that he'd called her Abby instead of Abigail or Miss Foster. "I'm a teacher. Kindergarten and grade one."

His smile widened and his eyes gleamed. "Of course you are."

"Meaning?"

"Meaning you look like a teacher. Sound like one, too." He tapped the rim of his glass. "Do you read?"

She smiled then. "I would hope so. Being a teacher and all."

His lips twitched. "I mean for pleasure."

"Constantly." The admission came quickly. Reading took her away from reality. Taught her new things and took her places she could only dream of. As a kid she'd always had her nose in a book.

"What did you think of the library?"

"It's amazing. Every wall is lined with books. They really need to be evaluated and that's beyond my expertise. I should have a friend of mine from Halifax come over. Even without the books, there are all those solid mahogany cases and the old silk settee and there's one particular pie-crust table that caught my eye."

She realized she'd gotten slightly carried away.

"So now you understand," he said softly. "The house is to me what the library is to you."

"Old and dirty?" She tried to make a joke but it fell flat, because his words rang true and they both knew it. He'd known exactly where to hit her for maximum impact.

She was still planning on putting it on the market, but

she understood the draw. There *was* something special about that library that called to her. It felt like . . . home. Damn him for playing on her emotions.

Loud voices came from the bar area and Tom's brows pulled together in a frown. When Abby turned around, she saw the waitress arguing with the man who'd been playing darts. "You're cut off, Rick. Sorry."

Rick's reply was succinct and made Abby's ears burn. "Friend of yours?" she asked quietly.

"You could say that." He sighed. "Rick Sullivan. I grew up with him. He hasn't been the same since coming back from . . . well, wherever he was deployed. No one's said." He finished off his beer and stood. "Maybe I've given you something to think about, anyway. And Abby?" He paused by her chair. "Don't forget to enjoy yourself a bit while you're in town. Do some shopping. Go out for a sail. See what the town has to offer. You might end up liking what you see." He put his hand on her shoulder as he passed by. "Good night."

"Good night," she murmured, her pulse hammering from the innocent touch. His assessment that she looked like a schoolteacher had stung and there had been none of the longing looks tonight that a girl knew meant a guy was interested. But it didn't stop the warmth that went through her at the feel of his fingers on her shoulder. Or the way his last words had been absent of any hostility or sarcasm. It had been a genuine invitation, a welcome to the town. An invitation she was almost inclined to accept.

She turned in her seat, watching him approach Rick, his size blocking the other man from view for a few seconds. She couldn't hear what they said, but a minute later they went up to the bar. Tom pulled some bills from his wallet and squared away the tab, and then they left together, Tom walking behind while Rick weaved his way to the door. He was a good friend, helping this Rick guy when it would have been just as easy to mind his own business.

A few minutes later Abby motioned for the waitress to bring the bill. Tanya came to the table to clear the dishes, but surprised Abby by saying, "Tom looked after your dinner and said to tell you welcome to town."

"He did what?" She hadn't expected that. And she might have thought he was trying to buy his way into her good graces but she got the impression that despite their rocky beginnings Tom had more integrity than that. It was a nice gesture.

"You're the one that's inherited the old Foster place, right?"

"That's me." She put on a thin smile.

"Big job sorting it out, I expect. Especially seeing as how it's been empty for so long." The woman patted Abby's hand—what was it with all the physical touching around here anyway? "You should head over to Breezes someday for breakfast," Tanya chattered on. "The old-timers over there will fill your ears about how that house is full of ghosts." She departed with a friendly smile.

Abby picked up her purse and sighed. *Ghosts?* She shook her head. Just one more thing she didn't need right now.

# CHAPTER 5

Abby took Tanya's advice and headed over to Breezes Café at nine the next morning, searching out breakfast and a Wi-Fi connection to do some research. Morning light poured through the wide windows, casting a cheery glow on the patrons. A local radio station played in the background. More than one person entered and was offered a wave and was called by name. If Abby was looking for Jewell Cove Headquarters, it appeared the café was it.

Once she'd ordered a bowl of oatmeal and a coffee, she booted up her netbook and opened her browser. With a sinking heart she realized Tom was annoyingly right. She ate rather absently as she went through the list of contractors in the area and the reviews for each one. At least on paper, he was the best around. Only one other company came close to impressing her, but when she gave them a quick call to see if they could provide her with a quote, she was told that they could maybe slot her in around October.

Tom had her over a barrel and, what was even more aggravating, he knew it. It was either hire him or sell it to him.

She was browsing through Tom's site, looking at refurbishment pictures, when someone cleared their throat beside her table. "Excuse me, Miss Foster?"

The man was probably in his early fifties, with a rough complexion that spoke of years spent in the wind and sun. His thinning hair was an interesting blend of gray and blond—what she thought might have been quite attractive at one point but had since been salt-bleached by the sea.

"I'm Abigail Foster." She held out her hand.

He shook it and his palm was rough. "Luke Pratt. I'm the mayor of Jewell Cove."

This man was the mayor? He looked like he'd just stepped off a fishing vessel.

"Won't you sit down?" she offered, pushing her nearly empty bowl aside.

"Thanks." He slid into the booth across from her and smiled. "How are you liking our town?"

She gave the only answer possible. "It's lovely. Small and friendly. Everyone seems to know who I am already." It was a bit of a backhanded compliment, she admitted to herself. A little anonymity would have been nice. But Pratt only smiled widely at her.

"And the house? It's a right beauty, isn't it?"

Was there a right or wrong answer to this question, too? "It's definitely something. A little worse for wear." She gave him a small wink. "A diamond in the rough, perhaps."

His florid complexion seemed to redden even more. "That's a fine way to put it," he agreed. "Your great-aunt Marian took a lot of pride in her place until she got sick. It's a shame that it's fallen into disrepair."

Abby suddenly remembered what Tom had said about the town pressuring Marian to turn the house into a museum. Was that the reason for the warm welcome this morning?

"I'm sure it's nothing that some paint and elbow grease can't fix." She lifted her chin a touch. "It was built to last, just like the Fosters, wouldn't you agree?"

Why she felt the sudden surge of family pride, she didn't know. But she met Luke Pratt's gaze evenly.

A spark of admiration glinted in his eye. "I would. It was Jedediah Foster's pride and joy—at least that's what the records say." A small smile touched his chapped lips. "We sea captains are made of sturdy stuff."

"Fisherman turned mayor?" she asked politely, a bit charmed despite herself.

"Captain Luke Pratt, retired U.S. Navy," he clarified. Was it just her, or had his shoulders straightened ever so slightly when he said it? "So Miss Foster, what are your plans for the house?"

Niceties out of the way, she affected a nonchalant shrug. "I haven't decided yet. I only just arrived yesterday."

"That's good news."

"It is?"

He rested his hands on the edge of the table. "Why settle on something so soon when there are options to consider?"

"And you're going to tell me about one of those options, naturally," she responded, curling her fingers around her coffee cup.

"Have you been inside the house?"

"Of course."

"Then you know how much history is there. The house is important to this town—as a landmark and a testament to the long history here. It would be perfect as a museum. Both to preserve the history and, of course, as a tourist draw to our town."

"Didn't you approach my great-aunt about this years ago?"

He sat back. Abby mentally thanked Tom for the

heads-up; this certainly wasn't due to any communication on Marian's part but Mr. Pratt didn't know that. Without intending to, Tom had given her the upper hand. Or at least helped her level the playing field.

"Well, yes. Not me personally, of course. But previous councils . . ."

"And her answer was always no."

"She might have said something about the house remaining in family hands."

Abby kept hearing that and it puzzled her each time.

He cleared his throat. "What we're proposing isn't to buy the property from you. It would still remain yours—just like Marian wanted. But we'd propose renting it from you. In keeping with Foster tradition, we would ensure that the articles inside were family pieces and not random articles brought in as indicative of the period. It would, in all ways, remain Foster House." He smiled. "Or as the locals know it, the House on Blackberry Hill."

There was that name again. "And would you be paying for the renovations needed to make it happen?"

He paused.

"Of course not." She answered her own question. "You want me to pay to fix it up and then hand it over to you, am I right?"

"We *would* be paying rent," he insisted. "The historical significance alone—"

"Which I appreciate," she relented. "Tell me, Mr. Pratt. Sentimentality aside, why didn't you just offer to buy the house?"

Sharp blue eyes met hers. "The town can't afford to buy it outright."

"Which is no surprise," she said. She admired his forthright manner, admired how he'd approached her today, even though she was starting to feel ambushed at every turn.

Then again, if Mayor Pratt looked like Tom this conversation might have gone very differently. She couldn't ignore the fact that last night their banter had felt the tiniest bit like flirting.

"I just arrived in town, Mr. Pratt, and I don't even know what needs to be done to the house. It would be premature to say I know what I'm going to do because there are too many unknowns." The man didn't need to know that she still figured selling it was the best idea. "But I'll keep your proposal in mind."

He nodded. "That's all I can ask," he said kindly. "I hope I didn't overstep by approaching you so soon . . ."

"Don't apologize. You were clear and to the point. That's refreshing."

Pratt slid out of the booth and held out his hand. Abby got up too and shook it. He gave her fingers a friendly squeeze. "You're quite like your Aunt Marian, you know. Not so much in looks, but you've got her backbone."

The way Abby was feeling about Marian's lack of contact with Iris's side of the family, she wasn't sure if she should take that as a compliment or an insult. She decided compliment, because it had clearly been meant that way.

"Thank you, Mr. Pratt. I'm sure we'll speak again."

He nodded and waved at a few locals as he left the coffee shop. Abby sat back down as the waitress came back to warm up her coffee. She wondered how Pratt had known to find her here. She could sense several pairs of eyes on her and tried to ignore the conspicuous feeling that crawled over her skin. No doubt someone had tipped him off and he'd hustled over here from the town hall or wherever the mayor's office was.

She looked back at the website she'd been browsing—Tom's—and knew she really didn't have a choice. Keep it, sell it, rent it to Jewell Cove—it had to be renovated before any option was viable.

With a sinking heart, she realized she was going to have to call Tom Arseneault.

Tom rested his hand on the railing of the deck overlooking the quiet cove as he waited for his burger to finish grilling. Other than the occasional car passing, there was no sound except the quiet lapping of water on the pebbled beach below. On a soft spring night like tonight, he was one hundred percent satisfied that he'd made the right decision, moving here. The cozy cottage was nestled in the trees and a grassy slope led down to the calm waters of Fiddler's Rock.

Josh was coming home to stay. Tom had been thinking about that a good deal since hearing the news. He didn't have a good feeling about this picnic his mother and cousins were planning. He agreed that he and Josh had to find a way to coexist. Jewell Cove was not a big town. They had the same family, a lot of the same friends. But throwing them together at some big welcome-home gathering might just blow up in everyone's faces.

He'd skip the whole thing if he could, except he knew someone would come out here and drag him if he tried it. The only thing to do was show up for a little while and try to stay out of Josh's way. Keep on the down low.

A car door slammed and Tom turned his head toward the front of the house. Had someone come in? He checked his burger, slid it onto the warming rack, and turned off the burner before going inside through the patio door. Just as he shut it behind him, there was a knock on his front door.

He opened it to find his cousin Sarah on his doorstep, looking her usual bright and cheerful self in jeans, a baggy T-shirt, and a perky ponytail.

"Sarah. This is a surprise. Are Mark and the kids with

you?" He looked over her shoulder, but she appeared to be alone.

"Nope, just me. Can I come in?"

"Of course you can." He said the words easily but he frowned a little. It wasn't very common for her to show up on his doorstep. She must want something in particular. He could pretty much guess what.

She stepped inside and he offered her a seat. "I was just going to have some dinner. I can put another burger on the grill if you want."

She shook her head and sank into one of his chairs. He realized his home was very different from her light and airy house overlooking the harbor. The cottage was all wood paneling and hardwood floors and sturdy furniture. The upholstery was dark and plaid—not a floral print in sight. It was snug and welcoming, and quiet and secluded. Just the way he wanted it.

"What brings you by, Sarah?" He kept his voice deliberately casual. "Everything all right with the family?"

"I've come to ask a favor," she said, smiling brightly. "You do know about Josh, right?"

"I heard."

"We're having a picnic on Memorial Day weekend to celebrate his homecoming."

"I heard that, too. Your mom called me yesterday."

"Oh."

It seemed very wrong that he and Josh should work so hard at avoiding each other. They had been the same age, with the same interests and friends. They'd played baseball together all through high school—Josh on the pitcher's mound, Tom at shortstop. They'd double-dated, spent summer afternoons at the beach, and once put a hole in his father's aluminum boat and had to swim for Aquteg Island before being rescued.

Now they were reduced to this.

He thought of Josh, all alone in his house in Hartford. Josh had been the one to take retirement from the service and set up their home, waiting for the day Erin would be back for good and they could start the family Josh had always wanted.

And then Erin had been killed three weeks before she was due to return. Tom hadn't always been a good friend or cousin, but he'd be a cold bastard to begrudge Josh the chance to come home and be with his family.

"I already promised to make an appearance, if that's what you're here for."

"Actually, I was hoping you would make us a dance floor for the party. Something like you did for Julie and Adam's wedding last summer, remember?"

A dance floor. It wasn't a bit of trouble. Some plywood and nails. It wasn't that. It was wanting to reach out to his cousin and make amends and being afraid he'd be slapped back. He turned his back on Sarah and walked to the wide bay window with his hands on his hips, gazing out over the water.

She went to him and put her hand on his arm. "Tom," she said quietly, "hasn't this gone on long enough?"

He didn't look at her as he answered. "What you're asking for isn't just a dance floor. It's not so easy to forget."

Her reply was clipped. "Well, someone needs to make the first move. Or does family really mean that little to you?"

He turned on her then, a little bit angry himself, because he wasn't sure why the onus always had to fall on him to make things right. Josh wasn't a totally innocent party, either.

"Don't you dare accuse me of that, Sarah. Not when you know better. We both know what I gave up in the name of family and brotherhood. Not that it did a damn bit of good." Tom had stepped aside when push came to shove and they all knew it. He hadn't stood in Josh's way.

"You let her go except for the one way that mattered most. In your heart. You said all the right things but we all knew why you moved out here. You're practically a hermit. You never date. You spend all your time on the job or in your woodworking shop. Please, Tom. Don't let this continue to drive a wedge between you and Josh when she's not even here anymore."

"It's not that simple," he relented, softening his words.

She shook her head, her eyes soft. "Of course it isn't. All I'm asking is for you to try. A visible gesture that you're willing to take this first step. I miss the old days, Tom. I want to see us all back together again, like it used to be."

"We're older now," he said, quieter. "We can't go back. It won't ever be the same."

For a few minutes they stood in silence, watching the softening light over the cove. A few ducks bobbed on the surface, their bodies sending ripples over the glass-like water. This was why he'd chosen this particular spot in the first place. The cottage had a way of quieting a busy mind and a hurting heart.

"You always were like a mother duck," he finally said, a smile in his voice. "If we all argued, you came up with a compromise. We got a scraped knee, you went for the Band-Aid. But you can't fix this, Sarah, no matter how much you try. That's up to Josh and me."

He saw her shoulders slump and he closed his eyes, giving in. Why could he never say no to the females in his family?

"I'll make your dance floor, and I promised Aunt Meggie I'd show up. The rest is up to Josh."

A smile spread across her face and she raised her arms and hugged him. "Thank you! I knew I could count on you, Tom!"

He chuckled as he gave her a quick hug and then set her back. "Don't get too excited. You had to know you'd wear me down. Now get going. Don't you have a family to look after or something?"

"We're meeting at Sally's for ice cream after ball practice. I promised Matthew one of her hot fudge sundaes."

He chuckled. "Just like we used to do when we were kids."

"Yeah, only Sally is much older now. You're welcome to join us," she added.

"Thanks for the offer, but I've still got dinner on the grill." Which was probably dried out by now, but it didn't matter much. The way he was feeling, the last thing he needed was to hang around with yet another big, happy family.

He walked her to the door and kissed her cheek before she left. But as she backed out of the driveway he frowned.

Everyone seemed to think that this big reunion was going to be perfect, but Tom got the feeling they were setting themselves up for disappointment. Even if he were willing to make a new start with his cousin, it was a two-way street. And he wasn't sure it was one Josh was willing to travel.

# CHAPTER 6

Abby's hands were sweating inside the rubber gloves, but she was doing so much cleaning that she didn't dare work without them unless she wanted chapped skin. For two days she'd scoured and washed and sometimes it felt like she hadn't gotten anywhere. So far she'd managed to make the master bedroom clean and fresh, as well as the bathroom with its old fixtures, stand-up shower, and luxurious claw-foot tub. Marian Foster had spent considerable money updating the house to modern standards while still maintaining a vintage feel to everything. Running water and electricity were readily available but to Abby everything still looked like she'd stepped back in time. Somewhat grudgingly, she had to admit she liked it. It gave the house character.

The hall and stairwell had been cleaned, the faded carpet on the steps vacuumed within an inch of its life, and she'd taken a whole day to work on the kitchen, wiping walls and cupboards from top to bottom. Her whole body ached. The next time someone asserted that housecleaning wasn't work, she'd set them straight in a hurry.

A new washer and dryer had been delivered and installed and a trip to the local department store had yielded small appliances like a new toaster and coffeemaker. It made no sense for her to remain in the motel indefinitely, so she'd made her first priority getting the house in a semilivable state. The work was long and exhausting, but with each clean wall and polished piece of furniture the place was starting to feel less like a derelict.

If only she could shake the uneasy feeling that washed over her now and again. It was cold and unpleasant and settled heavily on her shoulders. She told herself it was just foolishness and an overactive imagination. That it was because she was alone in the huge place. A couple of times she'd actually thought she'd glimpsed something out of the corner of her eye, only to turn to the movement and see nothing.

She had to get this place cleaned and on the market, because if she stayed here too long she was afraid she'd go all the way crazy.

The afternoon was spent vacuuming every possible corner of the library and polishing the wood with oil soap. As each gleaming surface came into view, Abby realized she couldn't put off making the call much longer. The house looked better as she cleaned, but it also highlighted flaws she'd missed during her first inspection. There was work to be done, work that she couldn't do herself. And for that she needed Tom.

She stripped off her gloves, took Tom's card out of her pocket, and grabbed her cell phone, dialing his number with her thumb. Might as well get it over with.

"Arseneault Contracting."

The deep voice was clearly his. It shivered along her nerve endings like silk. She swallowed. "Tom," she said. "It's Abby Foster."

"Well, well."

He sounded so smug she wanted to hang up and say to
hell with him. But she wouldn't give him the satisfaction.
She sniffed and rolled her shoulders, trying to relax. "I
was wondering if you were still interested in putting together a quote."

"Of course I am. Just a sec."

Abby heard what sounded like his hand going over
the phone, and then a muffled shout and a crash. "Sorry,"
he said, coming back. "We're just finishing a job and I
came inside to hear you better over the noise."

She put her fingers over the bridge of her nose. She
hadn't considered how convenient it was that his schedule
was open when everyone else's for miles around was
booked solid. "How is it you have all this time to fit me
in?" she asked. "Every other contractor I talked to is
booked right through the summer. Why not you, Tom? Is
there something I should know?"

"Every other contractor? So you shopped around and
chose me. I'm flattered."

"Don't be. Didn't you hear me? Everyone else was
booked. Let's call it a choice of necessity."

He laughed, the sound warm in her ear. "I heard you
just fine. Actually, I'm glad you asked. We had our latest
project go bust due to financing, and before that we were
set to do a big kitchen renovation down toward Camden,
but the marriage hit the skids and now they're fighting
over the house. Everything was put on hold."

"Oh."

"Well, my loss is your gain. Or my gain too, if you're
serious. Did you check my references? I do good work,
Abby. You can trust me."

Ha. Trust. This was the second time he'd asked her to
blindly believe him, and Abby didn't trust anyone these
days. She'd learned the hard way that people rarely kept
their word. Trusting was just a sure way to get hurt. Even

Gram, who'd been the most stable person in her life, had obviously been keeping secrets.

She pressed the phone to her ear. "I'd rather have some facts and figures to go by," she replied dryly.

"I can drop by tomorrow morning. We'll be wrapped up here by this afternoon and I can give you all the time you need."

There was no reason why his words should cause a stupid fluttering in her chest. No reason why the air in the library should suddenly feel close and cloying. But the idea of having a man like Tom Arseneault at her beck and call was enticing and made her feel a little giddy.

"I'll be here. Cleaning."

His low laugh rippled along the line. "It's quite a job, huh."

"You have no idea. It's a blessing I'm not an asthmatic."

He laughed. "It'll be worth it, Abby. We'll bring the old girl back to life, you'll see."

She didn't know what was more attractive—the idea of the restored mansion or the image of Tom Arseneault in his work boots and a plaid shirt. "I'll see you tomorrow, then."

"Tomorrow," he echoed.

As she hung up, she pressed a hand to her forehead. She needed help. Rugged carpenters weren't her type. For goodness' sake, she hadn't dated in so long she didn't even *have* a type. And the idea of restoring the house should make her relieved, not excited.

Still. Maybe tonight she'd paint her toenails. She had a new shade in turquoise she'd been dying to try . . .

Abby gave up on the pedicure. After a long day of scrubbing and scouring, she was too tired to cook so she ventured into Breezes again, greeted by the savory scent of pot roast, seafood chowder, and fresh bread. She recognized a few faces already and smiled as they nodded in greeting. Instead of taking a table and sitting alone, she sat up at the counter, perched on a wooden swivel stool with a rung back. The fastest thing to order was the chowder, and within seconds a steaming bowl was placed in front of her along with a plate holding the largest dinner roll she'd ever seen.

"This smells fantastic," she complimented the woman behind the counter. "Thanks."

"You need anything else, give a holler." The woman looked over Abby's head. "Evening, Art. Sweet tooth acting up again?"

"Maybe."

"I'll see what I can do. Be right back."

A man sat up to the counter a few stools over and Abby stole a look. Older than Luke Pratt for sure, probably in his sixties or more, with a friendly face and a slight potbelly. She smiled as he looked over, then turned her attention to her bun—really the size of a small loaf. She broke off a piece and spread it with butter. The real stuff—no artificial low-fat anything here, she realized. The sign said home cooking and they meant it.

"You're Miss Foster, aren't you?"

Abby supposed this would go on until she'd met everyone in the town, so she reluctantly looked away from her steaming chowder and smiled. "I am."

"You've got your great-aunt's smile. Art Ellis. May I?" He nodded at the stool beside her, and when she agreed he slid over, taking off his Bruins ball cap. "I used to look after the grounds up at the house before Ms. Marian took sick."

Her smile came easier. At least Ellis wasn't just being nosy, he actually had a connection to the house. "It's nice to meet you."

"You, too. Town's been buzzing with the news that you're here, but I didn't want to intrude. Thought you might be sort of a private-type person, like Marian was."

The waitress put a gigantic piece of apple pie in front of him, topped with a scoop of vanilla ice cream that was already starting to melt. "Linda, you're an angel."

"Our little secret," Linda replied with a wink. "And if you blame this on me and Margie asks, I'll deny it."

He grinned at Abby, then took a bite of his pie and sighed contentedly. "My missus would have a fit if she knew I was eating pie. Worries about my girlish figure. But Linda here makes the best pastry in town." He grinned, a sideways smile that made him look boyish, and patted his stomach. "Wouldn't want Margie to know I said that, either."

The smell of apples and nutmeg was heavenly. Abby sipped her water. "My lips are sealed."

He ran his hand over the thinning hair at the top of his head. "There's lots of speculation about you, Miss Foster."

She met his gaze. "Call me Abby. And I'm just as curious about the town as it is about me." She was surprised to realize it was true.

"It's true, then? That you never knew Marian?"

She didn't know why she was shocked that he should know that. "News travels fast around here. So you were the gardener?"

He nodded. "Of a sort. I cut the grass and kept the trees pruned, did odd jobs around the house. But the garden, that was all Ms. Marian. She loved her garden, especially the roses. She always had the nicest blooms. I'd hate to see the state of it now." He shook his head.

"It's a mess," Abby confirmed. "I don't think it has been touched since she stopped living at the house."

"A shame," he said, cutting through the flaky crust of

his pie. "After all the work she put in. The house probably isn't much better, is it?"

Abby smiled back. "I got the feeling that Captain Foster built it to withstand any storm, but it needs some attention," she conceded. "I need to have it assessed, but my initial impression is that it's sound."

"You should have Tom Arseneault have a peek at it. That boy knows what he's doing."

That "boy" had to be thirty years old and was the size of a barn door. "So I've heard," she replied dryly. Ellis didn't need to know she'd already asked Tom for a quote. Besides, she was sure the gossip mill would have everyone well informed about it all in no time anyway. "You know the house well, Mr. Ellis. I'd love to learn more about it. It's on Foster Lane, but more than once I've heard it called Blackberry Hill. Do you know why that is?"

Art sat back against the padded seat. "It's been called that for years. Blackberries grow wild all over that side of the mountain. You take a walk up sometime and check it out. Between them and the blueberries, the odd black bear's been known to show up now and again."

"I haven't gone up yet. Is there anything up there?"

Art nodded. "There's still one of the old barns from when it was the Prescott farm. That'd be your great-grandmother Edith's family." He leaned closer, as if sharing a secret, and damned if she wasn't drawn in. "When I was younger there was a rumor that the barns and buildings were hiding spots for spies during the war. But that's just a bunch of romantic talk. The Prescotts moved away after Edith and Elijah married and years later the old house burned in a lightning strike. The barn's still there, and the gate was put across the road because teenagers used to go up there and get up to no good in the barn."

"And you know this because?"

He grinned and his eyes twinkled. "Well, I suppose that would be because I was one of those teenagers."

She smiled as she looked down into her chowder bowl. Art Ellis could be a charmer too, couldn't he?

"But you need to talk to someone who knew Edith and Elijah," he said. He looked around the diner until he found who he was looking for. "Hey, Isabel. Come on over here a minute."

Abby's fingers tightened on her spoon. Good heavens, anyone who had known her great-grandparents would have to be at least ninety, wouldn't they? She spooned up more chowder, determined to eat before it got stone-cold.

"What are you going on about, Arthur? And it's Mrs. Frost to you," the sharp voice replied from a corner of the restaurant.

Mindless of the other patrons, Art let out a sigh. "Well, if you don't want to meet Marian's niece, fine by me."

It took a while for the elderly woman to shuffle her way over to them, but when she got there she didn't mince words. Her white curls bobbed as she nodded at Abby. "I'll sit over here, if you don't mind. I won't be sitting next to the likes of you, Arthur Ellis. Biggest trouble-maker I ever had in my class. Always teasing the girls." The white-haired woman used the counter to help lever herself up, and sat down with an *oomph* on the other side of Abby. She leaned ahead and wagged her finger at Arthur. "You were always more trouble than you were worth."

"You loved me and you know it," he replied. He gave Abby a wink. "They all loved me. I was a good-looking kid."

Abby took the bait. "I think you are probably right, Mrs. Frost. Charming, for sure, but a smart woman can see right through that, don't you agree?"

Isabel Frost laughed, a wheezy sound that made Abby

grin. "Your aunt Marian would have said just that," she confirmed. "And she probably did, many a time."

Once again Abby had been compared to her aunt, and in a positive way. She wasn't quite sure how to feel about that.

"Mrs. Frost taught most of the Cove until she retired in the eighties," Art explained. "She knew Marian. Knew Edith, too."

"Edith Prescott was beautiful," Isabel proclaimed. "She was a few years older than me, but I remember. Sweet and polite, bit of a stubborn streak, and with the most gorgeous hair. It was a hazelnut brown and so thick. And a beautiful bride, too. The day she married Elijah Foster she was radiant. Not a year later she had Marian. She was so happy then. Elijah doted on her and she had everything a girl could have wanted. We all lived for an invitation to the Fosters' for a party. And oh, my, they threw some grand ones."

Gorgeous, dark hair—could the woman in the photo on the mantel be Edith? The baby was probably Marian then. The records showed that Edith had died in 1945. Maybe, Abby considered, it was the only picture Marian had of herself with her mother. How sad.

Isabel's soft tone of remembrance continued. "The last party they threw was not a week after Pearl Harbor. It was a last hurrah, really. Elijah was gone after Christmas of '41, when he signed up with the Navy. Came back in '43 a changed man, with a limp and a cane for his troubles. Still, things seemed to come around for a while. Iris was born in '44. But then there was that tragic accident. The whole town was in shock. The war was just ending, you know. We were celebrating V-E Day and everyone knew Japan was next. Rumor had it that there'd been a little too much cele-brating up at the house and Edith fell down the stairs."

Silence surrounded them. It was so much more than

Abby had ever expected to learn today, but it raised even more questions. And the stairs . . . She suppressed a shiver, remembering the odd, oppressive sensation she always felt crossing by the bottom. It creeped her out a bit to realize that her great-grandmother had died there. *Ghosts* . . .

"A rumor?"

Isabel clasped her fingers. "No one ever said differently."

There was something about the way she said it, though, that made Abby perk up. Perhaps it was what *wasn't* said that was most telling.

"What about the children?"

Isabel folded her hands. "Elijah was never the same after Edith's death, they said. Became a bit of a recluse, either gone for work all the time or hiding away in that house. One of the maids had a particular liking for Marian, and she brought her up almost as her own. Iris, though, she was an infant, barely even walking. Too much for a widower to handle alone. The Prescotts were in Houlton and took Iris in with them."

That followed with what little Abby knew simply from family records. Iris had been brought up by her grandparents in the town close to the Canadian border. Abby swallowed around a lump in her throat, hungry for information but sad that it had to come after Gram's death. Why? Had she been ashamed for some reason? Angry at being cast out? There had to be more to the story. Families didn't just . . . split, did they?

"What about Elijah?"

"Had a heart attack in the sixties. Marian inherited the house and the Foster fortune with it. Art here can tell you a lot more about your aunt Marian. He looked after the grounds and did a lot of handyman work around there, didn't you, Art?"

"Sure did. She had her hands full lookin' after all the girls she helped." He frowned. "Some people didn't approve of what Ms. Marian did up there, but she was a good, kind woman." He smiled a little. "'Course, I'm a little biased, as that's how I met my Margaret."

There were so many stories waiting to be discovered, weren't there? Abby was surprisingly curious about the family she'd never known. Art and Isabel were so entertaining, Abby thought she could listen to the pair of them forever. And they didn't seem to mind that she was a stranger. They were quite welcoming when all was said and done. They accepted her at face value with an ease she'd never quite experienced before.

She wasn't quite comfortable with feeling so . . . comfortable.

Isabel patted Abby's hand. "You never knew any of this, dear?"

Abby shook her head. "I'm afraid I didn't know anything at all about the family."

"But Iris, you knew her?"

Abby nodded, tears clogging her throat. She hadn't realized how much she missed having a connection to family until just now. There was no one left. She was the last direct descendant of Elijah Foster, and this town was her only link to her family. For the first time, she saw beyond the resentment she'd felt since the legal notification of her inheritance. What Isabel Frost had given her today was a precious gift. She'd given Abby history. She'd given her life context. Even if it wasn't neat and tidy and happy, it was something.

"Gram never talked about her family. She always said some things were better left in the past," Abby ventured, when her voice was steady again.

Isabel frowned for a moment, but then the confused look was gone. "Well, it's a shame, but you're here now."

She patted her hand again. "What are you planning to do with the house?"

The words "sell it" sat on the tip of Abby's tongue, but she couldn't seem to make herself say them. She took a breath, realizing that what was going through her mind right now meant staying in town even longer than her revised plans. She couldn't deny that she was getting caught up in it—not just the romance of the house but also of its story. "The first thing I'm going to do is have it properly restored," she announced. Then, Abby promised herself, she was going to discover all the Fosters' secrets.

Saying the words out loud gave her a renewed energy. Even though she'd already asked Tom to work up an estimate, talking to Art and Isabel made it seem real and possible. She was suddenly quite hungry. She lifted her spoon and scooped up a mouthful of creamy broth. When Linda, the waitress, passed by again, Abby asked, "I don't suppose you have another piece of that pie back there?"

"With ice cream?"

What the hell. A few days ago she'd been determined to breeze in and out of town with a minimum of fuss. Now she was digging in her heels, ready to uncover what she could about the family she'd never known. She was going to need lots of energy to get through it.

"Why not?" she answered with a jaunty shrug.

As she dug into the warm sweetness of the pie, she got the feeling that she just might be biting off more than she could chew.

And that the challenge made her feel more alive than she had in months.

Abby got up at dawn and dug out her yoga pants and running shoes. In the days since her arrival she'd missed working out, though the heavy-duty cleaning had provided a substantial calorie burn. She'd been relieved to discover that both the fridge and stove worked and she'd cooked some simple meals for herself rather than going out to eat every night, which had helped. But she missed her routine. When she ran, the sound of her breathing and the rhythmic slap of her running shoes were calming, and the physical exertion made her feel strong and capable, completely in control. This morning it seemed the perfect way to gear up for a new start.

She jogged down the lane to the road and then turned left, starting up the winding incline. The May morning was cool but mild, the newness of the sun's light making the dew sparkle on the tall grass and wildflowers that had yet to open. A half-mile into the run, the pavement stopped and the road turned to dirt. A large metal gate blocked the road from any traffic, just like Art had said, but she skirted around it and kept on going. Legs burning, heart pounding, Abby could see the summit, not that far away now.

The sun rose higher in the sky and the only sound on the air was the birds singing in the scrub bushes and trees. She recognized the call of chickadees and the clear-as-glass song of the finches, marred only by the harsher squawks from starlings and crows. Just when she was sure her legs would give out, the path leveled. A gravel drive off to the right led to a rundown, abandoned barn. It leaned precariously to the side, as if it could slip at any moment into a pile of rotted lumber and shingles.

She gave a little shiver. The same dark feeling that washed over her from time to time at the house was here, too. The unstable structure was isolated way up here on top of the mountain. Private. No one nearby to hear a sound. No one would come to anyone's rescue.

That was crazy, though. She was in no danger. Abby shook off her thoughts and with a self-deprecating smile made a note to stop reading thrillers late at night. She was listening for footsteps in the dark and looking for things that simply didn't exist.

She grabbed her foot, stretching out her quadriceps as she inhaled deeply, intent on enjoying the incredible view from the top of her mountain. From the summit she could see the house, large and majestic, surrounded by trees and the back garden that was in dire need of love and attention after being let to grow wild for the last several years. Past the house she could see clear down to the town and the harbor, the buildings sparkling like multicolored jewels against the clear blue sky. The water narrowed around the tip of the bay but then expanded into the shining blue-green greatness of the bigger Penobscot. From there the ocean would go on for miles and miles, and even up here she could taste the salty tang of the sea air. It tasted like freedom.

She knew from the deed and the material from the lawyer that this land was all hers now as well. It had once been the home of Great-grandmother Edith's family. Elijah had bought a substantial section of the land from the family and built the mansion upon it. And when Edith and Elijah had married, Edith's family had sold the remainder of the property to Elijah and moved. Abby wondered if they'd seen Iris as a way to hold on to their daughter, and if that had any bearing on why Iris and Marian had been separated their whole lives. Maybe it had been too hard to let go, knowing their daughter had died so young.

Still, she couldn't imagine giving up this place so easily. It was a pretty piece of land with an incredible panoramic view. She wandered until she found an outcropping of rock and then sat, pulling up her knees, soaking in the morning. In the summer it would be thick with flowers and loaded with the wild blackberries that Art Ellis had told her about.

She wished she could stay longer, but Tom was coming

today and she wanted to get home and cleaned up before he arrived. Reluctantly she began the jog back down the mountain. The downhill slope proved more of a challenge for her knees and thighs than the uphill, and she was puffing and her T-shirt was wet through the back when she reached the lane again. She slowed to a walk, needing to cool down before hitting the shower. It didn't take long until she could see the whole length of the driveway, and the fact that Tom's truck was already parked next to her car.

Damn.

He was sitting on the top step of the small veranda, talking on a cell phone. When he saw her approaching he hung up and got to his feet, tucking the phone away in his back pocket.

He looked good. Faded jeans and work boots and a plaid shirt with the sleeves rolled to the elbows. And here she was, likely the color of a freshly cooked lobster with sweat creeping down the small of her back.

"You're up bright and early," she greeted.

"Too early?"

*Yes,* she wanted to answer, but didn't. "I ran the mountain. Sorry I wasn't here when you arrived."

He came down the steps. "It's no biggie. I made a few calls. Maybe I can have a look around and start making a list while you, ah . . ."

His gaze traveled down her body. "Clean up?" she suggested, feeling awkward but knowing there was nothing else to be done.

He nodded. "Yeah. That."

Of course she needed a shower. She felt a little weird about it, knowing Tom would be wandering through her house while she was getting naked, but she shook it off. "Suit yourself. I won't be long."

"Okay."

She unlocked the front door and led the way in. "Why don't you start with the downstairs? And there should be coffee on in the kitchen. I set it up to brew before I left. Milk's in the fridge. Help yourself."

"Thanks."

She scooted up the stairs before he could say anything more. Once in her room she grabbed some clothes and scurried to the bathroom, making sure to lock the door behind her. She turned on the shower and stripped while waiting for the water to get hot, feeling an odd sort of awareness about her nakedness. Wondering what it might be like if he walked into the bathroom while she was under the hot spray. As her pulse quickened she wondered what he'd look like if he stripped off *his* clothing. He would be big and brawny and beautiful. And he'd say her name in that deep voice of his . . .

Inside the shower stall she applied the puff with enough force to peel off her top layer of skin. It was utterly inappropriate for her to be having these sorts of thoughts about Tom Arseneault, a man she wasn't even sure she *liked*!

And who she was pretty sure didn't like her. She had to remember that part, too.

She huffed out a laugh to herself as she rinsed off the lather and reached for the shampoo. The sad truth was that despite any fantasizing, she probably wouldn't know what to do with a naked Tom Arseneault if she had him. It had been so long since she'd had sex she wasn't sure the old analogy of riding a bike would even hold true. Plus, if she were inclined to give it a try, Abby was pretty sure she should stick with someone a little . . . less potent. Maybe a banker or an accountant. She chuckled to herself. Someone with training wheels.

But the truth of the matter was, even if Tom wore a tie and glasses, Abby knew herself well enough to know that casual relationships weren't her thing. For her, sex was about trust. It was intimate, on a physical and emotional level. If and when she chose to be with someone again, she would be absolutely sure it was right.

She shut off the water and reached for the towel. She supposed that made her terribly old-fashioned but preferred to think of it as gun-shy. And one thing was certain. Tom Arseneault might be the greatest thing since sliced bread, but it was a long leap from where they were now to sleeping together. No matter how delicious he looked in his work shirt and jeans.

She gave a short laugh and reached for her underwear. Besides, it wasn't like he was exactly offering himself up for sex anyway.

# CHAPTER 7

Tom wandered through the downstairs, coffee cup in hand. The house did look much better now that it had been given a good cleaning. Abby must have worked her ass off to accomplish so much in such a short time. The woodwork and banisters were gleaming and the furniture polished. It made the good stuff look great and the bad stuff even worse. Like the floors and rugs. Despite a vacuuming, they really needed to be professionally cleaned. As did the draperies—if they could even be saved. The woodwork definitely needed some love—trying to match it was going to take some research.

On initial inspection, however, Tom was delighted to find the place was sound. The wiring and plumbing were good and there didn't appear to be any moisture in the walls. What they were dealing with here was aesthetics and not a lot of reconstruction, which was a pleasant surprise. The price and time factor would have gone way up if they'd had to start ripping out walls.

The veranda would have to be replaced, of course, and he'd have to check the roof and windows. The downstairs needed crack filling and painting throughout, and all the floors needed refinishing. The kitchen had a shocking lack of cupboard space, and he had some ideas how to improve on it, including replacing all the countertops with granite and adding a butcher block. He needed to inspect the fireplace flues as well, and ask if she wanted them opened and functional. The chimneys would likely have to be completely rebricked.

There was the issue of modernizing things, too. She could make the library into a den, add a wall unit for a television and stereo receiver, bring in cable, and surely she'd want Internet. Right now there wasn't even any phone connection. She had to be using her cell phone, and it must be costing her a fortune.

He stopped and stared out the kitchen window as it occurred to him that she had a fortune to spend on phone calls if she wanted. Rumor had it Marian had been a very rich woman. Where she'd gotten her money, no one quite knew. Certainly a substantial portion had come from Elijah's estate, but had it been that much?

The shower stopped running and Tom swallowed. Footsteps echoed dully on the ceiling above him and he imagined her running the towel over her long legs and full breasts. His coffee cup paused on the way to his mouth. The figure that had only been hinted at the last time they met had been in full relief this morning in the fitted running tee and snug yoga pants. Walking in the house behind her had been a revelation. The black material had showcased a fine, tight backside.

But he was her contractor, not her lover. She didn't even like him, for heaven's sake. She'd made it very clear that he was her last choice, not her first. Didn't stop his mind from wandering, though. After all, he still appreciated a good view. And the view had been very nice, indeed.

The bathroom door opened and he raised the cup the rest of the way to his lips. The brew was lukewarm.

"Tom? You can come up now. If you're ready to look at the upstairs, that is."

He didn't need a second invitation. He put his cup on a table and made his way up the grand staircase to the top. The scent of her soap drifted out of the bathroom and he forced his mind to focus on the state of the rooms. Abby came out of one bedroom and his mouth went dry. Her hair was darker now, still wet, and twisted up into a clip at the back so he could see the long, graceful column of her neck. She wore jeans and a top that was gathered just beneath her breasts, and then stayed gathered in some weird way that made her ribs and waist look tiny. Damn. Abby Foster had curves. Good ones. The kind a man would have to be blind not to notice.

Even a man like Tom, who had no interest in romance whatsoever. He was still getting over the last broken heart and it had been hellish enough. It was certainly not an experience he wanted to repeat.

"I've taken this room as my own while I'm here," she explained. "The furniture is gorgeous, isn't it?"

The bed was a walnut four-poster with a matching high-boy against one wall and a vanity table and chair next to a commode stand, complete with an antique china pitcher and bowl sprinkled with light blue rosebuds. The walls were the color of a robin's egg, and the duvet cover was pure white. It was airy and fresh with a hint of elegance. Sort of like her, he realized.

"It's very nice."

"The windows are a little drafty, but I like it. I don't even mind the floors. They aren't as scratched as the others. I think the scars on the wide planking add character."

"If you want to keep all the rugs, we should look into

finding someone who can professionally clean them for you. Or you can purchase new."

She looked up at him, the blue of her eyes brought out by all the other blue tones in the room.

"I don't know. I mean, I could sell it furnished or I could have an estate sale first. I suppose cleaning them would be good either way."

"I thought you hadn't decided what you were doing with the house."

"I'm considering all possibilities here." She put a finger over her lips. "I think I'd like to keep as much of the original as I can, you know? No matter what I decide. Come look at this."

She showed him to another bedroom, again with a four-poster, and then a third with more modest furniture. An embroidered sampler was framed and hanging on the wall. She hadn't managed to get that one cleaned yet and dust camouflaged the true character of the pieces, but he could see what she meant. It was rare to find such fine craftsmanship in furniture anymore. It had lasted because it was made to last.

The last bedroom had a smaller room joined to it, and there was no furniture inside at all. "It's like a nursery," she said, standing in the doorway. "A door from this hall but another door connecting it to that bedroom, too. Would a nanny or nurse have stayed in that room, do you think? Were the Fosters that rich?"

"Jed was," Tom answered. "He was rolling in it. And Elijah probably was, too. Have you checked out the attic yet? I'm sure it had to have been servant's quarters."

She smiled sheepishly. "I've been too chicken. What if there are mice or bats or something?"

Tom laughed as they moved past the nursery. "Hate to tell you, but if you've got a rodent or bat problem up there, it's going to be a problem down here." He stopped in front of a plain door by the back hall—the only door left unopened. "Want me to go first?"

At her nod, he opened the door, revealing narrow steps leading the way up into the third floor. The hallway at the top of the stairs was dimly lit, but a window kept it from being pitch-black. Tom went carefully, but he was pleased to discover the top level was as sound as the rest of the house. The wood floors were dull and it was all rather plain and spartan, but he didn't see any evidence of dry rot or bats. As for the mice, he was certain they were around. He'd recommend she get in the pest control man to take care of that, the sooner the better.

Taking in the layout, he saw that the top floor was made up of five smaller rooms and a cramped bathroom that everyone would share.

"Come on up," he called. "Nothing's going to get you."

He heard her steps following behind and smelled the fresh scent of her shampoo as she came up behind him. "It's so light up here!"

"More windows than you'd expect," he replied. "I'd say this was definitely servant's quarters. And probably where a lot of the girls stayed when Marian ran her home."

"People keep mentioning Marian's 'work.' "

He nodded. "Yeah, she ran a place for girls in trouble. For a very long time. Think about it. Up here on the mountain it's private, and she had the house all to herself. It was the perfect location."

"But why? Why that particular kind of house?"

He lifted one shoulder. "Who knows? All I've heard is that it was all extremely confidential. Only person who might know more is Art Ellis. He worked here back then."

"We've met. He's charming."

Tom laughed. "He's a terrible flirt."

"Don't knock Art. He recommended you."

He watched as Abby went from room to room, peering into the open doors at the contents inside. "Before or after you called me?" he asked.

She looked over at him, her face blank with innocence. "After. Does it matter?"

Tom was somehow glad she'd decided to ask him for a quote before talking to Art. She'd come to him on her own. "Not really," he lied.

"What on earth am I going to do with all this space?" She spread her arms wide. She looked enchanting when she did that, like a little girl inside a toy shop, wondering what to play with first.

"It's a lot of house for one person," he confirmed.

She dropped her arms. "The heating bills alone must be astronomical."

"It would have been colder up here in winter. Hotter in summer. Though the windows might have given a bit of a cross-draft for relief." He forced himself back to business. "There's not a lot of room above the ceiling, but we might be able to blow some extra insulation in there to make it more energy efficient."

She looked up at him with a smile, scanning the open area in the middle that seemed to form a type of common area. "Look at this sofa and table. And games! There's checkers and backgammon and decks of cards. Downstairs is so formal. This is the kind of place you could let your hair down and hang out with your girlfriends."

"Would you want to fix it up, too?"

"Of course. Oh, Tom, can't you just imagine what it would have been like to come up here, with all that natural light, and paint or something?"

"You mean next to the servants?"

"Oh, right." Her face fell at his reality check and he laughed.

"You're getting carried away. It looks good on you."

Damned if she didn't blush.

"What about this room?" she asked, opening a door to her left. The room was windowless and completely, utterly dark. Tom stepped across the creaky floor and felt around the inside wall for a light switch. Nothing. He reached into his pocket and took out a penlight, shining it into the room.

"Holy mother," he breathed. A cord hung from the ceiling and he stepped inside and pulled it, illuminating a single bulb in the ceiling. "Would you look at this?"

"You've got to be kidding," Abby said behind him. "Tom, that's a *sea chest*."

"It's . . . everything," Tom said significantly. The room was piled with chests and boxes. Maybe not filled with actual treasure, but he knew there'd be some gems in here nonetheless. "Marian must have stored all her stuff in here. This is a gold mine, Abby." He turned to her and grinned. "You wanted to learn about your family? I'm guessing a good part of it is in these boxes."

"It's a little scary. I mean . . . there's so much. Maybe there will be things I don't want to know, you know?"

"Every family has its skeletons," he replied. He wondered what she'd say if he admitted his own family tree had not only a town founder but a real pirate on one of its branches. "None of those skeletons can hurt you now, Abby. Everyone's gone."

He wished he could take back the words as soon as they left his mouth. Her eyes were sad as they rested on his face.

"God, I'm sorry about that. I didn't think." He tried to smile. "Of course they're not all gone. You must have your family back in Canada."

But she shook her head. "No, you're quite right," she replied softly. "I really am all alone. My parents and grandmother have been gone for a while now." Her expression of enchantment at discovering the treasure trove had disappeared. Now she just looked lost.

Tom tried to imagine his life without family. Even with the discord between him and Josh, Tom didn't know what he'd do without his brother or their parents, or his cousins, Jess and Sarah. Aunt Meggie mothered him like he was her own. No one should be completely alone.

"I'm sorry," he said quietly, feeling like a fool and not knowing what else he could possibly say.

"Not your fault," she replied. "My mom left us when I was little, but when my dad died of cancer, she got custody of me. We moved around a lot. I was in so many schools I never really settled anywhere, until I finally went to live with Gram when I was fifteen. When Gram went . . ." Her voice faded. "Well," she said softly. "It is what it is."

He hadn't realized that she didn't have anyone. But before he could scramble to come up with some suitable words, she shrugged off the heavy moment.

"Anyway, you're right. This *is* a gold mine. Did you know that I also talked to Isabel Frost last night? She knew Edith and Elijah before the war. How old is that woman, anyway?"

"No one knows for sure. Methuselah old."

Her light, lyrical laugh sent something wicked winding through his veins.

"I guessed over ninety. She'd have to be to remember Edith."

"You're right."

"She's sharp as a tack. I don't have family anymore, but I do have history. That's what this is." She blinked, pausing for a moment as if deliberating. "When I first got here I didn't want to know about Marian. I was too angry, you know? I told myself I didn't care about someone who clearly hadn't cared about me."

"What changed?" he asked.

A ghost of a smile tipped her lips. "I started to realize it might not have been all her fault. I'd like to know why my gram ended up so separated from the rest of her family. I'd like to find out all I can before I go, you know?" She swept out her hand. "And now this. It's like finding treasure."

She went forward and knelt before a solid cedar chest. He watched as she carefully lifted the lid and then peered inside.

"What's in there?" he asked, unable to stop himself from being curious.

"It's clothing," she said, leaning forward. "Oh, my gosh, look at this." She held up a long dress. The deep purple fabric shimmered in the light and even Tom, who was oblivious to this sort of thing, could see that it was beautifully crafted and impossibly old, the fringes hanging in layers. "It looks like it was from the twenties," she continued. "Can't you just see it? With one of those fashionable headbands over crimped hair, and loops of black pearls to go with it? Someone in the Foster family tree was a flapper, Tom!"

She rooted around more while Tom leaned against the door frame, simply watching the way her face lit up. It was so much better to see her this way than the way she'd looked when she'd admitted that her family was gone. He was smiling to himself when he heard her catch her breath and her hands stilled.

"Ohhhh," she breathed. "Oh, my."

"What is it?"

She turned her head and looked up at him, eyes shining. "It's a wedding dress. Maybe Edith's." She got to her feet and gently lifted out the gown. "It's so gorgeous," she whispered, holding it up to herself. "Look at the lace. It's a bit yellowed, but properly dry-cleaned it would lighten a lot. The sleeves and the sash, and oh, look at this lace panel." She grinned. "You were right. This *is* a treasure. I'm going to have to come up here and go through everything properly."

She turned in a circle, the skirt of the gown trailing in her wake.

It was an odd time and place for Tom to have the urge to kiss her. The attic was dusty and smelled a little like old newspapers, and the single bulb threw a harsh light into the storage room. But Abby looked so vulnerable and strong all at once, childlike in her enthusiasm but womanly too as she pressed the satin and lace to her curves.

She dropped the gown from her body and folded it carefully, laying it on top of the other items in the chest. His eyes were drawn to the curve of her hips as she bent to shut the lid. Because her hair was pulled back, her features were highlighted. Granted, she wasn't wearing makeup but he rather liked the natural, fresh look to her skin—it was very girl-next-door. She did fill out a pair of jeans quite nicely, not to mention the fitted top. All in all she was extremely attractive in an understated way.

Dangerous.

The lid latched, she turned around and faced him again, and the air in the attic was still as their eyes met. There was something else. Something he couldn't quite put his finger on, and the moment spun out, silent, their gazes locked until he was sure she was thinking about it, too. Curiosity. The temptation to touch.

And wouldn't that be a fantastic way to screw up a big potential contract.

He cleared his throat. "I'll bet if we looked, we could find a servant's stairway that leads right down to the old kitchens."

"Old kitchens?" Her nose wrinkled as she frowned. It looked adorable. She even had a few little freckles across the bridge, making her look younger than he knew she must be.

The tense moment passed and Tom let out a slow breath of gratitude, willing his thoughts to stay on task. "You haven't been down there yet, either? Where did you think they cooked the meals? Certainly not on the main floor in that tiny, cramped space. The basement will be where the old kitchens are. And the staff wouldn't have used the main staircase, either. Come on. It's got to be here somewhere."

They found the door behind a large set of bookshelves that were piled with games, magazines, and sewing supplies. For several minutes they emptied the shelves and then Tom braced his hands on the sides. "It's too big to lift. We're going to have to push it out of the way."

Inch by inch they moved it along the wall. Tom's muscles strained as he put his shoulder into it. Finally they got past the door hinges and he tried the knob. Locked.

"Dammit," he said, panting.

"Wait here. I'll be right back." Abby rushed off but within moments her feet pounded on the stairs again.

"Keys!" she announced, triumphantly shaking a ring holding a cluster of old keys. "I found them in a drawer downstairs. I'll bet one of these will fit." Breathless, she handed him the ring.

He hit pay dirt on the third try. The lock snicked back and the door swung open to reveal a small landing and then a staircase that turned and disappeared. He held out his hand. "You coming?"

"There are spiders in there."

"Probably. I'll kill them for you." He grinned at her. God, he loved old houses. And the little boy in him was thrilled with secret passages and sea chests, even if the only treasure uncovered so far was some old dresses. It reminded him of the old days when he and Josh and Bryce had thought to go looking for the legendary buried treasure at Fiddler's Rock. "Come on, Abby, where's your sense of adventure?" He wiggled his fingers.

She seemed to consider for a long moment, but finally put her hand in his. Her fingers were soft and cool to the touch. Her hand was a lady's hand, and something dark and forbidden seemed to curl through him as he led her through the doorway to the landing and the steps beyond. It was cool and dark in the stairway, utterly silent except for the sound of their steps and it felt ridiculously like sneaking around. It was the kind of hidden place that lent itself to forbidden kisses and late-night liaisons. The farther down they went, the tighter her fingers grasped his. This was the second time he'd held Abby's hand and he couldn't remember the last time he'd done something as simple as hold hands with a woman before Miss Abigail Foster came to town. When was the last time he'd been so very aware of a woman?

He wanted her house. He did not want her, he reminded himself. Except that he did. In the confined darkness of the stairway, he wanted to press her body into the cool wall and feel her slowly melt against him. He wanted to bury his fingers in her sweet-smelling hair and taste her soft, unpainted lips.

Jesus, he had to stop thinking this way. He planned to work for her. Besides, Abby wasn't the type of girl you seduced and walked away from, and after Erin, he wasn't ready to take the risk of something more. Especially on someone who had made it clear that she wasn't hanging around.

Unsettled, he led on until they reached the bottom of the stairs and were faced with another broad door. He reached inside his pocket for the key ring and searched for the right one.

With a breath of relief, Tom swung the door open and pulled Abby into the musty kitchen.

Abby's relief at being out of the claustrophobic column of the stairwell was brief. As Tom turned to lead her into the kitchen, her heart stopped. Over Tom's shoulder she saw a woman standing in front of the fireplace. Sad eyes watched her from a pale face. Dark hair curled around her shoulders and her simple, pale blue dress fell just to her knee.

Before Abby could make a sound, the image faded for just a moment. This was impossible. It had to be a trick of light, something in her imagination. Because the other alternative was that Abby was looking at a ghost, and just thinking the word was completely ludicrous. Yet as her eyes adjusted to the light in the room, the figure was still there, faint but there just the same. Standing there watching her with a look of expectation on her face. A shiver crept up Abby's spine as the moment spun out. The woman's expression changed. Her eyes flashed, her lips thinned, and the air in the room chilled in a cold, frustrated wave.

"Abby? Hey, are you listening?"

She whipped eyes back to Tom, still standing in front of her, staring at her strangely. "Are you okay? I said your name like three times."

Confusion tangled her thoughts. "Did you see that?" She looked back toward the fireplace but there was nothing there. She pressed her lips together. She hadn't imagined it. She *hadn't*. The feeling had been the same as when she'd passed the bottom of the stairs the first time she'd come in the house. Heavy and sad. Oppressive.

*Desperate*, she realized, and her stomach tumbled nervously. But how could that be?

"See what?"

And if she breathed a word of it to Tom he'd think she was out to lunch and rightfully so. She'd fall over laughing herself—if she hadn't seen it with her own eyes. She shook her head. "N . . . nothing. Looks like you were right. The stairs did come right down to the kitchens. It's cold down here." She wrapped her arms around herself.

"It would have been hot as hell with the ovens going, especially in the middle of summer," Tom remarked. "Damp down here now, though. I don't think Marian used it much from the looks of it." He pointed at the door at the other end of the room and frowned. "That was barred from this side so no one could come down. And the bookcase upstairs hid the only other way in." Tom went over to an old wood table and examined it. "Except mice, it seems. There are droppings here. You really do need to get someone in to take care of that. I'll give you a name."

The entries were barred from both ends, but Abby was sure she'd just seen someone, logical or not. And she got the feeling that that someone was Edith Foster. It was the woman in the picture on the mantel in the dining room. The dress was much plainer, but the face was the same.

If it was Edith Foster, it did indeed mean Abby was seeing ghosts.

Which was just flipping crazy. She hadn't just inherited a mansion, she'd inherited a haunted one. Holy shit. The old-timers were right.

Oblivious, Tom continued on. "If you plan on using this part of the house again, I'll have to factor that into the quote," she caught him saying, but she struggled to register the words in her brain.

"I don't know. I'll have to think about it."

"Are you sure you're okay?"

"It's just eerie down here. No wonder Marian closed it up. Let's go back upstairs."

Wasting no time, she led the way back through the

door, up the stairs and into the attic. Tom followed behind, more slowly as he stopped to lock the kitchen door and then the servant's entrance. It had to be Abby's mind playing tricks on her, that was all. The house was large and old and it had only taken one mention of ghosts that first night at the pub to set off Abby's overactive imagination. It had been a shadow, nothing more, probably from going from the darkness of the stairs into the watery light of the kitchen. Perhaps if she told herself that enough, she'd believe it.

Except there were other things she couldn't explain. Feelings, glimpses in her peripheral vision. The stairs in particular. And Isabel Frost's strange facial expression when she spoke of Edith falling down the stairs.

She spent the next hour going over plans with Tom, listening to his ideas for the kitchen and downstairs bath with half an ear, along with his promises to send along the names of local companies he could subcontract for the other necessary jobs.

But when he was gone she put on a pair of gloves, went outside and started pulling weeds from the back garden. She needed the sun and the feel of the warm breeze on her face to chase away the coldness of the basement.

There was more to Edith's death than an accidental fall. Abby had gotten that feeling by what Isabel hadn't said at the café, and she was doubly sure of it now. It wasn't even a matter of believing if it was or wasn't true. She'd seen it. And everything within her said that Edith had some unfinished business when she'd died and left a husband and two daughters behind.

Two sisters who were then separated for the rest of their lives.

# CHAPTER 8

Tom's quote came in, and while the number seemed unbearably large, Abby knew two things: it was fair considering the amount of work involved, and she trusted him to do the job he said he would. It was in the way he looked at things, touched them. He appreciated the house and what it represented, so she gave him the green light to get the ball rolling. Within twenty-four hours he'd begun ordering materials, booked the roofers, and had started fixing up the verandah—replacing the floor, railings, and spools.

Abby kept wondering if she'd see the mysterious figure again, but there'd been nothing out of the ordinary and she was starting to wonder if she'd imagined it. She'd gone through several of the boxes and chests upstairs but hadn't found any family clues—yet. The boxes had only been filled with clothing, table linens, and an old set of Royal Albert china, which Abby carefully carried downstairs, washed, and put in the china cabinet in the great hall. It was an enormous job going through everything, and she managed a box at a time in her spare moments, hoping that at some point she'd find something that told her more about the Foster family story.

Several of the renovation jobs would require subcontractors, and one of the first things to happen was a visit from pest control. Abby couldn't ignore the truth—she heard the scratching in the walls and saw the evidence. While the exterminator did his work, Abby made a trip into Portland, her car loaded down with rugs to be professionally cleaned. Once they were dropped off, she stopped at a department store and stocked up on linens—new sheets for the beds and towels for the bathrooms in colors that would coordinate with the new paint choices she'd made. Considerably lighter in her wallet and hungry, she had a fast-food salad before she headed back to Jewell Cove.

She spent the afternoon indulging in the luxury of shopping, wandering through town and finally taking the time to pop into several of the colorful shops on the streets above the harbor. There was the soap-and-scent store, Bubbles, where she splurged on several handmade bars: cranberry and lilac and, of course, the local blueberry. She went into the Leaf and Grind, a quirky little shop full of dark wood shelves, aromatic coffee beans, and glass jars of tea leaves lined up behind an old-fashioned counter. She treated herself to several kinds of loose tea and a new teapot and cups in cream and crimson, the perfect colors to complement the drawing room or library. At the pottery store she bought a gorgeous set of serving bowls for the kitchen, picturing them on the corner shelf Tom had suggested she add.

At first it seemed foolish to spend the money on such things, considering she wasn't going to remain in the house, but she rationalized the purchases because she'd want the house to show to best advantage when the time came to sell.

Arms filled with shopping bags, Abby stowed everything in her trunk before heading to the market to pick up a few days' worth of groceries. On the way there, however, she spotted one more store on the corner. It was hard to resist the mauve-colored building with the darker purple trim—especially when she looked up at the street name and saw that the store was appropriately situated on the corner of Lilac Lane and Main. The oval sign out front said TREASURES. She climbed the wood steps to the building and followed the flower-lined boardwalk path to the door.

The shrill buzz of a saw reached her ears, followed by a quick moment of silence and then the whine of a power drill. She paused at the steps to the wide deck that was under construction. Her lips fell open at the sight of Tom in a T-shirt, on his knees on the floor of the deck. He set a screw and then pulled the trigger on the drill, anchoring the decking board to the two-by-six beneath. As he reached into his pouch for another screw, the muscles beneath his shirt shifted. Abby licked her suddenly dry lips and debated whether she should turn and go back the way she came. But that was silly. Why should seeing him keep her from going into a store, for Pete's sake?

"Hi," she said, gripping the strap of her purse.

Tom looked up and pushed back the ball cap on his head. She noticed his slightly shaggy hair curled around the edge of the cap, giving him a youthful, roguish appearance. Oh, boy. She had to stop noticing things like that.

"Hey yourself." He smiled, putting the drill down on the deck floor. "Out shopping?"

"I didn't want to hang around while the Orkin man did his thing," she admitted. "I took the rugs to that place you recommended in Portland, and then thought I'd browse around town. I've been here over a week and I've hardly seen anything."

He watched her carefully. "No stop at the Realtor's?"

She shrugged. "Not much point until the renovations are completed, is there?"

He nodded briefly and sat back on his heels. "This's my cousin Jess's place," he said. "Just finishing a new deck for her and putting up a pergola on that side for her to display some summer stuff. Figured I'd get it done now that your veranda is usable and while I wait for materials to start arriving for your place. Speaking of, we should go over countertop and cupboard samples for the kitchen so you can decide what you want. That stuff has to be special-ordered so the sooner the better."

She swallowed, thinking about poring over granite and stain samples with Tom, standing close to him and smelling the spicy scent of his aftershave. Something had happened that day in the attic, something more than finding some clothes or discovering the back staircase. The air between them had crackled with attraction. Standing there looking at Tom now, his shirt damp with sweat, Abby could almost believe she'd imagined it all and more than once she'd considered that it was all one-sided. After all, Tom Arseneault was incredibly gorgeous. She'd have to be blind not to notice. He could probably crook his finger and have any woman in town. She bit down on her lip. He probably had a girlfriend. She had no business thinking about him that way, in a secret staircase or anywhere else for that matter.

She untangled her tongue and tried a smile. "We can do it whenever it fits your schedule."

"After I finish here, I'm all yours."

Now that was an intriguing idea. A pert comment sat on her tongue but she kept it to herself and asked, "What about Saturday? You want to come over to the house?"

He reached for a scrap of wood and tossed it on a growing pile beside the deck. "Saturday's good, but why don't we drive into Portland and hit the supplier's show-room? It's easier to decide when you can see things put together rather than trying to visualize it from a little chip, you know?"

Drive into the city together? She blinked as realization dawned. They'd be alone in her car—or his truck—together, maybe have lunch just the two of them. Like a . . . date, only not. The idea flustered her more than it should.

He'd stopped working and was watching her expectantly. She had no good excuse. It's not like she could tell him what she'd been thinking.

"That would be okay," she replied. "What time?"

"Ten? Is that too early? It could take us a while."

"Ten sounds fine." Ten meant that they'd be spending most of the day there. They'd definitely have lunch together.

She was totally making more of this than she needed to.

Tom stood up, tossing another scrap to the side. "Sounds good. Anyway, I'm due for a break, so come on inside and meet Jess." He put his drill to the side but left his nail belt on. Following him into the shop, Abby couldn't help but notice how the soft leather fit around his hips, making her mouth go dry.

There was music playing in the background of the shop, some sort of light Celtic tune with a fiddle that fit perfectly with the down-home, seaside feel to the place. Large windows overlooked the harbor, flooding the entire place with sunlight. There were shelves and tables everywhere, of varying heights and shapes, and at first glance it seemed a bit chaotic until Abby realized it was all laid out with great precision to maximize the floor space. Pigeonholes were stuffed with a rainbow of yarns while a nearby rack was host to ready-made items—scarves, shawls, socks, and a tiny clothesline that held baby booties with miniature clothespins. Knitted dishcloths filled a basket and beside that was a selection of needles, crochet hooks, and patterns.

Another area formed a children's corner, complete with craft kits, kites, stuffed animals, puppets, and puzzles. There were soaps in every shape, color, and scent Abby could imagine, and then candles—soy, paraffin, beeswax. Tapers and pillars and tea lights and others in covered Mason jars. Cinnamon and butter pecan and banana bread and chocolate chip cookie scents, jasmine and rose garden and lily. Closer to the cash register was jewelry, and one whole wall was dedicated to quilts. Several were hung on full display, while others were folded and draped over quilting racks. Beside the quilts were supplies—piecing squares, patterns, thread, needles, and one entire shelf filled with bolts of cloth.

And in the midst of it all was the most beautiful woman Abby had ever seen. She was tall, with hair as black as Tom's knotted at the nape of her neck in the kind of loose bun—a study in precise disarray—that made Abby envious. She'd never been able to achieve that careless bohemian, feminine look with her hair. The woman wore black leggings that ended mid-calf and a loose tunic that she'd belted around her waist. Sandals with metallic accents glittered on her feet. She was currently standing on tiptoe as she reached to put an item on a top shelf. "That's your cousin?" she asked Tom quietly.

"Jess. She's pretty, huh?"

"She's gorgeous." She smiled up at him. "Guess your side of the family missed out on those genes, huh?"

Tom laughed unexpectedly, making Jess turn her head, finally realizing they were there. "Oh, my gosh, I didn't even hear you come in! Sorry!" She beamed at them and hurried over. "I was thinking up a new candle recipe for tomorrow's class and totally got lost in my own head."

"Jess, this is Abby Foster. The new—"

"Owner of the house up on Blackberry Hill!" Jess finished for him. "Oh, goodness, how are you liking it? It's huge, isn't it! But beautiful, I bet. Tom said he's going to be helping you fix it up again. You made his year. He's been in love with that house for ages."

Abby's lips twitched as she looked up at Tom, who appeared slightly embarrassed. "Oh, don't be bashful," she teased. "It's not exactly a secret." She looked at Jess. "He put his foot through the veranda floor when he showed up, you know."

"And you called Bryce. We heard all about it."

"Don't be a brat," Tom said to Jess.

"Well, we did." She turned her brilliant smile on Abby. "Anyway, Tom will do a good job for you, he's the best carpenter around. And I'm glad to meet you at last. The whole town's been buzzing about you."

Abby hated being the center of attention, but right now she didn't seem to mind, especially when it came from someone as openly friendly as Jess Collins.

"This place is amazing," Abby remarked, still glowing in the warmth of the welcome. "Treasures is definitely a good name for it. You've got everything in here."

Jess beamed. "The family didn't think I could make a go of it, but we brought them around, huh, Tom?" She looked up at Tom with affection written all over her face. "Tom made all of my shelves and tables, you know. He believed in this place before the rest of the family did. And I haven't forgotten that."

Something significant seemed to pass between the cousins but after a moment it was gone. "Come on, I'll give you a tour. You should come back on the weekend. We're having a beading workshop on Saturday morning. Within an hour you'll have a gorgeous pair of earrings or even a necklace."

"We're headed to Portland on Saturday to shop for cupboards and a countertop," Tom replied.

"Right," Abby echoed. "Sorry. I really wish I could."

She was shocked to find that she meant the words. She'd never really been a joiner before. And she wasn't staying in Jewell Cove, so it didn't really make sense to foster any new friendships, did it?

Jess paused. "But Tom, Saturday is the picnic at Sarah's. You promised."

There was that look again. Abby's gaze went back and forth between the two of them. Tom's jaw tightened, Jess's eyes narrowed.

"You can't back out now," she threatened. "You promised Mom."

"No one will miss me." He shrugged.

But Jess shook her head and put her hand on his arm, stopping him from turning away. "*Everyone* will miss you." There was an accent on the word "everyone" that Abby didn't miss. Jess smiled at Abby but there was worry in her dark eyes. "My brother is moving back to town, and we're having a family picnic at my sister Sarah's. She's got fireworks and Tom's already built a dance floor."

"Jess," Tom said, his voice thick with warning.

"It's okay, Tom," Abby said. "We can do it another day. I'm free whenever. You should spend time with your family."

Tom's gaze fell on her. "If we left for Portland a little earlier, we could be back in time for supper." He glanced at Jess. "Would that make everyone happy?"

"As long as you show up. Abby, why don't you come along, too? The more the merrier."

"Oh, I couldn't intrude on a family thing. Tom can just drop me off at the house when we're done."

"Don't be silly. There'll be a ton of food, and it'd give you a chance to meet a few more people. It must be lonely in that old house by yourself, especially on a Saturday night. Besides, it would be good for Tom to—"

"Jess," Tom said sharply, surprising Abby. Jess's lips

closed in surprise and Abby got the sense that there was a whole other conversation going on beneath what was actually being said.

But then Tom's hand touched the small of Abby's back. "Why don't you come," he suggested, his voice rumbling in her ear. "I know I'm not the best company, but it's better than spending a Saturday night by yourself, isn't it? And like Jess said, you'll get a chance to meet some people. For the most part . . ." He aimed a telling glare at Jess. "My family is quite nice."

The warmth of his hand soaked through her light shirt and tingles seemed to run down to her toes. "If I do come, what should I bring?" she found herself asking. Lord, she really was weak where he was concerned, wasn't she? One little touch and she was ready to do whatever he asked.

"Just yourself," Jess insisted. "Trust me. There'll be lots to eat. My sister always goes overboard with these things, thinking she's feeding an army. We never complain because then we all get leftovers to last a week."

It was the first time Abby had been invited anywhere since arriving in town. There were always a few people who would say hello at the café or in line at the grocery store, but this was the first real overture of friendship. If the rest of Tom's family was as nice as Jess seemed to be, it would be an enjoyable evening. Why shouldn't she go?

"I guess I could come along," she replied, and Jess smiled.

"Great. Now shoo, Tom. I'm not paying you to stand around, am I?"

Tom raised one eyebrow at his cousin while she winked audaciously. Abby wondered if Jess was paying him anything at all.

"I'm going," he muttered, but before he went outside again he spoke to Abby. "I'll see you tomorrow. Now that the exterminator's been by, I'll start with tightening up the doors and windows. The roofers are coming next Monday to replace the roof." He smiled down at her then looked at Jess. "See ya, slave driver."

Jess linked her arm with Abby's and drew her away. "Come on, let me show you around. Upstairs is my workshop, and that's where I hold my classes. Down here is the main store, and I make most of the stuff myself. A few other local artisans sell on consignment, which helps me keep my stock up. And the quilts are done by a ladies' group with the proceeds going to charity."

The door to the shop closed and moments later Abby heard the dull drone of the saw. Jess was in the middle of showing her a display of felted hats when Abby had to ask.

"What were you going to say earlier? That it would be good for Tom to what?"

Jess didn't meet her eyes but instead fussed with a pile of fabric on the table. "Oh, he just doesn't date much, that's all."

"But it wouldn't be a date. Tom works for me."

Jess looked up. "It would be the closest thing to a date he's had for a few years, so we'll take it."

"A few years?" Abby stepped back. "But Tom's—" She caught herself just in time. The word "gorgeous" had been sitting on the tip of her tongue. "What I mean is, look at him. He's not exactly a troll."

Jess's musical laughter echoed through the rafters of the vaulted ceiling. "So you *did* notice."

Abby grinned. "Well, duh. I may not be interested but I do have eyes." *Liar,* a voice inside her taunted. She ignored it. "So why the dry spell?"

Jess's voice softened. "He got his heart broken."

Something twisted inside Abby. Big, burly Tom didn't date because he had a broken heart? But he always seemed so sure of himself. So confident and . . . She remembered how he'd looked down at her once he'd pulled his foot from the veranda. His attitude had been bordering on cocky. And then she remembered the way his fingers had tightened on hers in the servant's stairway.

Oh, dear. Knowing he'd been hurt shouldn't change anything, but somehow it did.

"What happened?" Abby found herself asking.

After a pause, Jess sighed. "She married someone else."

"Oh. Ouch."

"Yeah. But what are you gonna do, right?"

"Right," Abby replied.

"Anyway, I'm glad you're coming. We're all happy Josh is coming home. His wife was killed on deployment and he's really been struggling. Now he'll be around friends and family, you know? Make a new start right here at home."

"I'm sorry," Abby replied, feeling instantly sorry for Jess's brother—Tom's cousin. "How terrible. Were you all very close to his wife?"

Jess went still for a second, and Abby thought she looked not just sad but a bit annoyed. "Not particularly," she admitted. "Erin was gone a lot, and then they lived in Hartford. They didn't come home often."

Abby got the sense there was more to the story, but she wasn't about to pry.

"Listen," Jess said, her face lighting up as she changed the topic. "I know it's got to be lonely, being new in town and in that huge old house all alone. Tom and his workmen can't be much company. If you can't make the beading workshop, why don't you come out tomorrow night to my candle-making class? I still have space and it'll give you a chance to meet some local ladies and do something fun. You get to take home what you make and I always provide some snacks for when we finish. First lesson's on me as a welcome to Jewell Cove."

Abby nearly refused. After all, she wasn't actually staying in Jewell Cove for long but she got the feeling her protest would fall on deaf ears. Besides, the temptation to actually get out and have a social evening that had nothing to do with the house or grabbing a meal on the run sounded fun. "I think I'd like that," she found herself saying. "What time?"

"I close at six and we start at seven. Just take the stairs at the back and come up to the workshop entrance."

"Thank you, Jess. For the welcome and the offer."

"Anytime." She smiled and put her hand lightly on Abby's arm. "The cove's a nice place," she said, giving a squeeze. "Small town, of course, but I can't imagine living anywhere else. You'll see."

Abby picked up a pair of earrings and paid for them, then skirted past Tom without saying anything. On the way to her car she stopped at Sally's Dairy Shack and bought a chocolate dip cone, which she ate seated on a bench overlooking the marina. As she licked the drips from her fingers, she frowned.

If she wasn't careful, this town could wrap its way around her heart. She'd just have to make sure that didn't happen; to be ready to cut ties and move on. If she'd learned anything over the last ten years, it was that nothing good ever lasted.

She couldn't imagine Jewell Cove would be any different.

# CHAPTER 9

The next evening Abby dressed carefully in her favorite capri pants and a top in asymmetrical ruffles that was ultrafeminine and flattering. She wore her hair down, letting it fall over her shoulders in waves, and slipped on a pair of jeweled sandals. It was just as nerve-racking meeting a group of women for the first time as it was going on a first date and Abby couldn't help but want to make a good impression. She was so anxious about it she nearly considered staying home, curled up with one of the books from the library.

But she needed to get out for a bit, and knew she'd regret not going.

So she put on some makeup, grabbed her purse, and made her way down the hill into town, parking a few doors away from Treasures.

When she entered the back door, the noise was already at a fever pitch. Half a dozen women were in the room, chatting animatedly. The only familiar face was Jess, who was currently laying out supplies on a table. A long counter ran along one side of the room, with a series of hot plates plugged in along its surface. Abby clutched her handbag and paused in the doorway, unsure. But just then Jess looked up and a broad smile lit up her face.

Her dark eyes were warm and full of good humor and Abby thought for a moment that the family resemblance really did run through the cousins. Jess's eyes reminded Abby remarkably of Tom's when he was teasing.

"You're here!" Jess came over, giving her a quick hug.

Abby had no chance to guard against the contact, and let herself be hugged briefly before giving a light laugh and extricating herself from Jess's embrace. "I did."

"I'm glad. Come meet the other ladies before we get started."

Under Jess's guidance, Abby met Cindy White, mother of twins and wife of a local fisherman who considered Jess's classes her night away from the craziness at home. There was middle-aged Gloria Henderson, who played the organ at the Baptist church and kept her hair in a precise bob just below her ears. Abby also met Summer Arnold, who looked like she was in her early twenties and had a nose ring and a streak of hot pink through her blond hair, and Lisa Goodwin, another young mom, who worked at the bank and whose husband worked at the fish plant just outside of town. All of them gave her a warm welcome, but it was Gloria who gave her an assessing look, raised one eyebrow, and said, "Heard you hired Tom Arseneault to fix up the house."

"I did, yes. He started sealing my windows yesterday."

Gloria's smile widened. "Sealing windows." Her tone inferred a different job altogether. "Not hard on the eyes, our Tom."

What could Abby say? She'd be a liar to say she didn't notice, and they'd all know it. The room had quieted a bit and she realized a few pairs of ears were waiting for her answer. She smiled. "No, he's not," she confessed. "But that's not why I hired him."

"Of course not." Gloria winked at her. "Nice perk, though. His father was always a looker, especially when he used to mow the grass with his shirt off—"

"Gloria!" Cindy's shocked voice interrupted, but Gloria shrugged.

"Shoot, Cindy. Whole town knows I dated Pete Arseneault when I was eighteen. Apple doesn't fall far from the tree and I don't need glasses yet."

Abby laughed. "Anything I say is going to sound so wrong right about now. I think I'll just keep quiet."

"Smart girl here, Jess. She'll do." Gloria nodded as she issued her seal of approval.

"Should we get started, then?" Jess asked. "Tonight we're going to be making Mason jar candles using soy wax. If everyone will pick a workstation, we'll begin."


The glass jars were still hot and Abby could see she had a few bubbles in her wax, but she didn't worry about it. The room had warmed with all the hot plates going and the aroma of wax and scenting oils hung in the air. She was pleased. It had been fun, melting the wax and then using Jess's "recipe" to add the proper combinations of scents and dye. She had two candles to take home later, one a creamy white scented with warm vanilla and the other a spicy red cinnamon. She'd learned more about Jewell Cove in this one hour than she had all the rest of the time she'd been in town. It was a close-knit community, a little prone to gossip as most small towns were, and not without its troubles, but also supportive of one another when times were tough.

Now Jess had laid out snacks and wine and Abby found herself with a glass of pinot noir in her hand, dipping a cracker in a delicious red pepper dip.

"Having a good time?" Jess stopped by, her glass containing something clear and fizzy. Abby supposed as the hostess she was abstaining from the wine.

"Wonderful. It was really fun. And everyone is just so nice."

"They like you, too. Though everyone was fairly restrained. They don't want to scare you off. Lips might get looser as the wine flows."

Abby grinned. This had been restrained? "Thanks for the warning."

She answered numerous questions about the house, though she learned as much as she revealed as even the younger women knew of Marian and the home she'd run for years. Lisa Goodwin, the young mom from the bank, topped up Abby's glass and smiled sadly at her. "Your great-aunt was a special lady, Abby."

"You knew her?" Everyone in Jewell Cove seemed to think a lot of Marian. Abby found it slightly odd that a woman reputed to be so kind and giving could have shut out the only family she had left. Why had she never contacted Iris, or had the tables been turned? Lately Abby had started to think it might have something to do with the secrets that seemed locked up in the house. Maybe, in the end, Marian hadn't had a choice.

"I was one of the last babies born there. She took my mother in, you know."

Abby's heart took a jolt. "You? You were born at Foster House?"

Lisa laughed lightly. "I was, but it's not like I remember it," she said, and Abby laughed, too.

"Of course not."

"My birth mom couldn't stay at home once she found out she was pregnant. With Marian's help she put me up for adoption. I grew up right here in the Cove with two wonderful parents. I guess not long after that Marian closed it up. She was getting older and looking after the girls was a lot of work. And, well, society changed. It's a lot less taboo now to be a single mom."

"Still hard, though," Abby mused.

"Cheers to that," Lisa said, touching the rim of her glass to Abby's. "Honestly, I don't know how single moms do it. I can barely handle my son and my husband."

The hour wore on and Abby felt herself getting fuzzy around the edges. She really should have eaten dinner beforehand, she thought. The laughter was coming a little more readily when Summer, who'd been mostly quiet, treated the group to a sideways smile as she twirled one pink strand of hair around her finger. "I just wanted to give a toast to Jess for expanding her deck," Summer said, lifting her glass to their host. "Tom was working with his shirt off the other afternoon. It was quite the visual treat."

"Amen," Abby said clearly, then put her fingers over her lips. "Did I say that out loud?"

After a second of stunned silence everyone burst out laughing. Why on earth had she said that?

Cindy snickered. "I'll second that. Must be all that manual labor. A man like that must be good with his hands . . ." She looked up and flushed a little. "Sorry, Jess. Know he's your cousin and all, but damn, you know?"

Gloria tut-tutted. "And you're a married woman."

"Hey, just because I'm on a diet doesn't mean I can't look at the menu."

More laughs. "You have a boyfriend, Abby? Someone special back in Nova Scotia?"

Her throat tightened. "Not really."

"Well, then." Cindy sat back in her chair with satisfaction. "You should give our Tom a tumble."

"Cindy!" This time from Lisa. She looked at Abby. "Don't mind her. She's off the market so she spends far too much time setting other people up."

"Worked for you and Jason now, didn't it?"

Lisa grinned. "Indeed."

Abby took another long sip of wine.

Summer patted Abby's knee. "You've been initiated now, Abby. Don't take it personally. There's not a single woman in Jewell Cove who hasn't thought about Tom just a little bit."

And yet, according to Jess, Tom didn't date. Not since he'd had his heart trampled on. It must have been a doozy. It'd take a special woman to get him out of that dry spell.

She drained her glass and looked around. Someone like Summer, tall and pretty with a kind of quiet confidence and innate sexuality, perhaps. There was no ring on her finger after all. But definitely not someone like Abby. She was far too ordinary. And far too timid despite her occasional sharp tongue. A man like Tom needed someone more adventurous.

"Come on, Abby, what do you really think of Tom? And don't worry about Jess. She won't say a word, will you, Jess?"

Jess made a motion like sealing her lips and throwing away the key. Abby giggled, the sound oddly strange to her ears. She never giggled. "Oh, no. You're not going to sucker me into that." She recalled briefly how close the air had felt in the confined space of the stairway, and wondered what it would be like to be pressed up against the cool wall, pinned there by Tom's strong body. The very idea was quite exhilarating.

"And . . . we've lost her," Cindy mourned. "Earth to Abby."

She looked up, a little slow on the draw.

"That's okay," someone said. "Tom tends to have that effect on the female population of this town."

Abby really shouldn't have let anyone top up her wine. Jess rose and excused herself for a moment, and like some unspoken signal, the ladies got up and began cleaning up the remains of the snacks. Abby bit down on her lip. Did Jewell Cove even have a cab service? All the other women tonight had been smart and walked to Treasures. Abby couldn't possibly get behind the wheel now.

"It wouldn't matter anyway," she confessed to the room at large as she made herself busy, putting vegetable sticks in a plastic container. "I'm only in town until the house is straightened away and I can put it on the market."

"You're not staying?"

Abby shook her head. "I wasn't planning on it. What would a woman like me do with a place that big?"

Cindy grinned. "Marry Tom and fill it with babies."

There was loud laughter then and the chatter dissipated, covering Abby's hot blush. The evening seemed to be ending, so she kept her hands busy by tidying the rest of the food table until the last woman was gone and then she turned to Jess in the quiet of the workroom.

"I feel stupid," she admitted, "but I think I might need a cab."

Jess's lips twitched. "We don't have one in town."

"Oh." It was too long of a walk to Blackberry Hill, especially in the dark. "Jess, do you think . . ."

How humiliating. She was having to ask Jess for a ride home. Next time she'd just say no to the wine and stick with something fizzy, like Jess had.

Next time? She wouldn't be here long enough to make this a habit.

"I've arranged for a drive for you, don't worry."

"You did?"

There was a knock on the back door and Jess smiled. "Looks like your ride's here."

She opened the door.

Perfect. Just wonderful.

She'd called Tom.

\* \* \*

Tom couldn't keep the smile from forming the moment he saw Abby. She looked adorable in jeans and some sort of ruffled top. Her hair was down, and in the soft light of Jess's shop it looked like butterscotch. But it was her eyes that made him smile. Wide and blue but slightly unfocused from her indulgence in whatever Jess had served tonight.

"Someone call for a cab?" he asked.

"I can't believe you did this," Abby accused Jess.

Jess merely shrugged.

"You ready?" Tom asked, his hand on the doorknob.

He saw her pause. Was accepting a drive home with him so bad? She set her lips and lifted her chin. "Just let me get my candles."

She carried a still-warm Mason jar in each hand, her purse slung over her shoulder. At the door she turned to Jess and said, "You set me up. Regardless, thank you for a lovely evening."

Jess laughed, and when her gaze met Tom's her eyes were sparkling. "Come back soon, Abby."

Tom followed behind Abby, impressed by the calculated precision with which she took the stairs. Once at the truck, he opened her door, breathing in the aroma of vanilla and cinnamon, some sort of flowery scent coming from her hair, and the tang of red wine left on her lips. It was a heady combination and he felt the uncomfortable stir of attraction once more. He took one of the candles from her hand as she got up into the cab, their fingers brushing on the warm glass of the jar.

He swallowed, thinking Jess had been far too conniving tonight by asking him to play chauffeur. No matter how often he'd told himself that there was nothing between him and Abby, his simple physical reaction told him otherwise. Whether they'd acted on it or not, the spark was there. The little sizzle between them when their eyes met or fingers touched. He had no idea what to do about it. Ignoring it was probably the best course of action.

He started the truck and kept the radio on, making sure there was sound in the vehicle so that they wouldn't have to talk. But he should have known he couldn't avoid conversation. Abby turned to him as soon as they hit Lilac Lane and apologized.

"I'm so sorry she called you, Tom. I didn't ask her to, I swear."

"It's no big deal. I wasn't busy." Nope, he'd been sitting at home, staring at the television without really watching. Worrying about seeing Josh on Saturday. Wondering what he would say to his cousin. Wondering why the pain in his heart, the bit that had belonged to Erin for so long, suddenly felt awkward and strange, like it didn't fit anymore.

"It was totally stupid of me to say yes to wine. And what kind of town doesn't even have a cab company, anyway?"

Tom turned to look at her. Her eyebrows were pulled together in consternation, her hands clenched around the white and red candles. *Damn that Jess,* he thought. First the picnic on Saturday, now tonight. Honest to God, he loved his cousin but this was enough meddling already.

"Is that what she told you?"

Abby nodded gravely.

He stared at the road again. "We do have taxis. It's a small outfit, but we have them."

"Then why on earth did she . . ." There was a long pause in which Abby connected the dots. "Oh. Of course."

They turned up Blackberry Hill now and Tom's hands started to sweat. Jess had pushed the two of them together and they both knew it. What was even worse was that his

cousin had known that all she had to do was say the words
and he'd come running. Was he that transparent?

"Jess was just meddling," he said tightly. "Don't pay
any attention to her."

"It's so embarrassing," Abby said, sighing.

"Embarrassing to be driving home with me?"

Her head snapped up. "Oh, no, of course not! You're
the catch of the town!" She clapped a hand over her mouth.
"Shit."

He chuckled, uncomfortable with the words but enjoying how she seemed to lack the ability to self-edit after
a few glasses of wine. It leveled the field somehow. "The
catch of the town, huh? Says who?"

"Only everyone." He could feel her gaze on him as he
kept his on the road where it belonged. Who on earth was
everyone, anyway?

"All I hear is Tom this and Tom that. If people find out
you drove me home," she continued, "I'll be the envy of
every woman in Jewell Cove. So that makes me wonder.
Why *are* you still single, Tom?"

He swallowed. The wine had definitely loosened her
reserve, hadn't it? "Guess I'm picky who I spend my time
with. And here we are." Thank God.

He put the truck in park but Abby didn't move. Was
she waiting for him to open her door? He was about to say
something when he saw the color of her cheeks. They had
paled and her eyes looked enormous. She hadn't seemed
that drunk but you never could tell. "You're not going to
be sick, are you?"

She shook her head vigorously. "No, I didn't have *that*
much. I just . . . I forgot to turn a light on. The house is so
dark."

He stared at the hulking figure of the house, felt that
stomach-rippling sense of unease he'd felt in the basement kitchens the day they'd gone exploring. It had kind

of freaked him out, actually, and for just a moment he'd wondered if the old stories about the house being haunted held a kernel of truth.

It was all nonsense, of course, and he hadn't always felt it the past week when he'd been working around. But there were times when he'd felt . . . well, watched. And then he'd turn around and there'd be nothing.

The house really was intimidating, especially in the dark. It had to be odd, staying all alone in such a place. Everything echoed in the high ceilings and oversized rooms. "You want me to walk you to the door?"

Relief flooded her face. "Would you? I know it sounds silly . . ."

"Of course I will. Taxi service includes getting you to the door safe and sound."

He shut off the engine and the sound of their doors slamming echoed through the stillness. Somewhere nearby peepers sent up a quiet song. In the silence their footsteps seemed overly loud as they crunched on the gravel of the driveway. They paused on the newly repaired veranda while Abby struggled to find the key to the front door in the dark. Finally she got it in the lock and the heavy door swung open.

The unsettling feeling struck Tom again, so he stepped inside and flicked on the light switch.

"That's better," he said.

"Much better," she breathed, but he noticed she shivered a little.

Abby stepped forward and hung her purse on an ancient coat rack she had unearthed from somewhere. Tom couldn't help but think that he should turn around and go right now. Instead he stood still, in the doorway of the great house, wondering what the hell he was doing.

"Can I ask you something?" She turned around and tilted her head as she asked the question.

"Sure."

"Do you think there's anything to the stories that this place is haunted?"

He shut the door as insects were starting to slip inside, lured by the glowing halo of the hall light. Interesting that she would ask just when he was thinking the same thing. "Do you?"

She smiled a little. "You answered my question with a question. Maybe you don't want to reveal that you believe in ghosties? Probably not very manly."

"Ghosties?" He shook his head. Maybe Abby was drunker than he thought.

"I heard stories when I first got here, that's all."

"Are you afraid?"

"No."

"Well, then." He rocked back on his heels. Truth was, when it came to things like that he didn't know what to believe. He'd never seen an actual ghost, but there were times . . .

He clenched his teeth as he remembered. The day Erin had died he'd had the worst feeling. A pain in his chest he couldn't explain that had gone as suddenly as it had come. Hours later Jess had come to tell him the news while Sarah and Meggie had gone to be with Josh in Hartford. Tom had been full of grief but not surprised. Somehow he'd known. How was that possible?

And that was way too much to spill to Abby Foster tonight.

"Whatever . . . whoever it is, it's not angry at me. That's just it, Tom." She hugged her arms around herself. "Something was left unfinished here. I know it and it makes me uneasy sometimes."

"What was left unfinished?"

"I don't know. I think it has something to do with Edith, though. When I look up the stairs, it feels so heavy, so . . . I don't know how to explain it. It's going to sound crazy . . ."

He stepped forward, a bit relieved. It was no secret that Edith Foster had died after taking a fall down those stairs. "You do know Edith fell, right? I bet it's just knowing how she died that makes them seem kind of . . ."

Her wide eyes met his, utterly earnest. "Sinister?"

He swallowed.

"What if she didn't fall? What if she was pushed?"

"Oh, Abby . . ."

And yet there was that dark, heavy feeling again. God, she was putting ideas in *his* head now. This was what came from being brought up around a family of superstitious fishermen. He could tell himself it was utter nonsense until the cows came home. And there would still be a part of him that would believe.

"I felt it before I ever knew the story. That very first afternoon before you showed up. I got the oddest sensation when I stood at the bottom and looked up. Besides . . ."

She stopped, shook her head. "Never mind."

He frowned. This was really bothering her. "No, what? Besides what?"

She took a deep breath and met his gaze. "I've seen her, Tom. That day we were in the basement. I know it was her because she looked just like her picture in the dining room."

"You've had too much to drink," he said gently, trying to put her off, freaked out a little bit because he actually believed her. He'd been just as glad to get out of the basement as she'd been; there'd been a cold, odd feeling to it that he couldn't explain. "And you have an overactive imagination."

"Maybe." She put her hands together. "I thought maybe it's because . . . because I'm lonely and this place is so empty. That I don't have any family so I'm coming up with stuff in my head to make connections that aren't there."

Tom was on good terms with loneliness. He knew how to be a recluse with the best of them, but it didn't usually involve conjuring up dead relatives. It was good Abby went to Jess's tonight no matter what the outcome. "You just need to get out more," he suggested.

Her gaze dropped. "I'm not really good at that. I'm sort of . . . introverted. I'm okay once I get somewhere but nervous about going in the first place. I fake it and smile a lot, but I don't tend to open up easily."

"You seem to be doing okay tonight," he observed.

"That might be the wine talking." Her smile was sideways, and he couldn't help but smile back. She was probably right.

"So that's what you got into."

"Jess had a pinot noir that was really good. It was such a fun evening . . ." She laughed a little. "Next time I go to a class I'll make sure I have the number for the cab before I leave."

He nearly said not to worry, he could always come to get her, but bit his tongue. He really should go rather than stand here like an idiot. "You going to be okay now?"

She nodded. "I think so. It's just the dark. The worst part is going up the stairs, knowing they're dark at the top."

"I can put in a three-way switch so you can turn the hall light on from the bottom and vice versa."

"Really?"

"Of course."

"I'd like that."

"I'll get what I need from the hardware store and put it in right away. It won't take long to do." Not like there wasn't already lots of work, but it was a small job. He could bump it up the priority list.

Silence fell between them, while something else

seemed to fill the space that their words had occupied. Tom put his hands in his jeans pockets. "I should go . . ." And yet he made no move to leave.

She shook her head, making a wave of hair slide across her shoulder. "Yes, you have an early start tomorrow."

"Yeah." The word came out strangely husky, and his gaze fixated on the way a solitary curl kissed the hollow of her neck.

"Tom?"

"Hmm?"

She ran her tongue over her lips. "You really have to stop looking at me like that now."

"Like what?" How had she gotten so close to him? All he'd have to do is reach out and his hand would be on the soft curve of her waist. His gaze dropped to her lips, her lipstick long gone, but the natural color didn't need it. They looked soft and pink and as he stared at them she caught her bottom lip between her teeth.

She was nervous.

She was artless.

He took one step closer, so close he was enveloped in that citrusy-floral scent again, close enough he felt the silky whisper of her blouse against his fingers. When had he reached for her? When had she tilted her face up to his, her chest rising and falling as her breath quickened? Something he hadn't felt in a long, long time began to burn inside him. Not just curiosity. Not just desire. But satisfaction. A longing for it, a taste of it, as her pupils widened and the air around them stilled, waiting.

Abby Foster turned him on in a way he hadn't been turned on in months. He didn't want to dissect how long exactly. He wanted to be in the moment too badly, to stop thinking about everything that had gone wrong and simply feel what it was like to hold a woman again. A woman who had no knowledge of Erin or his past. Someone who took him at face value, rather than the way the women of Jewell Cove saw him. Pathetic and tragic, hung up on a dead woman . . .

He shoved the thought out of his brain as Abby's top teeth released her lip, making the soft flesh slide into fullness once more. Slowly, excruciatingly slowly, he closed the gap between them, until their breath mingled and her lips were only a fraction of an inch away from his.

"Tom," she whispered. He heard the tremor in it. It was as much a plea as a protest. He moved the final half-inch and touched his lips to hers.

Her mouth was slightly parted, soft and warm, with the tart bite of the wine still on her lips. He spread his hand on the small of her back, pulling her closer until their bodies brushed.

But it wasn't until she sighed and melted against him that he realized he'd made a big miscalculation.

Abigail Foster was far more than he'd bargained for.

# CHAPTER 10

Abby's body trembled as Tom stepped closer. She watched, fascinated, as his gaze dropped to her lips. Like a man who was about to kiss her. And God help her, every nerve ending in her body was electrified, watching his black eyes settle on her mouth with delicious intent.

"Tom," she whispered, longing to taste him, terrified at the same time. The wine was making everything fuzzy, it had to be. But even Abby was aware of the wistful sound of his name as it brushed the quiet air in the hall.

And Tom answered by closing the final distance.

He touched her mouth with his—gently, softly, lightly exploring as his arm came around her and pulled her closer to his body. But then his mouth opened more, deepening the kiss, and she caught the flavor of him as their tongues touched. Nothing had ever felt this good. Tom was a world away from the pain of her past, a brand-new page and she could write upon it whatever she wanted.

And what she wanted was a sweet, hot, magnificent kiss. And she wanted it from Tom Arseneault.

So she slid her hand behind his head, into the soft, dark strands of his hair, and pulled him down to meet the kiss equally while her body pressed against the hard planes of his.

Every square inch where their bodies touched came alive and the kiss took on a life of its own, a hot, demanding energy that felt glorious. A moan of pleasure sounded in the back of her throat and Tom's hands tightened in response. With pressure on her arms, he turned them around and she found herself against the wall, pinned between it and his gorgeous body. Willingly trapped as his hips pressed persuasively against her pelvis.

Any time now common sense would kick in, wouldn't it? He was getting too close, too . . . She couldn't think straight. As his jeans brushed against hers, all she could feel was need. Want.

His fingers ran up her arm, twisting in the broad strap of her blouse, shifting it off her shoulder to reveal the skin beneath. She should stop him. Stop this before it went too far, but it felt too good, was too unexpected to say good-bye to it yet. But it wasn't until that same hand grazed her ribs and slid up over the hard, pebbled tip of her breast that she caught her breath and felt the electric tingle of desire dart to her core, like a thread pulled tight.

"Oh, Tom," she whispered, tilting her head back in surrender as he kissed her neck. "Please don't stop."

He hesitated, his hand stilling on the side of her breast, and the thread of passion cooled, shifting into awkwardness.

She should have kept her mouth shut. Heat rushed to her cheeks. She should never have let herself get carried away. Never said his name. His fingers pushed the straps of her blouse back up over her shoulders and she no longer felt his lips on her skin. She closed her eyes, embarrassed by how quickly she'd lost control. She must have sounded so needy, sighing his name like that. Probably because she was.

"I should go," he said, taking a step back, his voice definitively cooler. "I should never have done that. I work for you."

It was a dumb excuse without an ounce of truth in it. She wasn't really his boss, after all. Her common sense hadn't intruded, but his clearly had.

The alcohol-fueled fuzziness in her brain was long gone. She couldn't blame this on the wine or anything else. What she could do, though, was try to salvage a little of her pride.

"I shouldn't have, either," she murmured, straightening her blouse and trying desperately to school her features. She'd never had much of a poker face. "I guess the pinot was better than I thought."

"You're a really attractive woman, Abby, but starting anything would be a mistake. It wouldn't be fair to you."

That was almost as good of a line as *It's not you, it's me.* For some reason it made her angry. Maybe because the dismissal came so easily to his lips. "Why? Because you're on the rebound?" She asked the question before she could help herself.

The change in his face was so instant that it made her step backward. Surprise, pain, anger. "Who told you that?" he asked sharply, his black eyes glinting at her in the bright light of the hall.

She hadn't realized one simple question could cause such an instant reaction. "Jess might have said something . . ."

"Jess should mind her own business," he growled, running a hand through his hair.

If she'd had any doubts about Jess's claim that he was suffering a broken heart, his reaction erased them completely. Whoever had hurt him had done a good job. "I think we've established that," she said quietly.

Despite the kiss and the fact that he'd started it, it was

abundantly clear that he wasn't *really* interested in her. She certainly didn't want to be some charity case at a family function, a pity-the-new-girl sort of hanger-on. "Listen, about Saturday . . ." She swallowed past the lump of awkwardness in her throat. "You can just drop me off here after we finish with the samples."

The fire in his eyes mellowed and he blew out a breath. "Don't be silly."

"I'm not being silly. You're not interested in this— whatever this is—and Jess is interfering, though why, I have no idea. Rather than be uncomfortable . . . I don't want to be a pity date or make things more uncomfortable between us than they already are."

"I didn't say I wasn't interested." His dark eyes burned into hers. "I said it wasn't wise."

She didn't know what to do with that. On one hand it made the butterflies in her stomach start winging around again. On another she'd agreed it was a mistake. She began to chew on her lip again and consciously made herself stop. The truth was, even if she were interested in Tom Arseneault, he was still hung up on someone else. That would only be asking for trouble.

"You're right. It's not the smart thing."

"Now that we've established that, there's no reason why you shouldn't come. It doesn't have to be a date."

"I'm not sure Jess got that memo."

"I'll make sure she understands. I'll remind her that she's the one who invited you." His agitation mellowed as he looked down at her. "If you'd go as my friend, that'd be great. I hate walking into these things alone. Really, Abby, it's me, not you."

She raised an eyebrow. There it was. Double whammy of letdowns tonight, then.

"I know, I know." He had the grace to look sheepish. "Worst cliché in history but it's true. Just because Jess doesn't know how to mind her own business, doesn't mean she wasn't right. I'm not—"

"Interested," Abby finished for him, her voice flat.

He shifted his feet. "Well, clearly I am on some level. I did kiss you."

"Why did you?" She tilted her head and watched his face. He had such an interesting face, a little dark and mysterious but with a glint of good humor and the strong set of stubbornness. How could she not be drawn to him?

The question seemed to send the tension humming between them again. And it wasn't relieved by his answer.

"I don't know. I just looked at you and . . . and I wanted to."

This time she did bite her lip. He'd wanted to kiss her, but was incapable of anything deeper. That spelled trouble in her books. She had to start looking at him as her contractor and not like . . .

Her mouth watered. Not like dessert.

"Come on, Abby, it's a long weekend. It's not right that you end up sitting here by yourself while there's a perfectly good party happening. Don't let Jess's interfering drive you away."

It wouldn't be Jess driving her away. And the truth was that while kissing Tom had been a brilliant experiment on her part, she knew it was nothing more. It wasn't just Tom carrying around a cart of baggage. She was a long way from trusting anyone. From opening up and letting anyone see the real Abby Foster. One kiss wasn't a cure-all.

But if she backed out now, how would it look? It would look like tonight's kiss mattered more to her than to him. She would look like a big ol' chicken.

"Make sure she knows," Abby said. "No matchmaking." She leveled him with a look. "And I'm staying away from the wine."

He chuckled a little. "Fair enough."

"And what I said earlier, about my great-grandmother . . . just forget it, okay? It's a combination of an overactive imagination and too many novels."

"Consider it forgotten."

"Okay. I'll still go on Saturday. Besides, no one but the two of us knows what just happened. We'll tell Jess that you dropped me off and went home. End of story."

"That what happened?" He grinned, and the atmosphere around them eased again.

"Exactly." She smiled back. Dammit, it was bad enough that Tom looked good enough to eat. It wasn't fair that she was starting to *like* him, too. It had been easier to dismiss him when he was boorish and aggravating.

"I should probably get going, then."

"Probably."

She walked him to the door, keeping her hand on the knob as he stopped on the veranda. "Thanks for bringing me home."

"Anytime. If you need anything . . ."

It felt like a polite, empty offer. The kiss still hung between them. No matter what they'd both said, how they'd backed off, the kiss couldn't be taken back.

He disappeared into the dark and moments later his truck started and the headlights came on.

Then he was gone. And when Abby turned around, she caught her breath and pressed her hand to her pounding heart.

It was her. Edith Foster.

Same gray-blue dress, same long hair that touched her shoulders. Same sad, pleading look in her eyes. She was here. Real but not real. Like Abby was seeing her through some sort of filter even though every detail was clear.

Her heart thudded in her throat as she asked clearly, "Edith? What do you want, Edith?"

There was no answer, but Edith turned and walked toward the stairs.

Abby's heart pounded so loudly she could hear it in her ears. When Edith paused at the bottom of the steps and looked back, Abby knew that she expected her to follow. And while Abby was completely freaked out at the fact that she was taking instructions from a ghost, oddly enough she wasn't afraid. She didn't feel threatened in any way. And so, with the fleeting thought that she must be losing her mind, Abby put one foot in front of the other and followed her great-grandmother up the stairs.

On the second floor, Edith paused and looked out the back window toward the outbuilding that had once been the carriage house and, later, a garage. Edith only paused a moment, her fingers against the glass before she turned back to Abby, her face profoundly sad. She then led the way into the bedroom with the smaller room linked to it. Abby was sure now that this room had been for babies. For Marian and Iris. Had the bigger room been Edith's? A nurse's?

Edith paused near one corner of the room and stared at her feet. Then she looked up, directly into Abby's eyes.

And then, just when Abby had been about to repeat her question, the figure melted away.

The room turned cold. Abby's heartbeat was still accelerated and she stared for several seconds at the spot where Edith had been. There was no doubt in her mind now that she was sharing the house with the ghost of her great-grandmother. And she was equally certain that there was something Edith wanted her to do. She wouldn't have led her up here otherwise. But what?

Abby went to the window in the larger bedroom, the one that overlooked the backyard, but with the lights on she could only see her own reflection in the glass. She wasn't calm enough to cut the lights and look into the darkness; considering the strange twist in the evening, who knew what she'd see if she looked out? Shivering, she retraced her steps back to the nursery, taking slow steps until she was in the corner where Edith had stood. Why had she stopped here, in this precise spot? What was she trying to say?

The floor creaked beneath her foot, audible in the complete silence, and Abby looked down at her toes.

Edith had looked down, too.

Abby's pulse started hammering again as she knelt on the floor, feeling along the wide planking. The piece of flooring was shorter here, maybe only three feet long. There was give along its length; it bowed slightly when Abby pressed her hands upon it and she considered trying to take the board up herself.

Tom would kill her, wouldn't he? She couldn't start ripping at original flooring. If she wrecked it, it could never be replaced. And yet there had to be a reason why Edith had stood just here, in this very spot.

She got up from her knees and sighed. This was insane. Besides, it was eleven o'clock at night. Whatever Edith wanted her to find would have to wait. She shook her head and went back down the hall to her room, put on her nightgown and brushed her teeth. No more odd sounds, no more Edith. It was like nothing had ever happened as she crawled beneath the covers.

But she left the downstairs lights on. Just in case. And lay awake for a long time while her imagination ran wild.

Abby woke up with sweat beaded on her brow. The sun was already up, streaming through the window, and she checked her watch—seven-thirty.

Her dream was already slipping away to the fringes of

her mind and her brain scrambled to gather the pieces and keep them whole. It felt important somehow. Edith had been there, and a tall, blond man who had made her laugh. But then Edith had been crying and there'd been another man, a darker man, holding a baby in his arms. Edith was screaming and the man had held the baby out from his body, as if he couldn't stand to hold it closer.

That was when Abby woke up, her limbs stiff with fear. Exasperated, she tried to reach into her mind for more detail. What had happened next? What had she missed? What did it all mean?

The slamming of a truck door jolted her out of remembering. Tom was here already. The dark, oppressive feeling of the dream mingled with the shocking memory of him kissing her last night. She sat up in the bed, the sheets pooling around her hips. Heard him turn the key she'd given him in the lock. Heard the front door shut behind him.

Abby sank back into the pillows, torn between jumping out of bed and still trying desperately to hang on to the tattered bits of the dream. There was something important she needed to remember. She wanted to cling to those last few moments, the last dregs of memory before getting up and facing the day.

Before coming face-to-face with *him*. Her dream finally evaporated from her mind, pushed away by the memory of last night. It was bound to be awkward between them. She could still feel Tom's body against hers, the way he kissed her like she was water and he was a man dying of thirst. It wasn't a big leap to fantasize about what might have come next. The big surprise was knowing she probably wouldn't have stopped him. All she'd been able to think about was getting closer to the hard, hot length of his body.

His boots echoed in the downstairs hall and she was

thrown out of that delicious bit of fantasy as his footsteps sounded on the stairs.

Up the stairs! And she was in her a nightgown!

"Abby?" he called. "You okay?"

Dammit. She was always up before he arrived. Always, ever since the first time he'd seen her sweaty and gross after her run. She made sure she was dressed and had her hair tidied and her teeth brushed. Now her hair was a tangled mess and she had morning breath and . . .

She opened her mouth to call out that she'd be right down, but before she could get out the first word, he appeared in her doorway.

"Um . . . hi." She pulled the sheet up to her chest.

"Hi."

The man wore work boots constantly. Abby realized she was getting quite attached to them. He hadn't shaved this morning and dark stubble shadowed his jaw, and his shirtsleeves were rolled up to the elbow. It would be much easier to not think about him if he'd stop looking so damned appealing.

"You feeling okay? You're always up before I get here. I was worried when you didn't answer."

Curse him for actually looking concerned. "I'm not hungover, if that's what you're asking." She cringed as she heard her sharpish tone. It was the interrupted dream putting her on edge, not a headache or any such symptom.

He grinned, lighting up the room. "You didn't have that much to drink. You were practically sober when I left last night."

Yes, she had been. Which meant that neither could place the blame of what had happened between them on the alcohol.

"I had trouble falling asleep last night, that's all." She'd lain beneath the blankets for a long time, thinking about the floorboard. And the more she thought about it the more she was sure there was something hidden beneath it. Why else would Edith have led her there if there wasn't something important to find?

The awkwardness multiplied in the room and she realized he'd quite understandably misinterpreted what she said. Naturally he'd think it was their kiss that had kept her up. She wondered if she would ever stop sounding like a complete idiot when he was around.

"I'm sorry." He backed out of the doorway and without thinking she leaped from the bed.

"No, it's not what you think." She felt her cheeks heat and pushed on, trying to explain. "It wasn't you, Tom. I mean . . . it doesn't need to be awkward between us, okay?"

And yet here she stood in a cotton nightie that ended several inches above her knees. Awkward was an understatement. She hurried to elaborate. "I found something last night after you left." Ignoring the fact that she was barely half-dressed, she brushed by him. "Come here, and tell me what you think."

She led him into the empty bedroom and went straight to the floorboard. "This is loose, here."

He knelt and felt around the board. "I can tack it back into place. Nothing to lose sleep over." He sounded genuinely puzzled.

"I don't want you to tack it into place. I want you to rip it up."

He stood and gaped at her. "What? Are you crazy?"

"I think there's something underneath it."

"Hopefully not rotted joists," he grumbled.

"I was going to try to do it last night, but I knew that if I wrecked the board it would be wrecking the whole floor."

"You're damned right it would." He frowned. "What makes you think that there's something underneath there?"

She already felt ridiculous for mentioning the whole "house is haunted" thing. If she told him about last night he'd think she was completely out to lunch. She shrugged. "Just a hunch."

"You're willing to chance wrecking this flooring on a hunch? I could never replace it, Abby. Not and have it match. You do understand that, right? If I wreck this one board, it means replacing the whole floor."

She looked up at him and nodded. "Which is why I didn't go looking for a pry bar last night. Will you do it? It won't get ruined if you do it."

He shook his head. "You are the strangest woman I've ever met."

"I know." It wasn't the first time she'd been called odd. She'd spent a good part of her childhood with her head in a book or in the clouds. Oddball came with the territory.

"If I say no, you're going to do it when I'm not here, aren't you?"

She smiled. "Probably. And then you'll be sorry."

He sighed heavily. "All right then. Let me get some things. Why don't you . . ." His gaze ran down the loose material of her nightshirt, which she suddenly realized was quite thin. "Get dressed."

He disappeared out the door and down the stairs. Hurriedly she dressed in a pair of denim shorts and a T-shirt and went to the bathroom to brush her teeth and pull a hair band into her hair. By the time he came back up, she was coming out of the bedroom looking perfectly tidy. The way she should have looked when he'd first arrived.

She waited while Tom used a small pry bar and claw hammer to lift the board, working it a bit at a time to keep from cracking the old wood. Impatient, Abby shifted her weight from side to side, trying to peer into the gap. Finally Tom lifted the other end and the nails let go with a squeak. "All in one piece," he said, relief in his voice.

"And you were right." He looked up, amazement marking his features. "There's something in there."

It was too crazy. Abby knelt beside Tom and watched as he set the plank to one side. A small box was nestled in the gap. Carefully Abby reached in and removed it, kneeling on the bare floor, ignoring how hard the wood felt on her kneecaps.

She lifted the lid on the box.

"Oh, Tom." The first item was a smaller version of the picture that was downstairs on the mantel. Edith and a baby. She turned it over and could still make out the slightly smudged ink on the back. "*Edith and Iris.* Tom, it's my grandmother." She touched the picture reverently. "She's beautiful, isn't she? And look at all that blond hair."

Tom knelt beside her. "What else is in there?"

Abby reached in and took out a lock of fine, pale hair, tied with a thread at each end. "Do you suppose it's Iris's?"

"It could be." He lifted a watch out of the box. "This is very nice."

"It's a man's watch. Elijah's, do you think?" Tom turned it over but there were no markings on it.

He shrugged. "It must be. But why would this stuff all be under the floor?"

Because Edith had wanted to keep it hidden. Abby knew that, but she didn't know why.

At the bottom of the box was a small packet of letters. Aware of the fragile paper, Abby unfolded the first one cautiously. "This one is dated 1943. That was when Elijah was in the Navy." Excitement ran through her words. Had she just found love letters from Elijah to his wife at home? "Listen to this."

She read the letter aloud.

*My dearest Edith,*

*As I sit here belowdecks, my thoughts are of you and how much I hated to leave you. This ship takes me far away from you and Marian, away to another world that seems impossible to imagine. The only thing that keeps me going is knowing that one day this war will be over and, God willing, I will be able to return to your side.*

She looked up and met Tom's gaze. "He did love her."

"Did you think he didn't?"

She shrugged. "I don't know. A few things people have said. A feeling. But this letter . . . it was written by a man who loved her very much."

She looked down and continued reading, her voice soft.

*I know we can't be together. I know how impossible it all seems right now. I have a job to do and so do you. But that doesn't stop me from telling you how much I love you and long to be with you again. You are in my every breath, and in my dreams I hold you in my arms. What we had . . . what we have . . . is too beautiful to be wrong.*

*Stay strong, my love, and when this is over I will see you again. Until then,*

*Always yours,*
*Kristian*

Abby looked up at Tom in confusion. "Kristian? Who on earth is Kristian?"

Tom looked down at the letter and back into her eyes. "Kristian," he said quietly, "is probably the reason this was hidden under the floor."

"Edith was having an affair."

"Looks like."

"But with whom? Who was Kristian?"

"Maybe the rest of the letters will tell you."

Abby sat down on the floor and crossed her legs. Something about the date at the top of the letter kept drawing her attention. In 1943, Elijah came home, just ten months before Iris had been born. Iris. Abby picked up the picture of Edith and the baby hidden with the stash under the floor. The possibility hit her square in the chest. Good God, had Iris been Kristian's daughter and not Elijah's? It would explain so much. And if Elijah had known . . .

Tom sat down beside her and took the letter from her fingers. "This is dated February of '43, and judging by the tone of the letter, it sounds like Edith's affair with this Kristian was already ending. Edith wouldn't have been pregnant with Iris yet, not if Iris was born in 1944. That is what you were thinking, right?"

She nodded, somehow let down. "I guess I let the romantic mystery of it all sweep me away."

"Oh, I don't know." His smile was slightly crooked. "This seems pretty crazy to me. At least you can't say the house is boring. In a place like this, family secrets are almost a given, aren't they?"

She smiled back, somehow relieved that the dates didn't add up.

"Why don't you read the letters in the garden? It's warm out and it'll get you out of the fumes."

"Oh, right. You're starting the painting today." She tucked the box under her arm and pushed herself to her feet. "And I've kept you from it."

"I don't mind. It was kind of exciting. There's a lot of history in these old houses, but most of it gets lost. I still don't know how you knew to look here, though. Heck of a hunch."

"I was walking around, thinking about how to furnish this room, and the board creaked. It kind of felt like there was . . . I don't know, no support under it." She smiled weakly, knowing she was a terrible liar. "What can I say? I read a lot as a kid. I used to dream up stuff like this in my imagination all the time."

She hoped she'd sounded convincing. Because admitting she'd followed Edith up the stairs and into the nursery before she disappeared would not exactly make Abby the picture of perfect mental health.

Tom seemed to accept her explanation as he too got to his feet. "Well, I'd better get to it. I'll get to that switch today, too. Don't want you to always be in the dark."

"Thanks, Tom." She was hugely relieved that things were back to seminormal after last night. While Tom was crazy-attractive and kissed like a devil, she knew deep down that their attraction could only end in heartbreak . . . for her. Even if Tom were on the market, she wasn't looking for a relationship. Relationships were messy, with emotions involved and the potential to be hurt at the end. And this *would* end. She wanted to find out about her family but after that the house was going up for sale. She had no reason to keep it.

Tom replaced the floorboard as Abby went downstairs and made some toast and tea for breakfast. She heard the tapping of his hammer, replacing the nails and locking away the secret compartment, now empty.

She sat in the garden among the tangle of shrubs and rosebushes and sipped her tea. Looking down at the box in her hands, Abby couldn't imagine the meager contents of the box would take too much time to go through.

She picked up the letters and untied the faded ribbon holding them together. The paper was thin but the words were easily discerned. As Abby read the stack, there was no doubt in her mind. Edith had been having an affair.

Each letter was filled with love and tenderness, and the emotions expressed on the written pages made her feel slightly like a voyeur, peeking into private moments.

At last Abby came to the final letter in the box. More worn than the others, the last letter was short and completely devoid of the flowery language Abby had come to associate with Kristian and Edith's romance; the scribbled lines caused her to put down her teacup and a chill washed over her skin despite the heat of the sun.

*I'm coming home. Wait for me,* meine Liebling. *The three of us will finally be together.*

Her brow puckered at the endearment that was written in what she suspected was German. Her gaze skimmed to the top of the page once more as a strange feeling washed over her. It was dated October of 1943.

Ten months before Iris's birth.

# CHAPTER 11

Tom loved the satiny feeling of wood beneath his fingers. It was almost like it was still alive and he treated it that way, deferring to each species' particular characteristics. Right now he was working with a smooth, hard oak, something rugged and timeless. His plans were for an entertainment unit, stained a dark walnut, with doors that would hide away the television and components. When closed, it would resemble a wardrobe and melt into the décor of the library without a problem.

Of course there was a chance she wouldn't want it, in which case he'd maybe sell it. That's what he did with most of his handiwork.

He kept telling himself that, especially when he started to feel rather uncomfortable about the fact that he was making a piece of furniture for *her*. Or when he started examining his motives for doing so. Did he have feelings for Abby? It appeared he did, on some level. He wouldn't have kissed her otherwise. Wouldn't be thinking about her all the time.

Still, it wasn't like he was in love with her. And the piece was as much for the *house* as it was for her, wasn't it?

He'd only ever made furniture for a woman once before, though, and that little fact nagged at him like a black fly bite that needed scratching. He'd been starting out then, learning his craft, and he'd made a coffee table out of pine for Erin. He'd pictured giving it to her and then making end tables to match and putting them in the apartment they would share . . .

He'd been pretty young and naïve back then. And when Erin had married Josh, Tom had taken an axe and found great pleasure in smashing the table to splinters, then burning it on the brush pile.

He frowned, looked at his measuring tape, and then measured again just to be sure before taking the piece of wood to the table saw to cut.

The shrill whine of the saw was fading and the discarded end thrown into a pile when he looked up and saw Rick Sullivan standing in the doorway to his workshop.

"Hey," he said, pushing his safety glasses to the top of his head. "What brings you out here?"

Rick appeared sober for once, and Tom was glad. Everyone in town knew that Rick had struggled since coming back from the Middle East. No one was allowed to hail him as a hero—he'd turn around and walk away from any group or individual who tried to portray him as one. He had a prosthetic where his left hand used to be.

But Rick only needed his right hand to lift a bottle, trying to drown out the demons who chased him. Tom had more patience than most with Rick because he understood how easy it could be to get pulled under when despair took over. That didn't extend to making excuses for him all the time.

Rick came farther inside the shop. "What are you building this time?"

"An entertainment unit. Just getting started on it, though."

"The Foster place must be keeping you busy." Rick picked up a piece of bird's-eye maple and examined it, then put it back down again.

"Pretty busy, yeah. But I still like doing this in my downtime. It . . . calms my brain."

Rick's gaze met his, and understanding flowed between the two of them.

"Thanks for the drive a few weeks ago," Rick offered, putting his right hand in his pocket.

"I didn't mind." Tom wasn't about to deliver a lecture on drinking. He knew if he did, Rick would turn around and walk out.

"We go way back, don't we, Tom?"

There was something in Rick's voice that made Tom pause. He looked over at his friend. Rick had let his hair grow a little after leaving the Marines, losing that jarhead look, and he didn't have the big build of the Arseneault men. Just a shade under six feet, he fit into the "lean and tough" category. Since coming home, he'd lost some of that wiry physicality, but the hard lines in his face remained. He looked like he'd seen far too much for a man his age.

"Way back to first grade." Tom grinned, pulling over a sawhorse and sitting on it. "When Jimmy Dawes cleaned my clock for touching his Spider-Man lunch box and you punched him and told him to leave me alone."

Rick grinned. "Jimmy needed to get over himself. Still does."

Tom laughed. "Pull up a pew, Rick, and tell me what's on your mind."

Rick grabbed a second sawhorse and perched on the seat. "Couple of things. First of all, is it going to be a problem if I come to this shindig your cousin's planning for Saturday night? She said no, but I knew you'd tell me straight."

"If Sarah invited you, she wants you to come."

"It's not Sarah I'm worried about. Jess hates me. And let's face it. You and me—we're friends. Josh and I are friends. Sara invited me to be peacemaker, I think."

"And you're not comfortable with that."

"The whole situation sucks shit, and we both know it. But Josh is . . . was . . . my best friend. I've never taken sides, but . . ."

"I think it's great you want to be there for him, Rick. God knows he won't accept any support from me."

Rick angled him a curious look. "Would you even offer it?"

"I don't know." Tom felt an old, familiar anxiety wind through him. "It's too weird. But I don't hate him, if that's what you're asking. I never did."

Rick nodded. "I know that. I think Josh probably knows that, too."

"Well, he could probably stand to see a friendly face, so I don't see why you shouldn't come. You don't even have to talk to Jess, though why she has a bug up her ass about you is more than I know."

Did Rick's cheeks flush the slightest bit? It was hard to tell with the early summer tan already darkening his face.

"I came for another reason, too," Rick said. He gave a half-smile. "Don't know why I need it because everyone in this town knows me and has since I was in diapers, but I applied for a job with Jack Skillin's charter operation. He wants references."

Tom could understand why. Rick hadn't exactly been a model citizen lately and any employer was taking a risk. It had nothing to do with his disability and everything to do with his very public drinking problem.

"You're asking me for a reference?"

Rick sighed. "Yeah, I am. You're one of the few people who still talks to me in this shit town. And before you say it, yes, I know why that is. I'm trying to get my drinking under control, Tom. I know it's a problem."

"You going to be working the boats?"

Rick huffed out a bitter laugh. "Nope. I get to work the sales shack. But it's something. I've got to do something or I'm gonna go crazy. Besides, working the dock means I'm around if my mom needs me."

*Finally,* Tom thought. He'd felt for a long time that Rick had too much time on his hands. He was like a powder keg waiting for someone to light the fuse, and now he was dealing with his mom's illness on top of everything else. "The drinking thing . . . is that going to be a problem on Saturday?"

"I don't always drink myself stupid," Rick said dryly. "I do know how to have a few and lock it down. I just choose not to most of the time."

Tom wasn't quite sure he believed him, but he was prepared to give Rick the benefit of the doubt, especially if he was finally looking for a job and trying to get his act together. "I'll back you up. You can tell Jack that."

"Thanks, man."

"Yeah, well, life's a hell of a deal, isn't it? We can all use all the help we can get." He got up and took the glasses off the top of his head, putting them on a workbench. "Come on up to the house. I've got a few sodas in the fridge and some leftover pizza from Gino's. We can sit out on the deck and watch the fish jump."

For over an hour they sat on Tom's back deck, feet propped up on the railing as the sun went down and the water of the cove morphed from peachy-violet to gray. They ate Tom's cold pizza, drank Cokes, and said little, letting the quiet night work its magic. Tom's thoughts went from Josh and Erin back to Abby.

Abby was about as different from Erin as she could get. Not just in looks, though there was that, too. She might be paying him to fix her house but she didn't need him. She was independent and more than a little strong-willed. Sweet, but at the same time he got the feeling that she always made her own decisions and didn't let anything stand in her way.

He thought of Erin buckling to parental pressure over the demands of her heart. The idea of the stubborn Abby doing such a thing made him laugh.

"What's so funny?" Rick asked, swilling the last bit of soda from the can.

Tom shrugged. "Nothing, really. Just thinking about people."

"Anyone in particular? That Foster woman, maybe?"

No one ever said Rick was stupid. Tom threw the crust of the last piece of pizza back into the box.

When Tom didn't answer, Rick leaned forward and put his hands on his knees. "Talk around town is that she's fixing that place up to sell it. Doesn't look like she's going to be around for long."

There was an unspoken warning in Rick's words. "Yeah, I'd be stupid to start something there, wouldn't I?"

"Hate to see you get the shaft twice, bro. What about Summer Arnold? She always had eyes for you, you know."

Tom chuckled. "Summer Arnold's not really my type. Maybe it's the nose ring and pink hair."

"Just hate to see you get your hopes up." Rick brushed crust crumbs off his jeans, and Tom noticed the awkward movement of his prosthetic hand. "You already got the crap kicked out of you by love," Rick said. "It's not worth it."

Tom was surprised at the bitterness in Rick's voice, but he couldn't deny the truth in the words. Abby had never made any secret of Jewell Cove being a temporary address. She'd be leaving. If he were a smart man, there'd be no more kisses in the foyer or any other part of that house.

The more he thought about it, the more he realized that making the entertainment unit was a dumb move. Abby certainly wouldn't care less, and after the renos were done, Tom wouldn't have a reason to be in the house again.

As Rick got up and said good-bye, Tom knew that the picnic at Sarah's was the perfect time to establish things as friends . . . no, as business associates. That was all there could ever be between them. He'd only been fooling himself to think otherwise.

Abby had felt a pressing need to find more answers ever since discovering the letters, so she spent one sunny morning in the attic, shoving the boxes and chests she'd already been through to one side of the windowless room. Books, clothes, old bedding . . . most would remain packed away for now until she could decide what to do with them. Some, sadly, were destined for the dump after too many years being shut up in the airless space. Those she put closer to the door, working up a bit of a sweat as the temperature in the attic rose and the physical labor of moving things around heated her up. But there were other boxes that she knew she'd come back to another day—books for the library, clothing to be examined for holes, different knickknacks, shoe boxes of black-and-white photos. Some were family treasures she knew she should keep. She understood now why there'd been pressure to make this place a museum. Besides its age, there were so many antiques and period items from the past that it made sense.

A museum would certainly fill the house with people, but that wasn't what Abby had in mind.

What this place needed was laughter. Friends. *Family.* It needed someone who could take it and make it a home. And that someone wasn't her.

Marian had felt the same way about the house, though,

and while Abby wasn't any closer to solving the mystery of the family split, she was starting to let go of a lot of her resentment. It was hard to hate a woman who had taken this big empty house and filled it with young women who needed her help, though Abby did wonder why Marian had chosen that particular cause. Abby swallowed, remembering how alone she'd felt in the weeks and months after her father's death when she was nine. She'd felt so lost; torn away from her home to live with a mother she barely knew, without her dad and without Gram's love and stability. She and Gram might have grieved together, but her mom hadn't wanted to hear her crying at night. At the time it had been easier to keep all her feelings locked inside.

Abby had longed to have a place where she was welcomed, accepted, understood. Her aunt Marian had provided such a place for girls in trouble, young women shunned because they'd made a mistake in judgment. It had been personal for Marian somehow. Abby could feel it even if she couldn't prove it.

The next stack of boxes were shoved into a far corner of the room and she pulled one down and plopped it on the floor in front of a three-legged stool she'd unearthed. She pulled off the cover and stared at a stack of journals and photographs. This was more like it. Real people, Jewell Cove's heritage in black-and-white. Abby flipped through the pictures first, examining each one with awe. There were some featuring upper-class women in elegant dresses, posing with the rose garden behind them. White tents had been set up for an elaborate garden party—the Fosters were really top-drawer, weren't they?

Another showed a cluster of men standing in front of a ship down at the docks—one of Elijah's shipping fleet, perhaps? There was one of Marian, holding Edith's hand on one side and clutching a bouquet of daisies in her other hand as she stared up at the camera, her dark eyes full of impishness. There were several more of Edith, and Abby touched the photos with trembling fingers drawn to one in particular. Even in the sepia tones, Edith's face seemed to glow as her hand rested on her belly, gently rounded with pregnancy. That had been Iris, Abby thought, pausing over the picture for a moment. Then she put it aside and picked up another.

This one was the household staff, all lined up in the great hall in full uniform. How grand it all looked, with the chandelier and wide, elegant woodwork and their spotless uniforms. The Fosters had maintained quite a staff, even during wartime. Abby counted a cook, kitchen maid, two housemaids, an older man who was out of livery but who had probably been a man-of-all-work or groundskeeper, and a smart-looking chauffeur who was young enough to have been called up and for some reason hadn't been.

His face called to her as she moved the photo in for a closer examination. Knowledge shot into her like a jolt of lightning. Not only was he young enough to have been called up, but the blond hair and cheekbones looked achingly familiar. Maybe it had been a long time, but there was no mistaking it.

He looked like her father.

Her fingers trembled as she stared at the picture. Abby's mind worked furiously through all the facts. The letters she'd found. Edith's affair. The lock of blond hair, the watch . . .

Looking down at the photo still clutched in her hand, it all added up: Elijah wasn't her great-grandfather. Despite the shocking revelation, a warmth and peace seemed to envelop the room, and she looked around, wondering if Edith was watching. Abby didn't see her, but she could feel her nearby, giving her approval. This was the mysterious Kristian. There was no doubt in her mind. Edith had

had an affair with the chauffeur. And Abby's grandmother was the result of that affair.

Her hand started to tremble and she put the photograph down on her lap. The letter he'd written while crossing the ocean . . . he must have finally been called up and gone off to do his patriotic duty. What a scandal it would have been—he was the help and she was married. That final letter in the box—the one that said he was coming home—Edith was going to run away with the chauffeur.

The ripples of that fact washed over her, trickling down into present-day circumstances. It meant that Abby was not an actual Foster at all. And yet here she was, sitting in the attic of the Foster mansion, owner of it all when none of it truly belonged to her. She hadn't a drop of Foster blood in her veins.

Had Marian known?

Was this why Iris had been cut off? Elijah must have found out somehow. Or perhaps he'd taken one look at Iris and had known that the pale-haired, blue-eyed baby couldn't be his. So Elijah had sent Iris away after Edith's death and brought up his only child, Marian. Of course. Elijah wouldn't have wanted to raise his dead wife's bastard. Not many men would, but Abby got the feeling that the stern-looking, uncompromising Elijah would find it particularly repulsive.

The pieces were starting to fit, but the answers only served to pose more questions. Abby went through the box, searching for clues. There were more pictures—bittersweet photos of Iris as a baby, all plump and pink and smiling. Marian and Iris together, Marian holding Iris in her lap, dark hair against light but clearly Marian was smitten with her baby sister. The children with Edith in front of the Christmas tree, a severe-looking Elijah standing behind them and just apart.

That was December of '44. Abby wondered what happened in the months between that and V-E Day, when everything irrevocably changed.

Tom stopped at the door of the storage room and poked his head inside. "Hey, Abby?"

Abby jumped at the sound of his voice. She swiveled on the stool, a hand pressed to her chest. "Whew," she breathed. "You scared me."

"Sorry." He grinned. "I tried calling up, but you didn't hear."

"Was there something you wanted?"

He took a step inside the room. There were boxes everywhere, separated into sections, and one open on the floor in front of her feet. "I'd like to start prepping the kitchen in a day or two, but that means packing up what's there. I thought you'd want to do that yourself so you'd know where things are and can find what you need to eat or whatever."

"Good idea," she replied, collecting the photos on her lap into a neat pile.

"What've you got there?" he asked, leaning forward curiously.

He saw her hesitate. Things hadn't been as awkward as they might have been after their kiss, but they hadn't exactly been comfortable, either. Especially since all he could think about was doing it again.

"Can I trust you?" She perched on the edge of the stool and looked up at him, her eyes wide. "I mean, this is the big-family-secret kind of stuff. Major skeletons in the closet. The kind of thing that would rock the small world of Jewell Cove."

He chuckled a little. "That sounds pretty big. But maybe it's not as big as you think. Our town's been the subject of lots of scandal over the years. Did you know that one of my ancestors on my dad's side was a pirate? He used to sail along the coast pillaging and stealing."

She smiled, clearly intrigued. "You're making that up."

"God's truth. Then he became a privateer during the Civil War. Made a tremendous fortune. Of course, it's long gone now. But there are rumors about there being treasure buried out on Aquteg Island, out past Fiddler's Rock."

She held out the picture, but as he put his fingers on it she hesitated. "Swear to me you won't tell a soul."

"I swear." She let it go and he looked down at the picture. It was a group of people—servants—in the great hall downstairs. "What am I supposed to be looking at?"

"The chauffeur in the back."

Tall, blond, upright bearing, nice livery. "What about him?"

Abby's voice lowered. "He's the spitting image of my father. The hair, the eyes, the shape of the cheekbones, and angle of the jaw are the same. I'm certain that this is Kristian—and that he was my real great-grandfather."

Tom's furrowed his brow. "Wait," he said, meeting her gaze. "The letter you read, the one in the box. It was dated February of '43. If this is really the Kristian from the letter you found—and we're assuming it is—the dates don't add up."

"I read the rest of the letters. The last one said he was coming back for her. It was in October of '43. My grandmother was born ten months after that."

"Wow," Tom said, handing her back the photo. "If you're right, that is quite a skeleton. Great-grandma Edith had an affair with an employee and she had his baby. But are you sure? No offense, but it sounds like a bit of a stretch. It's just a photo."

"Elijah and Edith were both dark-haired. My gram and dad were blond. Besides, it's more than simple coloring. If I showed you a picture, you'd see it. I promise. I'm positive."

She put the photo on top of the others and tucked them back into the box. "You know what this means, right? It means I'm not a true Foster," she said. "This house doesn't belong to me. It belongs to one of Elijah's relatives."

Tom shook his head and knelt in front of her, putting his hand on her knee for balance as he looked into her face. "It belonged to Marian, and Edith's blood runs in both of you. Marian could leave it to whoever she wished, so it is yours. In every sense. You have as much right to it as anyone, and don't you forget it."

Her eyes softened and he swallowed, forcing himself to stay where he was and not lean in the few inches to kiss her.

"Even if that's true, it sure raises a lot of questions." She bit down on her lip. "There are so many blanks. There's nothing after that last letter in 1943. What happened after that? What if Elijah found out the truth? What if . . ." Her voice stopped but the question hung in the air just the same.

"What are you thinking?" he asked.

"What really happened the night she died, Tom?"

"You think it wasn't a simple fall?" He rested back on his heels. An affair was one thing. But murder? He wasn't sure his imagination could stretch that far.

"I don't know what to think. But it would explain that awful feeling I get when I look up at the landing. And it would explain why things feel unfinished."

He let out a breath. His mind told him this was crazy. But for some reason he believed her. Maybe because at times he'd felt it, too—an edgy sort of energy in certain areas of the house.

"Who knows," he finally answered. "Is it possible

Edith's death wasn't accidental? Sure. But, Abby, you can't let what happened in the past drive you crazy worrying and wondering. Nothing can change it now."

After a pause, she put her hand over the top of his. "Thank you."

"For what?"

"For not laughing at me."

His hand rested warmly on the soft denim, her fingers on top of his. The old tension that seemed to tug between them was back.

"I wouldn't laugh at you," he echoed quietly.

"You wouldn't?"

"Of course not."

The moment spun out and it suddenly seemed as if she realized they were touching. She pulled her hand away and avoided looking in his eyes. "Listen, Tom . . . about the other night . . . I know we already talked about it, but let's just forget it happened. I don't want us to be uncomfortable together," she hurried to say. "And you're right. It probably wouldn't be the wisest course to become personally involved."

"Sure," he said, sliding his hand off her knee and standing again.

"I mean, I'm going to be selling this place eventually anyway, right? It would only complicate things."

Of course, who could forget that she was still determined to sell the house and move on? Wasn't it exactly what he'd told himself tons of times? "And I'm just the contractor," he added irritably. It was one thing to think it to himself, but it was another to hear her confirm it. And hell if he didn't hate that she was trying to pull away from him.

"Just the contractor?" She frowned. "When have I ever given you that impression? I would hope that you're my friend, too. Especially since I just unloaded on you."

Friends. They'd never been just friends, not since he'd kissed her in the foyer and realized he was farther along in his grieving process than he'd thought. It was all about Abby. The way she looked, sounded, felt beneath his fingertips. Even as he was telling himself to stay away, he couldn't help but want to touch her, be near her.

But just like Erin, Jewell Cove wasn't good enough for her. At least Abby wasn't tearing him in two by insisting that she loved him and then explaining why she couldn't be with him. She was one hundred percent up front that she was leaving the moment the house was on the market. He should be grateful she was keeping it simple.

Instead he felt like throwing something.

"Friends, sure," he answered.

She smiled sweetly. "Thank you, Tom. For understanding and not making it awkward. For . . . being here this afternoon."

Man, he had to finish this job and get away from this house. It would be the best thing for everyone to put some distance between them. Maybe she could forget about that kiss, but he couldn't.

He turned to leave but when he reached the doorway he turned back. "Abby?"

She looked up, so angelically sweet he had to force a smile. "Remember that the only person who can define you is you. You get to decide who you are, not some secret from the past that happened before you were ever born."

Her eyes brightened. "Thank you, Tom."

"You're welcome."

After he left he could still smell her perfume. The truth was he cared about Abby. She'd trusted him with an innocence that was both endearing and made him want to protect her from anyone who would hurt her—past or present.

It would be easy to fall in love with her, wouldn't it?

And from there get his heart broken all over again. And there was no way in hell he was going to do that.

Maybe the person he had to protect most was himself.

# CHAPTER 12

Josh Collins wouldn't hurt his sister for the world, but the fact that she'd singlehandedly planned the equivalent of a three-ring circus less than a week after his return to town made him want to throttle her.

He'd been in town a few days now but he'd yet to see his family. He'd made excuses like he was tired and he was settling in to his new place but truthfully he just hadn't been up to the hoopla. He knew he couldn't hide away forever, but tonight the last thing he wanted to do was go to a party. This wasn't some grand sort of homecoming or a hero's welcome. He was home because his life had gone down the toilet and he couldn't stand looking at Erin's father every damn day at work and then going home to their empty house at night.

Woo-hoo. Break out the firecrackers.

He'd much rather be boating on the bay right now. He let his mind drift. He'd venture down the coast, stop in one of those quiet inlets and cut the engine. Let the sound of the waves slapping on the hull calm his mind.

Instead he was standing at the top of Sarah's driveway, listening to the sound of music coming from the backyard, the rhythmic beat annoyingly cheerful. Someone laughed, the sound harsh and mocking. He didn't belong here.

But if he didn't show up his sisters and his mother would be breathing down his damned neck and asking if he was okay and was he depressed and had he seen someone and how doctors make the worst patients and he'd explode. Truth was, he wasn't okay. He was grieving. Erin was gone and he'd never be able to make things right. Or take back the things he'd said to her before she left.

So he took a deep breath, squared his shoulders, and started the walk down the driveway, around the corner of the house and into the backyard, carrying a six-pack of beer and a manufactured smile.

The sight of red, white, and blue banners and ribbons nearly wiped it off his face. Shit. They were going for the whole Memorial Day patriotism thing, weren't they? He closed his eyes and gathered himself. This was *Sarah*. She never did anything halfway. Ever. He should have expected she'd go whole hog.

"Josh!"

Jess was the first of his sisters to spot him and she bounced over, her eyes bright and her smile even bigger. "God, you're skinny. Sarah's going to have a field day fattening you up." She gave him a hug and said lightly in his ear, just loud enough for him to hear, "Are you eating enough? Have another muffin. Why don't you come for dinner?"

He laughed despite himself, grateful she was the first. "You sound just like her."

Jess raised an eyebrow. "She mothers everyone."

"Including you?"

"She tries." Jess laughed. "If Sarah had her way, I'd be married with a baby on my hip. Settled down."

Josh's smile faded even though Jess's had stayed pasted on her lips. "In your own good time," he said quietly, and their gazes met. Jess swallowed. Josh felt his fingers clench simply from memory. No one knew what Jess had really been through years ago besides him. Her asshole of an ex, Mike, had been an alcoholic and a mean one, and Josh had taken perverse pleasure in breaking two of the man's ribs as well as his jaw before making it clear that Mike would leave Jewell Cove and never come back.

He didn't blame Jess for being gun-shy.

"Josh!" Sarah had finally noticed him and came rushing up, a can of soda in her hand and a smile that made it hard to stay mad at her. Her cheeks were rosy and her eyes danced as she pulled him into a hug. She stepped back, handed her can to Jess, and grabbed his arms, looking up into his face. "Now you're back where you belong," she stated, satisfaction filling her voice. "I hope you're hungry. You're thin as a rail."

Josh rolled his eyes at Jess over Sarah's shoulder and Jess gave him a saucy grin in return. Making his way around the group, he shook hands with Mark and hugged the kids and popped the top on a beer while the latest Top 40 songs were cranked out of a stereo. Last in line was his mother, Margaret. Meggie to anyone who really knew her.

Her soft, dark eyes clung to his as she stepped up and put her hand on his face. "Good to have you home," she said simply, but of all the welcomes, it was hers that caught him square in the heart. The look she gave him was sad and understanding and he felt old beyond his years. They both knew what the others didn't. They knew what it was to lose a spouse. To mourn without a body.

"It's good to be home."

"Liar," she said quietly, smiling a little. "But you belong here, and it'll get easier."

"Will it?"

"Yes, it will. It just takes time. Everyone means well,

Josh. Just remember that when you're tempted to blow up at someone, okay?"

He looked down at her. "Me? Blow up?"

"You've got your father's temper."

"And my mother's stubbornness."

She grinned. "Sorry 'bout that. Now, I hope you're hungry. The food's out and the meat's on the barbecue."

He helped himself to a burger and potato salad and a few scallops wrapped in bacon. It wasn't so bad. Sarah's sloping backyard looked over the water and when he started to feel closed in he would watch the way the sun played over the surface as it got lower in the sky. The water always seemed to calm him the way nothing else could. He even made it through catching up with his cousin Bryce without a whole lot of awkwardness, meeting Bryce's wife, Mary, and their baby daughter.

And if he felt a pang watching the three of them together, he ignored it. The past couldn't be changed.

He leaned back in his Adirondack chair when a voice sounded in his ear. "Jesus, wouldja look what the cat dragged in."

The grin on his face was genuine as he tipped back his head and stared up at Rick Sullivan. "Well, goddamn. The standards in this place have gone way down if they let in the likes of you."

"You're tellin' me. Good to see you, soldier."

"Semper fi," Josh said, tipping his bottle in salute. "Pull up a chair, Marine."

Rick grabbed a lawn chair and put it next to Josh. As they gazed out at the water, Rick took a flask out of his denim jacket pocket. Josh tried not to stare as his childhood buddy anchored the flask in the crook of his left elbow and screwed off the cap with his right hand.

Not all of Rick had made it back.

Wordlessly they tipped up their respective bottles and drank.

"Hell of a thing," Rick finally said. There was no need for him to explain. Josh knew that such a statement covered any number of events. Rick's being wounded and losing his hand, Erin not making it back at all, the two of them sitting here now, forever changed yet somehow still the same. A history of several years all leading up to this moment.

"Ain't that the truth," Josh answered.

"You seen Tom yet?"

Josh scowled. "No, thank God."

"Hating him won't bring Erin back."

Josh had told himself that a thousand times. But there were things Rick didn't know. Things that could only be seen by someone on the inside of a relationship.

He didn't answer. Instead they sat watching the sun play over the waves of the bay. Josh was aware of Rick drinking steadily from his flask and something twigged inside him. How was his old friend really coping with being back home, with his disability?

There was a change in the air of the party. Josh couldn't put his finger on it but it felt like things got quieter, like someone was holding their breath. Slowly he turned and saw his cousin for the first time in several years. Since before he'd married Erin. Tom hadn't changed at all. Still big and brawny with his hair a little too long and his face in need of a shave. As boys they'd gotten into their fair share of trouble. There hadn't been this sense of competition. They'd always had each other's backs. But that changed the day Josh had seen Erin laughing up at something Tom said, her face glowing as if Tom had hung the moon and stars. Tom had looked like he hadn't a care in the world while Josh was burdened with trying to deal with the grief of losing his dad, being the new head of the family, finishing school, and being in the service.

For once he'd wanted something to come as easily for him as it had for good ol' Tom.

But it had ceased to be about Tom when he'd actually gotten to know Erin. He'd lost the chip on his shoulder and fallen head over heels in love with her. For a long time he'd considered what happened more his fault than Tom's. He wasn't proud of himself for stealing Tom's girl. Not even when Erin had insisted it was Josh she wanted to be with. He'd always borne a little bit of guilt—right up until he had proposed and Erin had accepted. And when Tom had stood up in the Rusty Fern and declared to the town of Jewell Cove that Erin was marrying the wrong man, it was the last straw.

Because he'd known, deep down, that despite what Erin said, there was something between her and Tom that Josh couldn't compete with. If Tom had really wanted her, he could have had her. Tom always got what he wanted and the thought of losing Erin had made Josh afraid—a weakness he hated.

Tonight Tom wasn't alone. A girl he didn't recognize was beside him, her hand on his arm while the two of them shared a laugh with Jess. She was pretty in an understated sort of way; not Tom's usual type by a long shot. Once again Josh felt like an outsider in his own family.

He got up from his chair, needing to burn some of his pent-up energy, and he found himself at the beer cooler again. He popped the top and took a long drink, trying to cool the resentment running through his veins. But it didn't work. After all that had happened, Josh was here alone, and Tom had a pretty girl on his arm. All the talk of Tom grieving was a pile of horse shit. Erin had only been gone six months.

For a half hour they managed to avoid each other,

though Josh was always aware of Tom and his mystery woman. They got something to eat and found chairs closer to the deck. Tom went to help Mark set up the fireworks while the woman sat and chatted to Bryce and Mary.

Tom had taken Josh's place in the family. And why not? Josh had barely been home since marrying Erin and moving to Hartford. His resentment deepened. The fear of confronting Tom had played a large part in keeping him away. Josh had his pride, after all. Now he wondered if he'd ever belong here again.

Abby had taken ten minutes to change for the party while Tom waited. They'd picked out a granite countertop and gorgeous dark walnut cupboards for the kitchen, and she'd completely fallen in love with some slate-colored ceramic tile. The whole kitchen was going to have a make-over and shopping for samples had been exciting. Right up until the moment she realized it wasn't going to be her kitchen at all. It would belong to whoever bought the house. That time was still a long way away, though. The more she discovered about her family, the more questions popped up. She was still trying to make sense of what she'd already unearthed in the attic. Trying to fit the puzzle pieces together. Something didn't quite add up and she couldn't put her finger on it.

Right now, though, she was in Tom's cousin's backyard, wearing a simple sundress and sandals, a light cardigan over her shoulders as the wind off the water cooled the air.

Tom never left her side for the first half hour. It was definitely feeling like a date as she first met his bubbly cousin Sarah, then his aunt Meggie, his parents Pete and Barb, and then a grinning Bryce and Mary and their gorgeous baby. Everyone was friendly and welcoming, but

Abby was on edge just the same. It felt like Tom was going through the motions. He never touched her, his smile seemed fabricated rather than genuine. She met neighbors and family friends, but one introduction wasn't made—not through mingling or as they grabbed something to eat.

Tom had not once spoken to his cousin Josh—the guest of honor. In fact, Abby was fairly certain Tom had avoided crossing paths with his cousin altogether.

She was about to ask him why when he said he was going to help Mark set up the fireworks.

Jess came over and brought her a serving of dessert—little jars filled with sponge cake, strawberries, and whipped cream. "You look like you could use this," she said, handing Abby a spoon.

"I do?"

"You're a little tense. Relax. You're doing fine."

"Jess, this isn't a date . . ."

"Sure it's not." Jess grinned and scooped up some of her shortcake. "Tom's been happier lately," she observed. Abby watched as he and Mark laughed over something as they anchored the fireworks into the dirt. Happier? And Jess thought it had something to do with her? Something warm seemed to run through her veins at the thought, but she tried to tamp it down.

"He's just enjoying working on the house," Abby replied. "We both know I'm just here until the work is done and I can sell it."

"You've decided for sure?" Jess sounded disappointed.

Whether or not she was having any moments of indecision was none of Jess's business; besides, she wasn't certain that Jess wouldn't go and tell everything to her cousin anyway. Perhaps with the best intentions, but Abby wasn't about to say anything that might come back to bite her later. "Well, nothing's written in stone," she replied. "But yeah . . . selling it seems to make the most sense."

After a few moments of silence she looked over at Jess. She was frowning at Josh and another man who was sitting with him. "What's the matter?" Abby asked.

"Nothing. I mean, I know Josh is struggling. I'm just not sure hanging out with Rick Sullivan is the best plan. Sarah was out of her mind to invite him."

Abby supposed she should be relieved that Jess meddled everywhere and not just in her and Tom's business. "Why?"

The wrinkle between Jess's eyebrows grew deeper. "Rick lost his hand overseas. He's dealt with it by drinking. A lot. I'd rather that not happen to Josh."

Abby looked closer. Now that she thought about it, she remembered Rick. He'd been in the Rusty Fern the first night she'd been in town. He'd given the bartender a hard time and Tom had gotten him to leave.

"Maybe she thought Rick would understand. Or that Josh needed a friend."

Jess's dark eyes were worried as they met Abby's. "I'm not convinced that's the sort of friend he needs. Rick's changed a lot, and not for the better."

There wasn't much she could say to that, so she asked the question that had been burning on her mind all evening. "Jess, why hasn't Tom spoken to Josh?"

Jess's face turned deceptively innocent. "What?"

Before Abby could repeat her question, they were joined by Tom's mom and dad, and shortly after, Tom. The words sat on her tongue, harder to hold in the longer the evening went on and still Tom and Josh didn't acknowledge each other. Tom even reached down once and took her hand in his, and for a second a delicious thrill slid up her arm at the contact. But she soon realized there was a tension in his fingers that had nothing to do with holding her hand. Instead of it making her feel closer to him, she felt even more isolated.

Twilight was beginning to settle in and the patio lanterns were casting the first bit of warm glow when Tom leaned over and said in her ear, "Come on, let me show you Sarah's roses. Maybe the garden will give you some ideas for the one at the house."

He led her across the lawn, but it just so happened that their route intersected with Josh as he went to put his empty beer can in a recycle bin.

For a long moment resentment seemed to sizzle, making Abby's tummy churn uneasily as her gaze darted between the two men.

Josh looked Tom in the eye before letting his gaze slide over to Abby. She didn't quite like the way he examined her, from the tips of her toes to the top of her head. Much like Tom had that first day, but this time the mocking stare felt . . . She held in a shudder. Not threatening. But definitely not friendly. Insolent. Tom's fingers flexed over hers and she forced herself to breathe normally. Things were tense enough without her letting Josh get to her. Tom hadn't wanted to come today, she remembered. Jess had insisted. Abby swallowed. They'd all known tonight would be tense, then. And no one had seen fit to warn her she was walking into a viper's nest of family drama. She lifted her chin. Josh would not intimidate *her,* however. That much she could control.

Josh finally looked back at Tom, the mocking smile still playing on his lips.

She heard the strain in Tom's voice as he spoke. "Josh. Welcome home." To her surprise Tom held out his hand. She was impressed with his self-control, considering all the hostility in the air and the fact that it was clear Josh was deliberately trying to provoke Tom.

Josh didn't answer. Instead he drew back and sucker punched Tom in the jaw.

Abby's heart hit her throat the moment that Tom hit the ground. Josh stood above his cousin, his fingers still clenched and his eyes blazing blue fire. In shock, her heart pounding, she knelt down beside a stunned Tom. "Oh, my God, are you okay?"

His black eyes met hers for an instant. "Yeah, I'm okay," he reassured her, sitting up. His hand rubbed the side of his face where Josh's fist had connected with bone. Tom looked up at Josh and his eyes burned with an intensity that was frightening. "The first one was free," he said, with quiet steel underlining the words. "The next one won't be."

Slowly Tom got to his feet. Oh, God, a fistfight? Abby pulled on his arm. "Don't," she whispered hoarsely. "Let's just go."

Meggie rushed up, Tom's parents right on her heels. "Josh! What on earth is going on?"

Josh leaned forward, his fingers still curled in a fist. Another dark-haired man moved in, gripping Josh's arm with one hand. The Rick person Jess didn't like. Better and better.

"I'm settling an old score," he replied to Meggie through gritted teeth, though his gaze never left Tom. "One that should have been settled long ago, right, cousin?"

Abby looked from Josh to Tom. An old score? What on earth?

"The score was settled," Tom answered tightly. "And you damn well know it. You won. Let it go, Josh. It makes no difference now."

He sounded so tired. So weary, and Abby was suddenly aware of the resigned expressions of everyone around them. Like they'd all expected the explosion. Tom turned to her. "Come on, let's get out of here." He took her hand

and to her relief started to walk away. The last thing she wanted was for him to get in some brawl and ruin Josh's homecoming—something that apparently meant a great deal to the rest of his family.

But Josh wasn't as willing to let it go.

"Asshole."

Tom's fingers tightened around hers for a moment. "Sorry," he murmured, before turning back to face his cousin. Oh, God, was Tom seriously going to hit him back?

But Tom only lashed out with words. "She's dead, Josh. It doesn't matter anymore. None of it matters anymore." Abby heard Tom's voice break on the last words and dread trickled down her limbs. *She?* This was over a woman?

"I damn well know she's dead!" Josh yelled, his voice echoing through the yard. Everything was still except for the music, which sounded incredibly out of place now. "She was my wife!"

Abby heard the anguish in the words and instantly felt sorry for Josh. How could she not sympathize with someone in such pain? But then she looked at Tom and a heavy feeling settled in her chest. His expression was no less tortured. Not just any woman—they were fighting over *Josh's wife*.

"Yes," Tom replied, his voice hoarse. "She was. She was your wife. She chose *you*. You can stop hating me for it now."

This, then, was the woman who had broken Tom's heart, the reason why he didn't date, the reason why he didn't get along with his cousin anymore. The woman who'd married someone else. She was still absorbing the information when Tom turned to her, his face utterly contrite despite the redness spreading along his jaw. "I'm sorry about this. We shouldn't have come."

"Oh, come on, Tom. Aren't you going to introduce me to your pretty friend?"

Josh's words were snarky, a deliberate taunt to set Tom off again. Something rebelled within Abby. Why had Tom brought her here? He had to know it wasn't going to go well. He'd been on edge all day. Even in Portland he'd been distracted. And right now she was feeling like she was nothing more to Tom than a statement. Like her being with Tom was his way of rubbing it in Josh's face. Josh was alone and Tom wasn't. And Josh was falling for it. It was easy to tell he was spoiling for a drag-out fight.

Anger burned. She refused to be used—by either of them.

She stepped up and held out her hand even though her heart was pounding. "Hello, Josh, I'm Abby Foster."

She kept her hand between them as she raised her eyebrows, challenging him. Someone had to have some common sense and it wasn't these two . . . boys.

He finally shook it. "Miss Foster." His cheeks even colored a little. The schoolteacher in her made her want to give them both a good dressing-down, but instead she withdrew her fingers from his and turned back to Tom. "I think I'd like to go now," she stated.

"I'll drive you home."

"No need. I can find my way back just fine. After all, I hear Jewell Cove has a fine taxi service." Her accusing gaze slid from Tom's face over to Jess. At least Jess had the grace to blush and look away.

"I'll drive you home," he repeated, stronger this time, and she knew better than to argue the point right now. One scene tonight was enough.

She turned her back on Josh and kept her eyes straight ahead, trying desperately to ignore the curious stares of Tom's extended family. When Tom's hand settled lightly at the small of her back, she had the urge to arch away from it. At the back gate Jess rushed up, her dark eyes wide with worry. "Tom, Abby, I'm so sorry. I guess we thought Josh would be on better behavior."

The apology didn't help. Abby felt angrier with each passing second. Angry and hurt. Jess had been so kind before. And Tom . . . she swallowed. In a short few weeks Tom had been her mainstay here in town. He was the only one she'd told about the house and her family and . . .

She blinked back the sting of tears. She'd *trusted* him. Both of them. She'd considered them friends. But friends didn't set up friends like that.

She turned on Jess. "You ambushed me," she whispered stridently so the rest of the family wouldn't hear. "You *used* me. You knew from the moment you invited me that afternoon in your store that this would happen."

"It wasn't supposed to be like that," Jess insisted. "Honestly, Abby. We just thought that if Tom brought someone, if Josh could just see it wasn't all about Erin anymore . . ." Jess looked genuinely distressed. "We thought it would make things easier. We never thought he'd punch Tom."

Tom took a step forward. "We?"

Jess's cheeks colored. "Well, um . . ."

"You and Aunt Meggie and Sarah, right? God, when will you three start minding your own business?"

Jess lifted her chin. "This feud between you two is ridiculous. It made sense that if he saw you moving on, maybe he'd stop being so angry about it."

Once again they were talking like Abby wasn't even there. She cleared her throat. "Know what? A heads-up would have been nice. Thanks a lot. Both of you."

Before either of them could answer, she strode off in the direction of Tom's truck.

He followed behind her, and she was already inside with her seat belt on when Tom climbed in behind the wheel. "Abby, I—"

"Just take me home," she interrupted coldly.

"But I want to explain."

She turned her head and stared at him as he pulled away from the curb. "Explain? You don't need to explain. The broken heart you nurse so well? It was because of your cousin's wife. And rather than let me in on what was going on and perhaps ask for a friend to go with you to-night for moral support, you played me. You acted like it was a date, being all nice and holding my hand and show-ing me the rosebushes—" Her voice broke off as she real-ized how foolish she sounded. She inhaled sharply. "When it was really just you rubbing me in your cousin's face."

He rested his hands on the wheel as he faced her. She'd never seen his face so dark and angry, not even the time he'd shoved his foot through her veranda floor. "So what's really bugging you, huh? That I used you or that it wasn't really a date?"

If they hadn't been sitting in a moving vehicle she might have slugged him herself. Had she wanted it to be a real date? Perhaps on some level she had. Otherwise she wouldn't have fussed so much with her clothes and she wouldn't have felt this queer curling through her stomach every time he touched her at the barbecue, even casually.

But that paled in comparison to this. "Don't take that tack with me, Tom Arseneault. I was set up and you damn well know it! You *used* me."

"Look," he tried to explain as they left the town behind them. "I didn't know Josh was still that angry. I know Jess is a meddler but I can't be mad at her. I had the same thought, which is why I went along with it. If you went with me, it would show Josh that I . . ." His fingers gripped the wheel tightly. "You know. That I've moved on."

"You can't even say it without hesitating because you know it would be a lie. You haven't moved on at all, have you? I'm not your girlfriend. You just wanted it to look that way." She made a sound of disgust in her throat.

" 'Meet new people,' my ass. You're just as bad as Jess. I thought you were my friends."

Oh, how pathetic and high schoolish that sounded but it was true. Since coming to Jewell Cove she'd made a few connections but it was Jess and Tom with whom she'd clicked.

"We are."

"No you're not." She stared out the window. "You're my contractor. A friend would have explained what I would be walking into, would have asked for a wingman. A friend would have been honest and given me the choice."

And that, she realized, was the thing with Tom. If he'd just come out and said what he wanted, what he meant, it would have been fine. It was like when he wanted the job. Once he'd explained that working on the house would be a dream come true, she'd been convinced.

But that wasn't his way. He didn't like showing his hand and she didn't like being manipulated.

"You can let me out here," she stated, as he slowed and turned the corner onto Foster Lane.

"I'll drive you in," he answered.

"No, really. I want to walk. Stop the truck, Tom."

For once he did exactly what she asked, stopping and putting it in park.

"Abby, I am sorry. Whether you believe me or not, I am."

She swallowed thickly. "Okay. Fine."

"Are we okay?"

There was no "we." The kiss the other night—had he been thinking about Erin then, too? Was he still grieving for her? He must be. His words hadn't been devoid of emotion tonight. She'd heard the voice crack. Wrong or right, the woman he'd loved had died. She felt herself start to soften just a little bit. But only a little. She was still really angry. And disappointed, she realized. In him. She truly hadn't realized how much she'd started to trust him until he'd given her a reason not to. And that was her mistake, wasn't it?

"Yeah, we're okay," she relented, her hand on the door handle.

There was a minute of uncomfortable silence. Abby opened the door and grabbed her purse, moving to get out.

"Look," he said, "I'm going to start stripping all the downstairs floors on Monday. It's going to get really dusty for a few days. I just wanted to give you the heads-up."

So that was it, then. No more explanation about Erin. No more anything. Back to the house again. Their one safe topic of conversation. For some reason it made her want to cry, but she wouldn't. She'd learned her lesson.

She made a quick decision. "I think I'll head back to Halifax, then. It'll be hard to move through the house when the entire downstairs is unusable, and I don't want to stay at the motel again."

"How long will you be gone?"

The truck idled and she felt Tom's gaze on her face. He actually sounded a little panicked at the thought of her leaving. How long? There was no question of her not coming back; there were too many questions she wanted answered.

But getting away for a few days sounded like a good idea, too. She wasn't running away, she told herself. It was just breathing room to let the dust settle. To put a little distance between her and Tom and let her get her head on right again.

"A week. Maybe two. You have my cell number if you need anything with regard to the house."

Which made it perfectly clear that their relationship— for lack of a better word—was back on strictly business terms.

"Abby . . . don't go because you're mad. I'm sorry I didn't tell you what you were getting into. We *are* friends. I made a mistake, that's all."

"I'm going because I have business to tend to." Which was a lie and they both knew it. She hadn't had any plans to leave until the last five minutes. And he had to go and make it even harder than it already was. When had she started to get so attached to this place?

She got out and slammed the truck door shut. He rolled down the window. "Hey, Abby?"

She looked up into the cab and felt that same little jolt of electricity she felt every time their eyes met. She hated that feeling. It made her feel weak and vulnerable.

"Will you text me when you get there? It's a really long drive. Just so I know you got there okay."

She nodded and turned away quickly, taking one step and then another away from the truck so he wouldn't see the sudden tears in her eyes before she resolutely blinked them away.

Tom had disappointed her tonight. Bitterly. So damn him. Damn him for doing that and then acting like he cared. There hadn't been anyone to care whether she came or went for so long. And she didn't want to rely on him. If there'd been any doubts, tonight had erased them all. He wasn't over Erin. And she couldn't have feelings for a man who didn't respect her enough to shoot straight and be honest. It wasn't much to ask.

Putting some distance between them was the best idea she'd had all week.

# CHAPTER 13

It didn't make sense that a rundown mansion that she'd occupied for less than a month should feel like home, but it did. Abby braked her car partway up the drive and simply looked, marveling at the changes only a few weeks had wrought. The white exterior seemed whiter somehow, perhaps because of the roof, the new black shingles shining in the June sun. The trim around the windows had been painted a creamy tan that mimicked the original colors, and the front columns had been treated to white paint while a darker stain had been applied to the porch floor. Even the overgrown ivy had been trimmed back, and already it looked far healthier. All in all the house was looking rather grand and even a bit welcoming.

Abby let off the brake and drove the remainder of the way to the house, anxious to get inside and see what other changes had taken place while she was gone.

The front lawn was freshly mowed, and as she parked and got out of the car she saw a huge urn of spiky grass, begonias, and trailing lobelia taking up one corner of the floor of the veranda. Climbing the steps, she spied a plastic stake in the planter holding a card. Curious, she plucked it from the holder and opened the tiny envelope.

*Welcome home.*

That was all it said but Abby knew in an instant who'd put it there. Tom. The realization sent something strange curling through her. She hated what he'd done. She'd told herself a hundred times that any fanciful thoughts she'd had about him were over. She supposed the urn was his way of apologizing for the party. A garden planter wasn't exactly romantic, but it was thoughtful and suited the corner perfectly. It was better than flowers. It was . . . personal. What was more disconcerting was that he'd somehow known she'd prefer it. She stared at the card again before tucking it into her pocket, where it rested warmly against the denim of her jeans. He was making it hard for her to stay mad at him.

She'd texted Tom to say she'd be back today, just to make sure that there wasn't any renovation going on that required her to be out of the house. In a way she'd half expected him to be here when she arrived, but this was better.

It gave her time to just be alone with the house. To allow herself to feel whatever it was she felt about it. Fear? No. Even with the unexplained occurrences, there was no fear. There was a sense of restlessness—no surprise there. She usually felt like she had one foot out the door no matter where she lived. She didn't want to stay anywhere too long, or get too attached. At least now she recognized why. She'd had a chance to think about it during her trip home. It was too easy to get emotionally invested. It wasn't worth the heartbreak in the end when things went sideways, which they always did. How many times had she heard promises that this was the last time they'd move, and how many times had she been let down? The simple fact was, throughout her life, the people she'd loved had left her in one way or another. And each time that happened, they took a bit of her with them. She couldn't afford to lose too many pieces.

The time away had reinforced that gut feeling she'd had ever since leaving Halifax. The city simply wasn't home anymore because there was nothing—no one—keeping her there. The whole time she was packing up her apartment, she'd wanted to be back here in Jewell Cove. Even with the mess of feelings she had for Tom, she'd been itching to return. To finish going through the boxes in the attic. To clean out the rose garden and see the flowers blooming again.

This house—the one she'd resented when she'd first arrived, the symbol of the family who'd cast her off—was starting to feel like a home. And she had no idea what she was going to do about that.

She slid the key into the lock and opened the door.

Tom and his crew had been busy.

The floors were absolutely stunning. The richly colored stain was varnished and shone like brand-new, leading into the drawing room and dining room before continuing through the great hall toward the library. The furniture had all been cleaned and placed back in the rooms. It was going to look fabulous when the rugs were back from the cleaners, and with things so close to perfect Abby realized that she'd have hurry up and order new draperies for the windows. With everything being spruced up, the old ones looked shabby now.

One of the tables from the library had been placed in the hall and on the top was a cordless phone sitting on its base. There was a label on the handset with the number written on it. If the phone was hooked up, Abby wondered if she now had Internet. It would be great not to have to use her cell phone for everything or drive into town for Wi-Fi. The data package charges for using her phone were so prohibitive. Not that she had to worry about money right now, but it still seemed exorbitant. She wasn't used to living with disregard for dollars and cents and didn't want to ever be that way, either. Having lots of it didn't mean she should be wasteful.

She took a few minutes to peek through the rest of the downstairs. The chandelier was missing from the hall, but a note beside the phone explained. *Found a guy who can convert the light. It's going to be great!*

Smiling, she tucked the note in her pocket with the floral card and moved on. The new pedestal sink had been installed in the downstairs half bath, the silver-and-gold faucet gleaming beneath a new light fixture. Best of all was the mirror, a rectangle of glass framed by an elegant swirl of what looked like distressed brass. There was a sticky note on the mirror and she leaned closer. *If you don't like it,* it said, *we can take it out.*

She wished she didn't like it, but she did. The old-fashioned elegance fit with the décor perfectly. More than that, the little notes Tom had left behind made it feel like he was right there, giving her a tour. They weren't love notes, but they felt intimate. Damn him. Just when she was determined to steel her heart, he had to go and do something endearing.

The kitchen was a mess; she'd packed everything in boxes and the cupboards had been uninstalled in preparation for the new ones. On the fridge was another sticky: *Sorry for all the mess. It'll be worth it. Promise.*

She crossed the hall to the library, an inexplicable warmth filling her as she stood in the doorway, anxious to see if there was another note for her. Maybe Tom wasn't here this evening but his presence was. It was in everything he'd accomplished in her absence. And he'd made sure of it by leaving his little missives in each room, making it impossible for her to forget that he'd been here, every

day, wandering through her rooms and bringing to life
the plans they'd come up with together. If it was an apology, it was a damn good one. Better than meaningless
words. Tom backed it up with action. It was hard to resist
that.

She swallowed against a lump in her throat. It was odd.
She'd never felt closer to someone, and still so far away,
too. No matter how hard she'd tried, she couldn't rid herself of the knowledge that Tom and Josh had been in love
with the same woman. Erin must have been some woman
to inspire such devotion—such passion—in both men.

Abby wondered what it would be like to have that sort
of female power. She couldn't compete with that, even if
she wanted to. The cold truth was that no one had ever
wanted her that much. No one had fought for her because
she hadn't been worth fighting *for*.

There was one last note in the library, a folded paper
on the sewing table she'd liked so much that very first
day.

*This room isn't finished. I have a surprise for you.*

A surprise? She spun in a circle, taking in the gleaming floor and polished furniture. It really needed a proper
sofa, something that fit the décor but was functional, too.
But what kind of surprise could he mean? They hadn't
talked about anything else.

Well, it wasn't for her to figure out tonight. Right now
she just wanted to crawl into a pair of sleep pants and a
T-shirt and scrounge for something to eat.

She'd changed and shoved her hair into a messy bun
when the phone rang, startling her in the silence. When
she answered it, Jess was on the line.

"You're home," she said. "Tom said you were due back
today."

"I just got back a half hour ago." Abby knew her voice
held a touch of reserve. The last she'd spoken to Jess was

the night of the party. They hadn't left things on nice terms.

"Have you eaten?"

It was nearly eight o'clock at night and she could hear her stomach growling. "Not yet," she admitted.

"Great. How about pizza?" Jess seemed like her usual self, as if nothing awkward had happened at all.

"Jessica, I—"

"If you're calling me Jessica, you're still mad." In contrast to Tom's inability to speak plainly, Jess was incredibly blunt. She was also perfectly sincere. "Honestly, Abby, I'm *really* sorry. We knew Josh was having a hard time but we had no idea he'd still be so angry. He and Tom were super close growing up. We just thought it would help mend fences. Promise."

"You still should have told me. I was so blindsided."

"I know. You're right. We were absolutely wrong to keep you in the dark."

Abby wanted to stay angry, but she knew Jess meant every word. Jess didn't feel the need to babble on, and her quiet agreement acknowledged Abby's rights to her feelings. Abby's hostility melted away. "Thanks for that. But as for pizza, I'm not really up to going out. I'm already in my pajamas. I'm just going to grab something from the freezer."

"No you're not, that's gross." Jess's voice was loud and clear. "Have you got wine?"

"There's probably a bottle kicking around here somewhere."

"I'm bringing pizza to you. Is there anything you don't like?"

"Anchovies," she answered easily, knowing steamroller Jess wasn't going to pay attention to any protests.

"Yuck," Jess answered. "No worries there. Give me half an hour. And don't eat."

She hung up.

Abby went around all the rooms and made sure she had all the notes, tucking them into her purse for safekeeping. The last thing she needed was Jess seeing those bits of paper in Tom's writing. She'd be sure to make something of it. Abby knew she should throw them out, but she secretly wanted to hold on to them. They were the closest thing to love notes she'd ever received. She was still mad at Tom, but the notes had gone a long way toward ameliorating her feelings. She would just have to keep a "fool me once, fool me twice" attitude about it and be smarter, that's all. No more confidences. Definitely no more kisses in the foyer. Or anywhere else.

She found a bottle of pinot noir that she'd stored in the fridge before the crew removed the cupboards. If she took it out now, it would have time to lose some of the chill before they were ready to drink it. Then she wandered for a few minutes, wondering if and when she'd see Edith again. The house had had a face-lift, but there was still a weird feeling as she walked through the rooms. Like someone was waiting.

Forty minutes later Jess pulled into the yard. To Abby's surprise, it turned out that it wasn't just Jess getting out of the car; her sister Sarah had come too, and carried a large pizza box while Jess held a bag which appeared to contain more wine and bags of potato chips. Abby's mouth watered at the sight of junk food. She could afford one night of splurging. Especially since all the cleaning and packing and moving had resulted in the loss of a few unexpected pounds.

"Hope it's okay Sarah came. She doesn't get out of the house much."

"Jess!" Sarah swatted her sister's arm. "Hi, Abby," she said shyly, holding out the pizza box. "We come bearing peace offerings."

Abby smiled. "Not necessary, but welcome just the same. Come on in."

It was the first company she'd had at the house and she felt a little excited as she led them inside and down the hall, feeling like a real hostess. "Holy hell," Jess exclaimed, her head twisted around as she tried to look at everything as they went through. "I've never been in here before. This place is huge."

"You get used to it," Abby replied. "And it looks a lot different today than when I left."

"Yeah?"

Abby took them into the library, the most comfortable room since the kitchen was out of commission. "Oh, yes. The floors weren't even stripped before I left. It looks completely different. There's a new roof and new paint outside, and the downstairs bath is all done. Just hold that a sec, will you?"

She scooted off to the kitchen to get a cloth and dashed back, spreading it on the table to protect it from the heat of the pizza box. "All the dishes are boxed up in the kitchen, but I'm betting that we can find plates and a few wine glasses if we dig a little."

It took a bit of searching but before long they had plates, utensils, and a roll of paper towel to serve as napkins. In lieu of a proper sofa, Abby plopped fat cushions on the floor for them to sit on and opened the box, releasing the tempting scent of dough, tomato sauce, and melted cheese.

"I'm so hungry, I could eat a horse," Sarah said, reaching for the first piece.

"How can you say that and stay the size you are? You just had dinner two hours ago!" Jess glared at her sister as she plopped a slice on her plate. "Come on, Abs, dig in."

Abby took a slice and bit into it. It tasted like pepperoni and cheese and belonging. The way she'd never really belonged before. She'd never had nights with the girls, never felt like she was so intrinsically accepted as she was here with the two sisters. It more than made up for any past transgression.

Sarah shrugged. "It was only chicken and salad. It didn't last long."

"Right. The last time you ate like this you gained forty pounds and had Matt—"

Jess halted and looked over at Sarah. "You're knocked up again?"

Sarah's eyes got huge as Abby watched the two of them. At Sarah's small nod, Jess's smile grew. "And everything's okay?"

"So far. Fourteen weeks," she said, smiling, too.

"What? And you didn't tell me?"

"We wanted to be sure . . . you know."

Jess nodded, her eyes twinkling. "Of course you did. Oh, honey. Congratulations."

Sarah looked over at Abby and explained. "We've been trying for quite a while to get pregnant again."

Jess reached for the wine she'd brought, wielded the corkscrew, and poured wine into two glasses. "No wonder you offered to be the designated driver tonight."

Sarah took a bottle of club soda from the bag containing the chips. "I was going to tell everyone at the party, but it didn't quite work out the way I hoped." She shrugged.

The party, where any announcement would have been upstaged by the Josh and Tom fireworks. "Congratulations," Abby offered, accepting a wine glass. "Sorry your big announcement got wrecked, though."

Sarah poured the soda into her glass. "I should have known better. Just ask Jess. I make all these grand plans but something usually happens to derail them. With Josh and Tom both there, I should have known that would be excitement enough." She scowled. "I really thought they'd be more grown-up about it. I can't believe Josh punched him."

"I can't believe Tom didn't clean his clock in return," Jess said, taking a sip of wine. "Tom's never been one to back down from a fight."

Just what Abby had thought. Unless Tom did feel guilty. "I felt like knocking their heads together, personally."

Jess snickered and Sarah grinned. "See? I knew there was a reason we liked you. We've been saying that for years."

Abby took a sip of the wine Jess had poured. "Does Josh really hate him that much?"

Sarah's and Jess's gazes met then they both looked at Abby. Jess spoke first. "We think Josh is more angry with himself. Or just angry in general and looking for somewhere to put it. Tom's an easy target."

Abby snorted a little. "I would think so. I'd be angry if I were Josh, too."

"Why? Tom didn't do anything wrong. Josh is as much to blame as Tom is."

Abby's lips dropped open at the unequivocal support for their cousin over their brother. "But this Erin . . . she was Josh's wife."

"Yeah, but she was Tom's girl first." Sarah looked sideways at Abby.

The bottom seemed to fall out of Abby's stomach. "What?"

"You didn't know? He didn't tell you?" Jess smacked her forehead with her hand. "No wonder you were still so angry! Our cousin is so stupid. He never comes right out and says what he means anymore."

"I've noticed that," Abby remarked dryly.

"Well, he did get burned. Like the night Erin and Josh

got engaged and he made a fool of himself at the Rusty
Fern. We were all there."

"Erin was dating Tom?"

"Oh, yeah. She was vacationing here with her family
that summer before going off to basic. Tom was young
too, and full of piss and vinegar as our mom would say.
We all knew he was sweet on her. And then Josh came
home from school and swept her off her feet."

"Tom didn't fight for her?"

Sarah wiped her fingers on her paper towel. "He and
Josh had grown up like brothers. Bryce, too. We'd been
through a lot as a family that year. Our dad died in a fishing accident and Josh was a mess. When Tom knew Erin
felt the same way for Josh, he stepped aside. Problem was,
he'd fallen in love with her anyway. I think a part of him
hoped the thing with Josh would burn hot and fast and
flame out. Or that Josh would go back to med school and
that would be the end of it and Erin would come back to
him. Only it didn't work that way. Erin spent Christmas
with our family that year. It was barely four months after
they met, and Josh proposed."

"That's fast."

Jess smiled. "They were happy. But Tom . . . he hadn't
gotten over her. The night of their engagement announcement he got drunk, stood on a table, and told everyone
that Erin was marrying the wrong man. That she could
have done better with him and how he'd had her first anyway. It was quite an uncomfortable few minutes until
Bryce came in and told him to get off the table or he'd
take him to jail, brother or not."

Abby tried to imagine Tom standing on a table in a
drunken state and making that sort of announcement. Not
Tom, who kept his emotions hidden. Who hid behind a
slick exterior of charm without really showing his true

self. Even the night he'd kissed her, he'd hedged. He'd only done it because he wanted to. No deeper explanation. Just an impulse. Abby suspected the closest she'd gotten to seeing the real Tom Arseneault was probably the fire burning in his eyes as he told his cousin the first punch was free.

"That doesn't sound like something Tom would do."

"Oh, the old Tom would. He's changed since then," Sarah confirmed. "Josh and Erin got married and Tom retreated to his cottage out at Fiddler's Rock. We hardly saw him for a long while. We really thought that once they were married, Tom would get over her. But he didn't. He put all his time and energy into his business. Seriously, you're the first woman he's shown any interest in at all. We took it as a good sign."

"Kind of backfired." Abby sipped at the wine. Goodness, Jess really did know how to pick them. First the pinot at her shop and now this lovely bold shiraz. "This is really good, Jess."

"Drink up." She raised her still-full glass. "And cheers. To new friends and new babies."

They touched glasses and laughed, a new comfort level settling in around them. Friends. Twenty-four hours ago Abby wouldn't have thought it. But Jess and Sarah had an easy way about them that was hard to resist for very long.

By nine-thirty the pizza was down to two lonely slices and Jess had opened Abby's bottle of wine. Abby was still on the floor, leaning back against a chair munching on potato chips as she watched the two women with affection. It had been the best evening. She didn't really want it to end. "Know what? I think we should have a pajama party." It was a crazy suggestion. She hadn't had a sleepover since she was twelve years old.

Jess giggled. "I'm on the downhill slide to thirty and

you want to have a slumber party? Are we going to get into your parents' liquor cabinet and sneak out the windows to meet boys?"

Abby grinned. "I think the ship has sailed on the liquor. And sneak out one of those windows and you'll break your legs. Sarah would have to drive us to the hospital."

"We have a doctor in the family. Besides, maybe Josh will take a shine to you, Abby."

"No way. I'm not getting in the middle of those two again."

"In the middle?" Jess put on an innocent look. "But if there's nothing between you and Tom . . ."

"That's what Tom said," Sarah confirmed, waggling her fingers for the chip bag. "Nothing between you at all."

It stung that he'd said that to them and Abby set her lips in annoyance.

Jess leaned closer. "Unless he lied. Look at her, Sarah! She's not saying anything. Come on, Abby, out with it!"

"If that's what Tom said, then it must be right," she hedged. And if she didn't want there to be anything between them, why did his blithe dismissal of their kiss get on her nerves so much?

"You're a terrible liar. Something has happened, hasn't it?"

They both stared at Abby, looking for the juicy details.

"He just kissed me, that's all."

The resulting whoops through the room made her grin crookedly. "Oh, shut up."

"When? Where?"

"The night he drove me home from your candle-making class, and in the foyer," she answered.

"And how was it?"

Sarah swatted Jess on the arm. "You don't have to answer that, Abby."

"Yes she does!" Jess put down her wine glass.

"It was . . . nice," she answered weakly. "But you guys, it was just that one time and neither one of us is in a position to start anything. For one thing, I think I know better than to get hung up on a guy who is still in love with another woman."

"A dead woman."

"Jess!" Sarah swatted her again, her eyes wide.

"Well, she is," Jess answered. "Maybe that's crass but it's true. And until someone comes along that pulls Tom into the land of the living . . ."

"What about Josh?"

"One stubborn man at a time, please."

Abby snorted. "What about *you*, Jess?"

For the first time, the glib, fun-loving expression faded from Jess's face.

"I said something wrong, didn't I? God, what a buzz-kill I am."

Jess looked up, her lips curving just a bit, though her eyes remained distant. "First of all, I can't believe you said 'buzz-kill.' And as for me, well, I got burned too, that's all. I try not to let it make me jaded. I'm just waiting for the right time and the right guy. Until then I get to be Fun Aunt Jess."

"The right guy's out there," Sarah said warmly, squeezing Jess's shoulder.

Abby felt tears spring into her eyes as the emotional moment drew out. Then she laughed and swiped her fingers under her lashes.

"Shit, I think we're drunk, Jess."

They started laughing, even Sarah.

"Please stay," she said to the women. "I haven't had this much fun in . . . never mind how long. Sarah, can't you call Mark and tell him to get the kids off to school tomorrow?"

"He does owe me," she replied. "Jess?"

"Is it really true that each room has a four-poster?"

"Most of them do."

"Then why the hell not?"

They stayed up longer, nibbling on chips and sipping more wine as they chatted. When midnight drew close, Abby led them upstairs to the bedrooms and showed them where things were in the bathroom. She lent them T-shirts to wear as pajamas. When the lights were all out and she was under the covers she let out a contented sigh.

As her eyes drifted closed, she realized something really important.

The house felt happy tonight. The bedrooms deserved to be full and there should be laughter and maybe even tears. She understood now why Marian had chosen to open her home rather than live here alone.

How on earth was she going to bring it back to life?

*Marry Tom and fill it with kids.*

As if.

# Chapter 14

Abby woke when the sun was just beginning to filter through the curtains. She checked her watch—just after six.

Jess and Sarah would still be sleeping, but Abby knew that she was awake for good. Quietly she got up and slipped into shorts and a tank top. She wanted to run the mountain. She'd missed it during her weeks away.

The air was crystal clear as she shut the door behind her and let her muscles warm up as she walked to the end of Foster Lane. Once there she began to jog, drinking in the scent of grass and wildflowers and the unmistakable saltiness of the ocean. On one of her mornings, she'd discovered a path that looped around the summit, bypassing the barn and leading up to where the old Prescott house had been. All that was left now was the stone foundation. It made her a little sad, but it made her feel connected, too. Her family had lived here. She wished she'd had a chance to know them.

The path also afforded a wonderful view of the town below. The rainbow of buildings glowed in the early morning light and Abby could imagine the smell of fresh bread coming from the bakery, almost taste the signature chocolate croissants they made. Nothing went better with a hot latte from the coffee shop next door.

Down the street, Breezes Café would smell like coffee and bacon. Men in hats and sun-bleached T-shirts would be at the marina, preparing their boats and fishing rods for a day on the water. In a few hours the shops would open, the wood-and-screen doors letting in the fresh breeze, clacking against wooden door frames as tourists wandered in and out. The water truck would crawl down Main Street, a local teen working the wand to water the hanging baskets hung on lamp posts.

When had she become so invested in the day-to-day goings-on in this town? She paused at the summit and caught her breath. It wasn't supposed to be this way. She was supposed to remain unemotional, unattached. But there was something about Jewell Cove that spoke to her. She couldn't put her finger on it. Didn't want to. But as she inhaled deeply and started running again, she realized that she was going to miss this place when she left.

She arrived back at the house just after seven, opening the door as quietly as she could so as not to disturb her guests. She needn't have bothered. Sarah and Jess were already up and, from the sounds of it, in her kitchen. She shut the front door and made her way down the hall, following the sound of voices and general shuffling and clanging.

There was a frying pan on the stove and Sarah had a spatula in her hand while Jess was scooping frozen orange juice concentrate from a can straight into glasses.

"Good morning."

Sarah beamed. "Good morning." She looked at Abby and grinned. "Up early, I see."

"I went for a run. I might be a little sweaty."

Jess muttered something unintelligible, but it might

have sounded a little like "people being a mite too cheerful this early in the morning."

"Little hair of the dog, sis?" Sarah waved the wine bottle.

"Don't gloat," Jess grumbled. "You know I'm generally a one-glass-only person. I don't know what came over me."

"I'm entitled to gloat. After six weeks of morning sickness and feeling hungover every day, it's a relief to wake up hungry and not nauseous."

Sarah took the spatula and flipped a perfectly round pancake.

"That smells really good," Abby said.

"You had a bag of mix in your pantry box."

"And I couldn't find a pitcher to mix it in, but I did find a can of this in your freezer." Jess brandished the juice concentrate.

"I'm a terrible host. I should have been here to cook you breakfast, not the other way around."

Sarah laughed. "We're friends now. Friends just make themselves at home."

"Maybe," Abby said, digging around in the dish box for three more plates. "But since you brought pizza last night . . ."

Sarah paused on her way to the fridge. "No one is keeping score, you know."

Abby didn't think she'd ever met anyone more generous than the Collins sisters. She'd already forgiven them for the barbecue incident. Yes, they'd made a mistake by not letting her in on the plan, but their intentions had been good.

"I'm sorry I yelled at you that night," Abby said quietly, knowing they knew exactly which night she was referring to.

"You were entitled." Jess ran water into the glasses and

started stirring. "No need to apologize. Are you still mad at Tom?"

She shrugged. "A bit. I mean, we went there together. If anyone should have explained, it should have been him."

"Especially after . . ." Sarah let the words hang meaningfully.

Lord, she'd told them about the kiss last night, hadn't she? Her face burned as she handed plates around and went in search of forks. "Yes, especially after the whole kiss thing," she answered, her head stuck in cardboard as she dug at the bottom of a different box.

"What whole kiss thing?"

She froze, her fingers on the coveted utensil tray and her butt sticking straight up in the air as his voice came across the kitchen and everything else went silent.

"You're just in time for pancakes," Sarah announced, covering the quiet.

Abby dug herself out of the box and came up with a smile, blowing a stray piece of hair out of her face. "Good morning."

He stood in the doorway with his hands on his hips. He looked good, better than she remembered. Today he wore a dark gray T-shirt with the usual jeans. He was all lean hips and broad shoulders.

"Good morning. To you too, cousins. Surprised to see you here." He addressed them all, but his gaze was glued to Abby, and a little crooked smile on his lips told her he was happy to see her.

"Slumber party," Abby announced cheerfully. "I got back last night."

He looked in the sink and saw the empty wine bottles. "Indeed. No one fit to drive, I assume?"

"Oh, Sarah wasn't drinking. She—"

The startled look on Sarah's face stopped her. "She was, uh, drinking club soda. She planned on driving, but

I convinced them to stay. We were having too much fun."

Sarah hadn't told everyone yet. And since she'd put off making the announcement, Abby knew it was Sarah's news to tell, not hers.

Sarah had recovered and shook her head at Abby. "It's okay," she said. "I might as well start telling people anyway now that the cat's out of the bag." She looked up at Tom. "I'm pregnant."

Abby's heart melted even further as a soft smile spread across Tom's face. He hugged Sarah, lifting her off her feet. "Congratulations. Now you be careful, you hear? It took you long enough to get this way. Don't want to shake anything loose."

"I will, promise. Let me down."

Tom was looking at his cousin with such affection that Abby had to look away for a moment. As much as she didn't want to admit it, hearing the whole story last night about Erin changed things. She got out a fourth plate and fork and handed it to him. "Have a pancake."

Sarah plopped one on his plate and smiled, but Tom held Abby's gaze. "What whole kiss thing?"

Of course he wouldn't let that go. "Oh," she covered, hoping she sounded convincing. "Just a movie we watched last night, that's all."

The gleam in his eyes made her think he wasn't convinced, but she turned away and grabbed her own breakfast. If he didn't believe her, he'd have to prove she was wrong. And blood ties or not, she got the feeling that Sarah and Jess would back her up.

But Tom let the subject go and the four of them took the simple meal out to the sun porch on the back of the house. Abby couldn't help but stare at Tom's arms as he wrestled with the tight windows, easing them up and letting in the early summer air. The chatter was deliberately light and Abby praised the work he'd done in her absence. "I like the mirror. It should stay," she said, sliding a sideways look at him as he cut his pancake with the side of his fork.

"And you don't mind about the chandelier?"

"No, I'm glad you found someone. Does this mean we can start on painting the upstairs now?"

"Yes. We don't have anything else until the cupboards and countertops come in. The painting crew is coming later this morning."

"We should get going so you can get to work," Sarah said, picking up plates.

Breakfast had definitely filled a hole, but Abby knew she'd kill for a cup of coffee and she was out of both grounds and milk. "I'll get that, Sarah." She turned to Tom. "Is there anything you need in town? I know I can't use the kitchen much, but I'd like to get a few things to tide me over. Like coffee."

"I wouldn't say no to coffee," he replied. "I didn't bother with it this morning."

In no time flat the girls had the kitchen tidied and Tom was already covering the furniture in the spare bedroom with sheets and taping off the trim. Abby left at the same time as Jess and Sarah, and when she came back, two more trucks were in the yard. She was a little relieved. After all she'd learned about Tom, she wasn't sure she was ready for one-on-one time. She was still letting all of the information settle so she could make sense of it.

She'd misjudged Tom. He'd done the noble thing and stepped aside when all was said and done. If he'd loved Erin—and he must have—it couldn't have been an easy thing to do.

Abby put on a pot of coffee and gathered up some

gardening materials she'd found in the garage. She poured a cup for herself in an insulated mug and then called into the hall, "Hey, Tom, coffee's on. Help yourself."

She stepped outside into the moist summer air that smelled of grass and leaves and rosebuds.

Marian had tended this garden with love and care. Now it was time for Abby to do the same.

The whole damn day had been torture.

He'd come earlier than the guys today, hoping to catch a few moments alone with Abby. He owed her an apology, after all. And not the half-assed one he'd given her the night of the barbecue. It had been especially clear when she was gone and he was working in her house alone.

He'd missed her.

But instead of a warm and sleepy Abby, he'd found his meddling cousins invading Abby's kitchen like a couple of teenagers. Hell, they'd even had a slumber party. And then his crew had shown up and they'd started painting. He had fans going now, trying to minimize the fumes. George and the boys had already left in their trucks, so the only chance Tom had had all day to speak privately to her was now, when he was finished for the day.

She was still out in the garden.

He stepped outside, wandering around to the side of the house where the pathways meandered, all leading to the lattice arch and the profusion of rosebushes that surrounded it. She'd been busy. The bushes were neatly trimmed back, the deadwood pulled out, and she'd built a brush pile down over the side hill, away from the other trees. She'd pulled so many weeds from the flower beds that her wheelbarrow was rounded with them. Now that the garden was cleaned out, Tom could see the perennials that had withstood the test of time. Too choked to grow properly, the green stalks of lilies, irises, and phlox became clear. A lilac bloomed in one corner of the garden, and along one side she'd pulled away tall grass to let the rhododendrons have their space, their brilliant pink and purple flowers announcing the arrival of early summer.

It was going to be gorgeous when she got it done.

Abby knelt on a foam pad and sat up, stretching out her back, oblivious to him standing there. The stretch exaggerated the curve of her breasts and the long column of her neck, and then she pulled off her glove and rubbed her neck with her fingers, closing her eyes and tilting her head to one side.

Tom thought about rubbing it for her, working out the tight muscles and the kinks. She'd looked at him differently this morning. The last time she'd been so angry. So hurt. Not that he could blame her for that. But this morning it had been different. She'd teased him, acted like nothing had happened. He wondered if he had Jess and Sarah to thank for that. Wondered exactly how much they'd told her about him, and Erin, and Josh, and what a messed-up situation it had been.

While he watched, she put her glove back on and went to work on another patch of weeds. What would he say to her, anyway? How could he explain about Erin without sounding like a complete jerk?

He knew what she thought. That he'd gone after his cousin's wife. That he hadn't was merely a technicality. He'd hovered on the brink, unbearably tempted. Maybe he'd never followed through, but in his mind and in his heart he'd done it a thousand times and he hated himself for it.

He could never explain it all without tarnishing the memory of Erin. She was gone. He'd be damned if he'd put an ounce of the blame on her now.

Abby deserved better. So he turned around and walked away, out of the garden and back to his truck.

The early-summer evening was slow and lazy as he drove into town, past Memorial Square, and parked along the vibrant waterfront. Pockets of people clustered around vendors and storefronts, spilling off the narrow sidewalk onto the plush grass. Someone's rosebushes were blooming nearby and the scent filled the air, mingled with the smell of fresh fish straight off the boat. They were familiar aromas, ones he'd smelled for as long as he could remember. At least some things never changed. Jewell Cove would always be exactly what it was. The tourists would come and go, people would move in and move away, but there was a stasis to it that was strangely comforting.

He'd been inside among the paint fumes all day. The last thing he wanted tonight was to go home to an empty house and cook. A quick meal in the great outdoors sounded too good to pass up.

He put in his order at Battered Up, the canteen next to the charter boat sales shacks. As he waited for fish and chips, he wondered if Rick had gotten the job he'd applied for with Jack Skillin's operation. A boy, probably sixteen or so, was hanging up life vests at Jack's hut, getting ready for the next day's tours. Inside another shed, a middle-aged woman was tallying receipts for the day. This time of year this side of the dock got crammed with tourists looking for a day of deep-sea fishing or whale watching, for a chance to see humpbacks, minkes, or the rare and highly protected right whale.

When Tom had been a teenager, he and Bryce and Josh had gone out of the bay with their dads a lot. They'd packed a lunch and their gear and spent the day on the water, catching pollock and cod and mackerel, getting a glimpse of seals and whales and the odd blue shark or sunfish.

Those had been good times. He missed them, more than he cared to admit.

His order was called and he grabbed packets of ketchup, tartar sauce, and vinegar before searching out a vacant picnic table. He found one on the far side in the shade of a tree, a stone's throw away from the Three Fishermen Art Gallery. The brick-red building had warm beige trim and a scalloped screen door that was a work of art in itself. As Tom cut into his fish, he saw two young women come out carrying bags, their leather sandals slapping on the concrete walk. They were pretty, probably early twenties, with their hair up in the artfully arranged disarray that was a complete mystery to Tom. They looked over at him and smiled, and one of the girls nudged the other with an elbow.

Tom treated them to a polite smile and then looked away.

In months past he might have met their gaze a little more boldly, said hello. Maybe he hadn't officially dated, but he hadn't lived like a monk, either. He'd just been discreet about it.

But now there was no temptation. He thought he might know why and he didn't like it one bit. Abby Foster and her house were supposed to be a good thing for him—professionally. Definitely not a romantic complication.

He finished his meal in silence, but when he got up to put his plate in the nearby garbage can he paused awkwardly, halfway up from his seat at the picnic table. Josh and Jess had been coming his way but now halted as they realized he was there, their hands filled with rounded plates of clams, chips, and coleslaw.

It was bound to happen. In a town this size they were going to run into each other from time to time. They couldn't go on giving each other the silent treatment or throwing punches and accusations. Tom pushed himself away from the table and looked at Jess, then Josh.

"Nice night," he said benignly.

Josh said nothing but Jess's eyes were sympathetic. "It is. I don't have any classes tonight so I thought it would be a good time to grab some dinner with my big brother."

Her free arm was tucked around Josh's.

"How's the pergola working out, Jess?"

"Great. Sure you won't join us, Tom?"

Tom looked at Josh's clenched jaw. There was making an overture and then there was pressing your luck. Josh still hadn't said a word. Things were not going to be forgiven so easily, then. At least he wasn't sniping out insults and no fists were flying. Tom supposed it was progress of a sort. Peaceful coexistence he could live with, he supposed.

"No, thanks, Jess. I've already finished and I've got some work to do at the house. Thanks for the offer, though."

Jess nodded. "Well, when you see Abby tomorrow, tell her I said to drop by the shop any time. We had fun last night. I kind of hope she stays in town, you know?"

Wasn't Jess the cool and brave one, pushing Tom's buttons with one hand while holding the pressure cooker of Josh's resentment with the other. Tom remembered the look on Rick's face a few weeks back and nearly smiled. Maybe someone like Jess was exactly what Rick needed to get him back in line.

"I will," he said, making his legs move. He went to the garbage can and tossed in his paper plate and napkin. But he still had to pass by them and something had to give. Someone had to make the first move.

He looked at his cousin as he came in line with them. "Josh," Tom acknowledged simply.

Josh's lips were a thin, harsh line, but he gave a brief nod. "Tom."

Tom raised a hand in farewell and made his way back to his truck. Oddly enough, the brief exchange with Josh just now bothered him far more than the passionate outburst at the party. Maybe it was remembering those fishing trips they'd taken as boys, but the truth was he missed how things used to be.

Never had it been more clear that nothing would be the same between them again.

# CHAPTER 15

Abby felt the sensitive tingle and tightness before she ever got out of bed. Yesterday's gardening had been a big mistake. Now her lower back ached, the backs of her legs were tight and painful from bending over all day, and a glorious sunburn bloomed on her forehead and cheeks. Her chest, shoulders, and arms were pink too, though not nearly as tender. She pressed her palms to her face and it was hot to the touch.

How could she have been so stupid? It was June, for Pete's sake. She should have slathered on the sunscreen before she'd ever gone outside, and put on a hat.

But she'd been so very aware of Tom that she'd forgotten how to be sensible. And then she'd gotten so wrapped up in the garden work she hadn't thought about it again.

Slowly she crawled out of bed and started a cool shower. The combination of stiff muscles and the tight sunburn made it hurt to move. Using the puff with her soap stung her sensitive skin and she caught her breath as she bent to pick up her towel. She took the stairs slowly, one step at a time, holding on to the rail. Who knew that bending over to pull a few weeds would be so hard on her hamstrings and hips?

She was halfway through her first cup of coffee and putting cream cheese on a bagel when Tom arrived for the day's work. He knocked and then called out when he opened the door, a sequence that had become a habit, she realized. At least today she wasn't still in bed.

"In the kitchen," she called out.

She put the knife in the sink and turned back around as he came through the kitchen doorway.

"Holy hell!" Tom's jaw dropped as he stared at her.

She wanted to crawl into a ball of embarrassment. "Is it that bad?"

He nodded. "I could make jokes about lobster season . . ."

"I forgot sunscreen yesterday."

"You don't say." He stepped forward. "It looks painful, Abby. Are you okay?"

She nodded but there was a lump in her throat, both from his concern and feeling stupid. "I hurt everywhere," she confessed. "My legs and back are killing me from bending over so much and my cheeks feel like they're on fire."

"Do you have any aloe gel? You should put something on it. It's not going to be pretty if it blisters."

She shook her head, mortified at the idea of her face peeling. Even more attractive.

"I might have some spray-on stuff in the truck in the first-aid kit. Hang on."

He disappeared only to return a few moments later with a can of antiseptic spray in his hand. "Here. Hold out your arms. They're not nearly as bad as your face, but you should have something on them."

She held up one arm and watched as his gaze focused

on her skin, spraying a cool layer of mist over the surface.

"Now the other one."

She should insist on doing this herself. But it was too tempting to let Tom take care of her just now. No one had ever really taken care of her in years—except maybe Gram, before she got sick.

He stood back and met her gaze. "What about your . . . neck?"

"It's fine. I think my hair protected it from the worst of the sun," she answered.

But instead he only stepped closer, aiming the nozzle at her collarbone where the slightly pink skin was visible above the collar of her linen shirt. "You silly, silly girl," he said quietly. And he aimed the can and hit her square in the chest with the cold spray.

"Ah!" she cried out at the sharp contrast in temperature. "Hey!"

A wicked grin curled up his cheek. "Did I get it all? How low does it go, Abs?"

Her face and limbs weren't all that was hot. Tom's concern was moving toward teasing now. And his gaze had dropped to the neckline of her top, where the thin linen touched skin. Her breasts tightened under the thin fabric.

"Not *that* low," she managed, trying to sound stern but knowing she was a damned liar. The suggestive tone in his voice was all it took to make her body react.

She wanted to stay angry. Wanted to be sensible about the fact that he came with even more baggage than she did and she shouldn't be looking in his direction. But he made it impossible. He was just too *Tom* for that to happen. It was pointless to deny it.

He laughed, a deep, sexy rumble inside his chest, and sprayed some of the antiseptic into his palm. He rubbed his hands together and then came close, so close that she was forced to back up against the wall where her cup-boards used to be.

He held up his hands and smoothed the palms, his fingers, over the tender skin of her face.

The medicinal smell of the liquid should have killed anything arousing between them. It certainly wasn't some sweet-smelling massage oil or chocolate-flavored body butter . . . good God, where were those ideas coming from? And yet, despite the sharp scent it was his hands, his fingers, which sent her into a slow melt. The way his palms ran from her cheekbones over her jaw, how the tips of his fingers trailed down the curve of her neck.

Like a caress.

A strange look passed over his face, one Abby couldn't decipher, but it was so serious, so conflicted, that her heart did a bump in response.

"I'm sorry," he finally said quietly, his fingers hesitating but remaining lightly on her skin.

She knew he wasn't talking about her sunburn or anything else. He was apologizing for the party, and this time she knew he truly meant it. This time she understood why he'd done it.

"You should have told me," she whispered. "I would have understood, Tom. You let me believe that you'd . . ."

"I know," he said, but still his fingers traced the curve between her neck and shoulder.

"Why?"

His dark gaze met hers. "Because I'm an ass. Because I wanted to forget about Erin and Josh and just pretend to be a guy inviting a girl to a picnic and not feel guilty about it."

"But you didn't deserve what he said. Jess and Sarah told me . . ."

"Jess and Sarah don't know everything, Abby."

Of course they didn't. How could they? Tom kept his

cards close to his chest, didn't he? He wasn't the kind to spill his guts, even to family. She understood that—probably better than he could imagine.

Abby squeezed his arm. "Of course no one knows *everything*. Everybody has their secrets. But you never say what you really mean. It's like you're afraid for people to get too close. Like with the house. Like the party. Why is it so hard to be honest?" In the back of her mind the words "pot calling kettle" echoed, but she ignored them. With Tom she'd always made her wishes crystal clear. Whatever else she'd kept to herself didn't signify.

"I don't know." He swallowed and she saw his Adam's apple bob. "I don't know why it's so hard to be honest with you."

Her heart stuttered. Only with her? "Maybe it makes you feel vulnerable."

"Maybe it does." He took a deep breath and let it out. "What do you want to know?"

They hovered in the moment, a pause that felt like once this moment was over things wouldn't be the same between them. She desperately wanted him to kiss her again. To kiss *her,* not some ghost from his past. And he was waiting for her to say something.

"Were you ever with her after she and Josh hooked up?"

"Define 'with her.' "

Abby swallowed. "Did you sleep with her?"

"No."

Relief flooded her body. She would have thought less of him for that.

"Kiss her?"

His gaze clung to hers. "Yes," he answered, utterly honest and not looking away.

A million questions sprang into her mind. When? Why? How many times? "Is that why Josh is so angry with you?"

"Josh doesn't know about it. And telling him won't accomplish anything now. He's been hurt enough."

It almost sounded like Tom was trying to protect his cousin. Or maybe he was just protecting himself.

She lifted her chin for one last question. "Do you still feel guilty about it?"

"Every damn day."

She should be turning away, avoiding what was bound to be complicated and messy.

"I lied. I have one more question." Her heart seemed to sit in her throat as she licked her suddenly dry lips. "Are you ever going to kiss me again?" she asked softly.

"I shouldn't." He sighed. "I promised myself I wouldn't. You complicate things for me, Abby." Yet even as he said it, Tom's fingers tightened on her shoulder, his head dipping closer to hers. Then, just when she thought she'd surely die of anticipation, he surrendered to the need they were both feeling and kissed her.

He tasted like morning coffee and man and she gave herself up, leaning her head back and opening her mouth wider in surrender. God, but the man knew how to kiss so that her knees turned to jelly. She forgot about her sunburn and how horrible her face must look and the tightness in her legs and pressed her hands to his chest, focusing instead on the feel of hard muscle beneath her palms.

Tom's hands reached behind, cupping her bottom and pulling her close against him, the intimate contact sending a forbidden thrill rippling through her body.

"Won't the other guys be here soon?" she murmured, tilting her head to one side as Tom grazed light kisses down the side of her neck, making goose bumps pop up on her skin.

"Not for another hour or so. They're picking up the paint for the hall and stairway."

"An hour . . ." she whispered, suddenly realizing that

her fingers were playing over his T-shirt while his hips rubbed against hers.

This wasn't just a kiss. This was foreplay.

"An hour," he confirmed roughly.

She slipped her hands beneath his shirt, feeling the warm skin of his back before sliding them over his ribs and across his abs. He was so hard all over, and she let her fingertips explore each ridge and ripple until his breath grew ragged.

"Tom?"

His lips were by her ear and his warm breath sent delicious shivers down her spine as he answered, "Hmmm?"

"Are you thinking about her now?"

She knew the question could halt everything in its tracks. But she had to know. No matter where this led, she did not want to be a stand-in for Erin. She'd rather stop it right now and save herself a boatload of regret.

Tom straightened and gently cupped her cheeks in his palms. "I am not," he answered. "I see you. I want *you*. You're driving me crazy and I don't know what to do about it."

A purely feminine thrill rippled along her spine. "I want you, too," she whispered, shocked to find it was true. Her fingertips played over the sensitive skin of his ribs and down over his hips, then slid beneath the back waistband of his jeans, just an inch or two, but enough to pull him more firmly against her.

"Dammit, Abby." He let her go and reached behind his head for the neck of his T-shirt, pulling it off in one masculine motion that kicked her libido into overdrive.

Summer hadn't been kidding. Shirtless, Tom was a fantastic specimen of perfection.

"It's only fair," he said, his voice somehow rough and silky at the same time as he reached for the buttons of her top. In no time he had it spread open and pushed it off her shoulders. Self-conscious now, she stood before him in cutoff shorts and a white bra. She was so out of practice. So unsure of what to do, wondering if he expected her to make the next move or if he would just take the lead . . .

Tom reached for the cotton and Abby held her breath. Slowly he unclasped it, sliding it off her breasts, revealing her to both his eyes and his hands.

He cupped her breast in his hand, their eyes met, and everything changed.

There was an urgency now, a desperation in both of them, as Tom claimed her lips once more in a scorching kiss. As he explored the inside of her mouth with his tongue, his hand, large and deliciously callused, shaped her breast. She had a fleeting attack of nerves before pleasure wiped all coherent thoughts from her head.

Needing to touch him, Abby experimented by rubbing her hand along the ridge of his zipper. He made a sound in her mouth, the vibration rolling through her like a drug.

That sexy sound only increased the urgency of the moment. Would they do it right here? On the hard tile of the kitchen floor? There was no counter, no table, no nothing other than a TV tray and a patio chair for furniture. Tom's hand slid from her breast to her bottom, pulling her flush against him.

He looked at her again and she reveled in the realization that his eyes were black with desire and hunger and it was all for her. He swept his arm beneath her legs and lifted her into his embrace. Their abandoned clothing lay on the kitchen floor as he took the stairs to her room.

He put her down on the white duvet and untied his boots, shoving them off his feet and leaving them by the bed.

The first hot contact of his mouth on her breast made her cry out. Her eyelids slammed shut as she arched her shoulders, pressing herself more firmly against his lips.

The weight on the mattress changed as he knelt beside her, gently teasing her skin as her heartbeat rocketed through her body, pulsing at sensitive points. His teeth scissored lightly and she gasped, surprised at the pain/pleasure response. But as Tom reached for the button of her shorts, something more crept in, speaking louder than her libido. Doubt. She froze.

"What's wrong?" he asked quietly, his fingers halting on her zipper.

"Nothing," she answered back, and he pushed the zipper down. Slid the shorts over her hips until she was clothed only in the plain bikini panties she'd put on after her shower.

"You're beautiful," he murmured, lying propped up on his elbow. He stroked down her arm with a fingertip, then across her belly to the band of her panties. "So goddamned beautiful."

Oh, God. Her eyelids grew heavy, hypnotized by the soft touch of his hand and huskiness of his voice.

"Abby."

She opened her eyes.

"We can go as slow as you want," he said, making her feel all liquidy and jacked up at the same time. "There's no rush."

"I don't . . . I mean I haven't . . ." She tried to focus on what she was saying rather than the feel of his hand as it slid lower. But her body took over and she arched up to meet his touch. "It's been a while," she breathed.

Which was the understatement of the year.

"For me, too," he said. "Do you want me to stop?"

That he would even ask made her want to weep. Where had this tenderness come from? It had stopped being frantic and hot and was quickly becoming something more. Something . . . important. She shook her head.

Tom slid his fingers to the waistband of her panties and drew them down her legs.

She was completely naked. Shyness overtook her until Tom's gaze settled on hers. "Slowly," he said, his voice low with promise. "It's better slower."

He stood by the bed and took off his jeans but paused to reach inside his wallet for a condom.

Abby's misgivings kicked in again. He said they'd go slow but everything seemed to be moving too fast. Looking up at him, she felt a pang in her chest—this man was someone she could really care about. Someone who had the power to ultimately hurt her. She couldn't do this. She didn't know how to be easygoing about making love, and what else could this be? No promises or commitments had been made. She braced up on her elbows.

"Stop," she whispered. "I was wrong. I thought I could do this, but I can't. I'm sorry."

A muscle ticked in his jaw. She shouldn't have let it get this far. She should have known she wasn't ready. She reached for the blanket at the bottom of the bed and scrambled to cover herself, to feel less naked. It didn't work. Her body was covered but the rest of her felt horribly transparent.

He tucked the condom back into his wallet. Reached for his jeans and pulled them on, but left them unbuttoned so that the tiny vee of skin below his navel was still visible. It was sexy as hell. She still found him irresistible, she realized. Even though she wasn't ready, she wished she was.

"I'm sorry, Tom, it's all . . ." she started.

His brows pulled down in a dark frown. "Why on earth do you keep apologizing?"

"I just . . . I led you on, made you think that . . ."

He cursed and the frown deepened. "Abby, it's fine. If

you're not ready, you're not ready," he said, putting his hands on his hips.

She swallowed, looked up. "I'll just shut up now." She didn't know what else to say. Sex wasn't something Abby took lightly. Her one and only attempt at a casual relationship in the past had left her feeling unsatisfied and empty. She'd awakened in the morning all alone, like she wasn't worth staying for. Abby never wanted to feel that way with Tom. The fact that he seemed that important frightened the hell out of her.

He came closer and sat on the bed. Wordlessly he handed her her discarded sleep shirt from the top of her hamper and she pulled it on, feeling only slightly less exposed beneath the flimsy cotton.

He reached out and tucked a stray piece of hair behind her ear. Gently he touched her cheek. "You are amazing and I'd be a liar if I said I wasn't disappointed. I want to make love to you, Abby."

The delicious heat spread through her limbs again at his words.

"I've made a lot of mistakes," he continued. "I'm not a good man in a lot of ways. But I hope I treat women with respect. I would never force you to do anything you didn't want. It's okay if you're not there yet."

Women. Whether before Erin or after, he'd been with women. Plural. Of course he had. Chances were he didn't place the same monumental importance on sex that she did. He wanted to make love to her but had he thought past that part? Of course not. And neither had she. Nothing had changed. She was still only temporarily in Jewell Cove and they both knew it.

But Tom could do this and walk away more easily than she could. She'd be that girl he met one summer. A pleasant memory. It wasn't like that for her. Sex would always mean something beyond the physical. It had to be about love, not lust. Maybe that made her old-fashioned, but there it was. There was something between her and Tom. It was lust, not love—how could it be? He might be able to walk away in one piece. She wasn't so confident that she could.

"I'm sorry," she murmured. More sorry than he imagined.

"Don't be. I would never want you to feel pressured into something you're not ready for."

He was killing her with his consideration. "Thanks, Tom."

"Don't thank me too much. I could still really use a cold shower."

Their gazes met and the sheepish smile on his face didn't quite reach his eyes. They were still edgy and black and exciting.

He got up and grabbed his boots. "Since I'm not going to use your shower, it's probably a good idea if I get started on the day's work, if that's all right with you."

Feeling awkward, Abby nodded. "Yes, fine. I thought I'd do a little more exploring today, anyway." That was, after all, the reason she'd come back. She wanted to find out what happened to Edith. Who Kristian was. And most of all, what had happened to drive Marian and Iris apart for the rest of their lives. The answers were in this house somewhere, and she kept letting Tom and his family distract her from that purpose.

"Let me know if you discover any deep, dark secrets," he teased. "I'll be in the kitchen. I want it to be completely ready for when the cupboards are delivered."

When she heard him reach the bottom floor she got up and pulled on her shorts and chose a different shirt from her closet, not wanting to go back downstairs as she was. Her hair had come loose from the band, so she went to the bathroom to fix it. When she caught sight of herself in the mirror she was horrified. Her hair stuck out in frizzy bits and her cheeks were terribly red from the burn. Whatever had prompted Tom's response this morning, it sure hadn't been her looks. She was a mess.

Maybe he hadn't really been seeing her. Maybe he'd been thinking about Erin after all.

Or maybe not. Maybe he hadn't cared what she looked like. Maybe he was genuinely, sincerely attracted to her.

She touched her fingertips to her sunburned cheek, remembering the gentle way his fingers had caressed her skin. She'd been the one to put on the brakes. Maybe, just maybe, Tom was having as hard a time getting her off his mind as she was with him.

As the sound of his hammer rang through the house, she frowned. The last thing she needed was to get emotionally attached to anything here in Jewell Cove—including Tom Arseneault. Because when push came to shove, in the end she *was* putting the house up for sale. And she *was* going to leave and go back to her very safe life and her very safe job. The idea of doing anything else was simply too scary.

# CHAPTER 16

*I would have made love to her.*

The knowledge permeated Tom's thoughts over and over again. Each time it struck him like a punch to the solar plexus, stealing his breath. If Abby hadn't put on the brakes he would have kept going, would have felt her soft, hot skin beneath him on the pure white duvet, would have heard her soft moans as he moved inside her.

He'd wanted her that much.

That was a surprise.

An even bigger surprise was realizing that even with the separation of two floors between them, he still did.

The crew showed up with materials, and then Tom sent them out on a rush repair job in town. It left him with too much time to think. As he cut in around the ceiling of the kitchen with his paintbrush, he knew this morning had nothing to do with his feelings for Erin. It had been all Abby. It was her independent streak mixed with her vulnerability, her sharp tongue tempered by sweetness. She wasn't like any woman he'd ever known. It had been her wide eyes and soft lips and the way her scent curled around him. Finally touching her skin had been like putting a match to paper.

The big question was, what was he going to do about it?

A younger, rasher Tom would have said pursue and not thought twice about it. But there was something about Abby that made him pause and take greater care. It was in her eyes this morning when she'd asked him to stop. When she'd said she couldn't go through with it. It occurred to him that Abby was probably keeping secrets of her own, and why shouldn't she? Everyone had a right to their own secrets.

With the edges painted, Tom refilled the paint tray and went to work with the roller, applying the paint in an even white layer over the ceiling. There was also the small matter of Abby's questions this morning about him and Erin. He'd answered honestly, but there were things she didn't know. Things that no one knew. When he'd met Erin he'd been a simple carpenter on a crew while she came from old money. The summer they'd met, Tom had fallen hard, and by the time he realized that he was Erin's chosen form of rebellion against controlling parents, it was too late. He'd already fallen in love with her. And what had started as a way to thumb her nose at her parents had become more for her, too.

She'd gone slumming just to anger her folks, who had kept the leash pulled just a little too tight. In the end, though, the pressure had been too much and Erin had buckled. It was Josh who'd gotten the parental stamp of approval. Josh, the doctor. Josh, more polished and worldly and a much better prospect to parents who settled for nothing but the best for their little girl. They hadn't been crazy about her joining the army, but let it go because in a few years she'd be the respectable wife of a doctor who was in practice with her daddy, rather than scraping by with an ordinary carpenter living in a two-bedroom cottage on the beach.

As much as he'd loved her, it had made Tom angry that she hadn't fought harder for them. He would have given her everything. He could have given them a great life if she'd only been brave enough to take it.

That bitterness had lasted far too long. Tom hated that it had driven a wedge between himself and his cousin. Erin had at least been honest when she came to see him just before she left that September. She'd told Tom that even though she cared for Josh and he looked better on paper, she loved Tom more.

It had been torture. Knowing came with a heavy price—years of loneliness, a half-life—all for nothing. Because the sordid truth was that Erin had come to him one last time, begging him to be with her, and Tom had turned her away.

It was the last time he ever saw her.

His maudlin thoughts were interrupted by a cry coming from the hallway; a desperate, keening sound that made the hairs on the back of his neck stand on end. He put the paint roller down as alarm washed over him. There it was again . . . and he was certain he heard the word "no."

He crossed the kitchen in long strides, heading for the hall, panic making him rush. He saw Abby right away, standing at the top of the landing, weaving unsteadily. Her body gave a strange jerk, her hand slipped on the banister, and she leaned forward almost drunkenly. Heart in his throat, he raced up the steps two at a time and barely caught her as she collapsed. With the weight of her limp in his arms, he started to tremble as consequences ran through his head. If he hadn't been there, she would have tumbled right down the hard wooden stairs clear to

the bottom. A fall down those hardwood steps could kill
a woman . . .

The blood drained from his face. Just like Edith.

Abby opened her eyes, staring at him with such a
stricken look that panic rushed through his limbs. "Shh,"
he comforted her, holding her close, the adrenaline rushing from the residual fear of knowing that a split second
later and she could have been badly hurt. "It's okay. I've
got you, Abby. You're safe."


After wasting fifteen minutes idly pacing her room and
listening to the sounds of Tom working downstairs, Abby
knew she couldn't avoid him forever. This was her house,
he was her contractor. What was she going to do, stay
upstairs all day? She laughed. Yeah, like that would
work. No, what she needed to do was just get it over with,
Abby thought as she gathered her resolve and left her
room, wondering what on earth she was going to say to
Tom. She'd figure it out as she went.

As she reached the open hallway overlooking the
foyer, Abby stumbled and caught herself on the railing.
The moment her hand touched the finished wood, she
was flung into her nightmare, the one she'd had weeks
ago but never finished.

Suddenly another scene came to life before her eyes.
Instead of her gleaming hardwood floors, the hallway
was covered in a dark red carpet from the stairs to the
railing above the foyer. Creamy gold wallpaper replaced
her soothing modern palette. A glance through an open
doorway showed her bedroom, decorated in yellow and
green. It was her house, yet subtly different. Everything
was off.

Especially the air, which smelled of scotch and cigar
smoke, fear and desperation.

The next moment, Abby could feel herself moving toward the stairs, unable to control her motion, the sounds of her breathing loud in her ears. Her heart seized with fear as she made out a figure standing at the banister. What was going on?

And suddenly she was at the top of the stairs. Tears streamed down her cheeks. A terrified child with brown curls stood behind her, eyes wide with terror as she clung to her skirts. On the floor was an open suitcase, clothing scattered over the floor as if the latch had been violently ripped open. And in front of her was a man, his face cold and cruel in the shadows.

*Elijah!* Abby recognized the man from her dreams. Shocked, she tried to say something, anything, but she was frozen, trapped in the scene like she was reliving a memory, only the memory wasn't her own.

She couldn't breathe. Elijah was holding a baby in his hands, a look of violent rage on his face. The baby was strangely silent, not even crying in the chaos crashing around her.

*Please, Elijah, please! Let me have my baby. Let me have Iris!* Abby heard herself say. Only it was Edith's panicked, pleading voice. Thin at first, as if from far away, and then closer, louder, until it screamed in her ears. *I'll do anything, I swear. Just please, give me the baby! Don't take her away from me!*

She reached for Elijah's arm, crying as she begged for him to leave her child unharmed. Insisting that Iris was innocent in all of this and it was her fault.

She moved toward him, hands outstretched, asking for the baby.

And his arm pushed her away as he called her a dirty whore.

That was how it had happened. With weeping and begging and violence. As if in a dream, Abby felt her great-grandmother's pain and desperation as her own. A cry escaped her lips in shock and pain as a hand tightened on her arm, the fingers strong, digging into her flesh, shaking her. Cold rushed through her body, freezing her to the spot, and she felt the world sway. She *was* Edith. And she was the one in danger.

Elijah shoved her away with a thrust of his arm. She heard herself cry out, the dream fading into reality. As Abby felt Edith fall, she was dimly aware of the sound of footsteps rushing toward her as her hand slipped on the mahogany banister and she lost her footing.

An odd buzzing sound filled her ears as she slid down, down, down . . .

A pair of strong arms caught her.

"It's okay. I've got you," she heard Tom say.

When he lowered them to sit on the floor, she began to cry. Abby wasn't sure what had just happened. She only knew that she'd felt things, seen things, heard things, that were shocking and traumatizing and . . .

She was going out of her mind, she thought wildly. This kind of thing didn't really happen. Oh, God . . .

Her body started to shake.

This was how Edith died.

Abby remembered the rage on Elijah's face as he shook his wife. She'd think about the how of what had just happened later. Right now she was simply going to hold on to a warm, full-of-life Tom Arseneault.

"What is it?" he asked gently. "You've got to stop crying. Please, Abs. Please don't cry anymore, it's killing me."

She took a shuddering breath and sniffled. "I'm sorry . . ."

"Don't apologize. Just tell me what's wrong. You nearly fainted just now. I saw you going and—" His voice broke off on a crack of emotion.

"I felt so strange," she whispered, her breath hitching,

"and there was this buzzing in my ears . . . And you caught me. If you hadn't I'd . . ." Her breath hitched and she shuddered. She would have fallen head over heels down those stairs.

"Have you eaten today?"

"I don't remember."

Her head rested in the curve of his neck and his T-shirt was wet from her tears, clinging to the skin of his chest. She pushed away, just a little so she could look into his face. The next words were so hard to say, but she had to tell someone. "Edith was pushed the night she died, Tom. Elijah killed her. He was threatening to send Iris away and they fought. It was terrible. She kept pleading with him and he pushed her and she fell."

"Come on, Abby. There's no way to know that for sure. Not now. It was decades ago." He rubbed her arms with his hands.

Abby swallowed. "I saw it, Tom. I saw it all happen."

Tom froze. "Wait a minute," he said slowly. "Are you saying you saw Edith again?"

Abby nodded her head. "Yes, well, no. I mean, I saw her again. The night of Jess's candle class."

They both remembered what happened that night. And what had happened the next morning. He squeezed her fingers, making her look up at him. His gaze searched hers. "The loose board upstairs. It wasn't a coincidence, was it?"

She shook her head. "No, it wasn't. I saw her, Tom. She took me right up the stairs. Stopped and looked out the back window for a minute and then stood in the very spot where that box was hidden."

"And then what happened?"

"She disappeared." She blinked up at him, uncertain. If she hadn't seen it for herself, she would think she was crazy. Did Tom? Or did he think she was making it all up? If he didn't believe this, he'd never believe what just happened. "You believe me, don't you?"

He rubbed a hand over her hair. Did he believe her? Tom wasn't sure, but he knew Abby and she wasn't crazy and she wasn't a liar. He shrugged. "There's a lot of superstition among fishermen, and I've heard my share of stories. Who am I to say? If you say you saw her, I believe you."

A warmth filled her then, a feeling so wonderful and pure that she nearly cried again. She hadn't expected his unequivocal support.

"That day when we found the box of letters? I'd been dreaming that morning, just before you arrived. I saw bits and pieces of what happened then but couldn't put it all together. But just now, when I touched that railing . . . it was like I was there, too, Tom. *Like I was her.* I can't explain it. It's crazy. But this whole thing is crazy. I just know what I know. And what I know is that Elijah shoved her away and she tumbled down these very stairs."

Her eyes were deep and sad. "No matter what she did, she didn't deserve that. She was a mother to those two babies. She loved them and they had to grow up without her." Abby began to cry again, thinking of her own family, as Tom murmured words of comfort and held her close. She wrapped her arms around his middle, needing his warmth.

"Are you all right now?" Tom's raspy voice was warm in her ear when she'd finally quieted. She didn't want to let go. The moment she did, everything would change. Not in any big, earth-shattering way. But once this moment was gone, it would be gone forever, and she wanted his arms around her just a little longer.

"I'm fine. Sad, but fine."

"You should eat something."

"I will, I promise."

He took a finger and tilted up her chin. "That's not a promise I believe you'll keep. I've been working in the kitchen, remember? I know there's nothing here besides half a box of crackers. Why don't you wash your face and we'll get some fresh air. Find you something in town."

So much had happened that she wasn't sure she could keep her balance let alone feel like showing up in public. "Don't you have work to finish up here first?"

"I'll come back early tomorrow and finish up. Day after that we'll be installing your cupboards. Before you know it, this place will be in tip-top shape."

Abby swallowed. And then there would be no excuse left. She'd have to see a Realtor and put it on the market.

There was something she wanted to do first, though. Especially now.

"Tom, do you know where Edith was buried?"

He nodded. "In the Foster plot in the Jewell Cove cemetery. Elijah's there too, and Marian. It goes right back to Jedediah."

"Would you take me there?"

"Now?"

"Yes, now. I want to take her some roses from Marian's garden. And then I promise I'll eat something."

"I'll take you. Go clean up and I'll pack up here."

"You're sure?"

He nudged her with an elbow. "You seriously think I'm going to let you drive in your state?"

"I'm not exactly helpless."

"No, you are definitely not helpless. In fact, I think you're probably tougher than you realize. Just indulge me. I'll feel better knowing you're safe. After all, what are friends for?" But his eyes were soft with worry as he touched a finger to her cheek.

# Chapter 17

The Jewell Cove Cemetery wasn't actually in the cove at all, but on the outskirts, up a long dirt drive that looked like little more than wheel tracks. A set of wrought-iron gates marked the entrance into a field. It seemed an odd place for a cemetery until Tom explained that there'd once been a church just to the south of it that had burned down sometime in the sixties. The church had been rebuilt closer to town, but the cemetery had stayed.

Abby hopped out of the truck, her hands full of fragrant rosebuds from Marian's garden. The graveyard was definitely out of the way, but it was one of the most peaceful resting spots Abby could imagine. Cushioned by the crest of the hill, the cemetery was free of traffic sounds. There was just the wind through the leaves and grass and the sound of birds in the trees. A mourning dove had already started a plaintive song nearby. If Abby had to pick a place to rest, this would be it.

"Most of the town has relatives in here," Tom said, leading the way through slowly. "My grandparents are over there, as well as their parents and brothers and sisters." He pointed at headstones bearing the Arseneault name. "Over here is the Collins family. Josh's dad, Frank—my uncle. He was a fisherman, lost at sea."

Abby paused. There was a spot for Meggie beside him, her name already there with the date left to be engraved. A love that deep and abiding seemed incomprehensible somehow, and yet right all the same.

"The Foster plot is over here," Tom said quietly, leading her down a worn path. She glanced at headstones along the way—some newer, others so old they were tilting and the engraving was hard to make out. Even though it was off the beaten path, the whole place was well tended, with freshly cut grass trimmed uniformly around the markers. Tom stopped and Abby looked at the headstones. George and Elizabeth. Jedediah and Martha. Robert and Richard, the two sons killed overseas. Abby wondered if there were even bodies there or if the markers had been placed simply in memory. Burton Foster—had he been a cousin? Louisa, died an infant. Elijah. Edith. Marian.

All the bloodline and spouses except Iris, who hadn't been a Foster at all, and her son. The line had died with Marian.

Abby stepped forward and arranged the roses around the base of Edith's headstone. "She was there that night," she murmured, her hand gently tracing the carved words on the headstone. "Marian was there the night Edith died. Do you think she remembered it? I hope not. I just hope Marian knew how much her mother loved her."

Tom came forward too, squatted down beside her and picked up a stem that she'd dropped. He put his hand on the granite and sighed. "I think Marian knew. Edith made a mistake, but you're right, she didn't deserve this. You can't help who you love. At least Edith had the guts to follow her heart. I used to wish Erin had been willing to risk everything for love. And when she finally was, I would have given everything for her to take it back."

Abby paused at the tight thread of pain in his voice. "What do you mean? When she chose Josh?"

He shook his head, pushing his hands against his knees. They cracked as he stood up. "She was going to leave him. That's what no one knows. Not even Josh."

"She was going to leave him for you?"

Abby stood up now and looked at him. He was staring out over the waving grass of the nearby field. "Did Sarah and Jess tell you about the night Erin and Josh got engaged? About what I said?" At her silent nod, Tom continued. "See, the thing about that night at the Rusty Fern is that even though I was drunk, I was right. She shouldn't have married Josh. Later Erin confessed to me that Josh checked all the right boxes. I wasn't good enough for her family."

"That's ridiculous." Abby dismissed the idea. "You're wonderful. You have a successful business and you're honest and loyal and hardworking."

He smiled but there wasn't much heart in it. "Thanks for saying that, but I was a lot younger, trying to get the business off the ground, a manual laborer with a fixer-upper cottage, and Josh was a doctor with better manners than his rough-around-the-edges cousin."

Abby's heart ached for him. "So she let you go and put the military and miles between you. Like Kristian did with Edith."

"Only Kristian didn't have a choice, did he? He had to go. I chose, Abby. When Erin came to me right before she deployed the last time and asked me to leave everything behind and be with her, I refused."

Abby's chest squeezed. Erin had come back and asked Tom to run away with her? What a horrible position to be in. Happiness, but at such a cost.

"You refused because of Josh."

"I refused because I knew we could never truly be

happy, not with Josh between us. How could I let her divorce him and be with me? He was like my brother. I couldn't do that to him. I either had to hurt her or hurt him. I told her to go home and make it work. That she'd made her choice. I told her to . . ." His voice caught. "To start a family like Josh wanted."

"Do you regret your decision?"

His dark gaze settled on her, accepting the inevitable guilt. "What do you think? Instead of running away with me, instead of going home, she ran away to another tour. And she didn't come home again. I have to live with that every day."

He turned away and began walking to the truck while Abby stood, dumbstruck, in the middle of the cemetery. That was what Tom was carrying around? Because of his decision, the woman he'd loved was dead. That was how he saw it, wasn't it? He was blaming himself.

She went after him, crushing a cluster of purple violets as she rushed to catch up. Tom had been there for her more than once, and most of the time she'd given him a hard time for simply being private. Who could blame him now? No wonder he didn't want to show how he really felt. He'd been burned too often and still bore the scars.

"Tom, wait . . ."

She caught up with him about ten feet from the truck and grabbed his arm. "Tom. You have to stop blaming yourself. You can't live that way."

"If I hadn't turned her away, she wouldn't have gone overseas again. She would have been safe . . ."

"And you would have been miserable." She considered for a moment. "The night at Sarah's, Josh said some pretty nasty things. You could have come back at him with this." Especially in the heat of the moment. As ammunition went, it was pretty good.

"He lost his wife, Abby." Tom stared at her like he

couldn't believe she was suggesting something so stupid. "I couldn't hurt him that way. Not deliberately."

Her heart ached for him. "You," she said softly, "are surprisingly loyal and compassionate."

"I'm not!" He shouted it out and the words echoed through the woods behind them. "Don't you get it? I was tempted, Abby. So tempted. I kissed her that night and we almost . . ." He ran his hand over his hair. "I was guilty of everything in my mind and in my heart."

"This is crazy. You feel guilty for not being with her, you feel guilty for betraying your cousin when you did no such thing, you just feel guilty for everything! Did it ever occur to you that you don't need to take responsibility for every little thing? Surely Josh deserves some of the blame. After all, you had her first." Not to mention Erin's part in all of it. She'd been the one to pit cousin against cousin.

Tom's eyes blazed. "He'd been through his own challenges. He'd lost his dad and was dealing with trying to hold the family together."

"So it's okay that he moved in on your girl?"

He closed his lips.

Abby furrowed her brow, feeling a spurt of anger toward this apparent saint of a woman who'd driven such a deep wedge between Tom and Josh. "Do you know what I don't understand? I don't understand how one woman can love one man and marry another and still inspire such devotion in both of you!"

She began to stomp away, feeling less sorry for Erin by the moment and annoyed that Tom and Josh had both been completely wrapped around her finger.

"Why, because no one has ever loved you like that?"

The words cut into her deeply. She caught her breath, frozen to the spot. They were words spoken in anger, lashing out because of his own pain, but they were weap-

ons just the same. Apparently he had no problem deliberately hurting *her.*

She turned around, determined not to cower away from
tough conversations any longer. "Yes, because no one has
ever loved me like that. I've never been in love before. I
sure as hell haven't been loved the way you and Josh love
her. But I do know that if someone loved me as much as
you loved Erin, nothing in the world could have forced
me to let them go."

Whether she was perfect or flawed, Tom was going to
love Erin until his dying day, wasn't he? It was a splash
of cold, sobering water. "I feel sorry for you. You have a
lot to give someone, but until you let go of her it's just
a waste."

For long seconds Tom just stared at her. The mourning
dove's cry echoed through the cemetery and over the
meadow. Abby's words hit him with the force of a truck.
He'd opened up to her, trusted her, and she still didn't
understand. He knew he was being cruel, but he lashed
out anyway.

"Wise words from someone who admits to never having been in love." Again his words hit their mark, and
seeing her wince, Tom felt like an even bigger ass.

"Everyone has their own pain, Tom. It's not limited to
you and your situation. Don't think you know me, because you don't."

"Does anyone?" He stepped forward. "Does anyone
really know Abigail Foster?"

Standing in the cemetery talking about love and Erin
and Josh and Abby, Tom felt a surge of anger that had
nothing to do with the past. He wanted to reach over and
demand Abby let him in. Demand that she really trust
him.

She met his gaze evenly. "No. No, they don't. And that's just how I plan to keep it."

Tom gave a bitter laugh. "Well, honey, isn't that the pot calling the kettle black. You talk about me 'letting go' of the past when you're too afraid to even let anyone in at all."

Silence filled the cemetery; even the dove halted its song. Now Abby knew she'd made the right choice by stopping whatever had been going to happen between them. She could never compete with Erin's ghost. And at this point, making love was a big enough deal that she didn't want to squander it on someone who would be thinking of someone else.

"So what now? You run away again?" Tom accused.

"There's nothing to keep me here, is there?" Abby paused as the words sank in before saying quietly, "I'd like to go home now."

"I promised you dinner."

"I don't think either one of us is in the mood for that right now. I have a frozen pizza. It'll be fine."

Tom made a move as if to protest further.

"Please, Tom. Just take me home."

He brushed by her and went back to the truck, opened the door and stood next to it. Moments later they pulled into her driveway. Tom shut off the ignition and turned to face her. He was still annoyed, she could tell. And something more. Something deeper below the surface than simple anger.

"I believed you when you were sure no one would. I have been there for you, and maybe I should remind you that you were the one who put a stop to whatever it was that was happening between us in your bedroom. If you think I could do any of those things if I didn't care about you in some way, you really haven't bothered to know me at all."

Abby was pissed off that Tom could manage to make her feel so small. To feel like she'd somehow wronged him, but more than that she was tired. Today had been too emotional, too stressful. She might have her own fears and misgivings but at least her heart wasn't tangled up in someone else's.

"It doesn't matter, does it? You're so far from over her. And that's too big a risk for a girl like me. I've known it all along, okay? So let's just call this what it is. A bit of a mess when all is said and done. And probably best to leave it all here since I'll be putting the house up for sale before too long."

Silence descended on the cab of the truck.

"Fair enough," Tom finally said, his face stony with attempted indifference. "Truce, then? There's not much point in arguing."

Or anything else, Abby thought, disappointed. A truce between them seemed so . . . bland. Being with Tom might be messy, but she'd kind of gotten used to it. He challenged her but that wasn't necessarily all bad. She'd started looking forward to it.

But it wasn't all good, either. "Truce," she replied, putting her hand on the door handle.


The kitchen was done, the cupboards and countertop and the new tile floor installed. With the last of the draperies on order and the painting complete, there was nothing holding Abby back. She'd gone to the Realtor in town and within twenty-four hours the house had been listed at a price tag that she personally thought was astronomical. She also knew it was worth every penny, especially considering all the renovations Tom had done. What had once been a landmark was now a showpiece unmatched on the mid-coast.

All that was left now was for Tom to put up the refurbished chandelier and there would be no reason to see him again. She didn't need to stay in town to sell the house. That's what Realtors and lawyers were for, after all.

She was in town the morning the FOR SALE sign went up and ran into Jess at Breezes. Jess was carrying an extra-large paper cup with a tea bag string hanging from beneath the lid. When she saw Abby a smile lit her face. "Hey, stranger," she said, meeting Abby on the sidewalk. "Missed you at the last candle class."

"Sorry. It got really busy at the house, getting it ready for the Realtor."

"You're still bent on selling?" Jess sounded disappointed, and her lips turned down in a small frown.

Abby tried to make her voice light; after all, there was nothing sad in the news. It was what she'd intended to do all along. She was going to go back to Canada. She had a job waiting next fall. An apartment.

Maybe that would put enough distance between her and the feelings that seemed to crop up ever since she'd set foot in Jewell Cove. Feelings like warmth and belonging. They made returning to her life in Halifax sound supernaturally boring. "Sign's going up this morning. I expect to be flooded with offers by two o'clock."

Jess's eyes clouded with worry. "So soon . . . I thought maybe with things between you and Tom . . ."

Abby swallowed. "There is no me and Tom, Jess. There never really was." Why were the words so hard to say?

"Maybe if you hung around longer."

"He's still in love with Erin." Abby kept her voice low; after all, she'd learned quite quickly that there were big ears everywhere in a place this size. "You must know that. I couldn't compete with her even if I wanted to."

Jess sighed. "I wish they would both move on. Neither one of them is happy."

She didn't need to say the name for Abby to know she meant Josh. Abby looked at Jess and asked something she'd been wondering for a long time now. "What was it about her, Jess? For Tom and Josh to fall so hard, to ruin their friendship? I don't get it."

Jess fiddled with the tab of her tea bag. "I don't really know. She was beautiful, and physically strong, but there was a vulnerability about her, too. A 'little girl lost' vibe. I think they both responded to that. I think she was the sort of woman that makes a man want to take care of her, you know?"

Abby did know. "I hope I'm not that way," she mused. "I can take care of myself."

Jess smiled. "Yes, you can. I think we all realized that the moment Tom put his foot through your veranda and you called Bryce. But you miss the point. Just because a woman is self-sufficient doesn't mean she won't make a man *want* to take care of her. Two very different points of view."

"You think Tom wants to take care of me?"

Jess sent her a knowing look. "I think Tom wants to take care of everyone. And I think the fact that you don't necessarily let him is good for him. I wish you'd reconsider. Even if you sell the house, I wish you'd stay. You belong here."

Abby swallowed thickly. "I can't." The truth was, she didn't know how to really belong anywhere. She'd learned at a very young age to rely on herself and no one else. At least that way she wouldn't put her hopes—her faith—in any one person and they couldn't let her down.

She blinked as that simple truth slammed into her. If she kept running she never had to get too close to anyone, never have a home to call her own. Neither would anyone have the power to disappoint her. To leave. What would happen if she put down roots here? If she let her heart get involved? Tom would have the power to break it, wouldn't he? And he probably would. She'd be a fool to let that happen.

"Are you okay?" Jess's voice broke through her thoughts.

"Yeah, fine, just thought of something I need to do, that's all." She forced a smile. "Besides, you probably need to get to the shop."

"Tom cares for you, Abby. I can see it all over his face when he looks at you. Maybe he doesn't realize how much, but I wish you'd give him a chance."

Her words stung just a little bit. "I have my own reasons, too, Jess. I'm sorry."

"Me, too. Will you promise me one thing, though?"

Oh, boy.

Jess put her hand on Abby's arm. "Will you promise not to leave without saying good-bye to me? To Sarah? She's finally told everyone the news and I'm throwing her a baby shower." Jess's dark eyes—the ones that reminded Abby so much of Tom—pleaded with her.

Abby's throat swelled up with emotion. Intentional or not, she'd made connections here. "That sounds like fun," she replied. "Now scoot. I need to grab some breakfast."

Jess was gone with a wave.

Inside Breezes, Abby sat alone, listening to the conversations going on around her. One family of tourists was talking about going on a whale boat excursion. A group of ladies were meeting for coffee and animatedly discussing the latest book they'd read in their book club. Abby listened to that one closely, smiling as they debated which hero had more heroic qualities—Darcy or Captain Went-worth. A couple of old-timers were deliberating the cost of purchasing a new tractor and one very pretty young lady was at the counter ordering the makings of a very nice picnic basket. Abby lifted her hand and waved as a few familiar faces came in. The waitress, Linda, brought her a chocolate-filled croissant even though Abby hadn't ordered it, because she knew it was her favorite.

A pang resonated through Abby's heart.

Of all the places she'd lived in her adult years, this was the first place that truly felt like a home.

She drained the last bit of coffee from her cup and left a twenty on the table. She was going to miss Jewell Cove deeply. More than she ever imagined possible.

# CHAPTER 18

With the house officially on the market, Abby figured her time to finish going through the final possessions in the attic was limited. She'd already organized the storage room into things for the historical society, things to get rid of, and other items she wanted put into storage. There was just the back corner left—a half-dozen cardboard boxes and one small chest.

The summer heat was cloying in the windowless space, and Abby made short work of the boxes, which contained mostly clothes. Most she would donate, but a half-dozen dresses were particularly pretty and she put them aside, wondering if she dared have them dry-cleaned. Vintage stuff was getting more popular.

But it was the chest that gave her trouble.

It was locked. And she had no idea where to find the key.

She retrieved the ring she and Tom had used to open the servant's stairway, but none of the keys fit, and she suspected the lock was rather rusted. Deciding to risk injuring the chest, she trotted back downstairs and got a knife and also a claw hammer from a small toolbox she kept on hand. If she couldn't pick the lock, maybe she could pry it open.

It took ten minutes and substantial cursing, but she emerged victorious with the lock successfully picked. She lifted the lid, an arthritic creak sounding from the old hinges.

Her first glimpse of the chest's contents was disappointing. She didn't expect to see a haphazard collection of personal items strewn without any care or organization.

Abby frowned, staring down into the mess. Everything she'd found so far had been folded, wrapped, placed just so. Items had been deliberately and carefully packed. But not this. In the mess she made out a hairbrush and comb, the handle of a mirror. She picked it up and saw half the glass was missing—she'd have to be careful of that. A dusting-powder box was tilted on its side; Abby picked it up, leveled it out, and carefully lifted the pale pink lid adorned with painted lily of the valley.

The soft floral scent rose in the air and she put the lid on her lap so she could pick up the puff. The powder was half gone . . . Abby swallowed. It was strange. It was like someone had simply dumped the contents of a vanity table into one chest without consideration.

She found the broken mirror piece and set it aside. There was a beaded clutch purse, empty, and a tiny bag with makeup inside—Pan-Cake foundation, an eye pencil, and a tube of brilliant red lipstick. A novel with a bookmark two thirds of the way through—*A Tree Grows in Brooklyn*.

It bore all the signs of a life interrupted.

There were hair ribbons and a jewelry box filled with costume earrings and necklaces. A soft velvet bag, heavy—which, when opened, revealed a waterfall of real jewels. A rope of creamy pearls, a teardrop diamond pendant, and an exquisite emerald choker with matching chandelier earrings.

Who in their right mind would pack these away and put them in a corner of an attic? If they were indeed real—and she was nearly certain they were—they were worth a lot of money.

Marian's things? Or her mother's?

She went through more of the chest until her fingers touched a leather book cover. She prised it out and brushed off the surface. It had once held a lock, she realized, but the lock and key were missing and the metal hooks were bent at an odd angle, as if they'd been pried open.

She opened the cover.

*Diary of Edith Foster, 1943–*

There was no end date.

She turned the yellowed pages, drawn in to the voice of her great-grandmother. It was clear how much Edith loved Marian—the opening pages were filled with daily activities and latest accomplishments. It was equally clear that Edith was not as contented with her autocratic husband, who took a strong view on a wife's vow of obedience. Abby sensed the relief Edith had felt when Elijah joined up after Pearl Harbor, and how the atmosphere of the house lightened in his absence. Beneath the harsh light of the single attic bulb, Abby drank in the pages describing how the love affair between Edith and the chauffeur blossomed, and how he was kind and gentle, a welcome relief after Elijah's cold, stern ways. He made her laugh, Edith said, and made her feel beautiful and special. Abby was half in love with him herself as she read on about their affair, the clandestine rendezvous, and the way he snuck peppermints to Marian when he thought Edith wasn't looking.

And then, in late 1942, Edith had discovered a terrible

secret. She'd interrupted a secret meeting in her parents' barn at the top of Blackberry Hill. She'd been so confused at first, listening to the strange language the man spoke. Then Kristian answered him in the same tongue and she realized she didn't really know him at all. She made out enough to know that he was speaking German—and that he was talking about the names of different coves and inlets along the coastline.

Abby paused, her hand over her mouth, and then began reading again, turning the pages with crazy speed as Edith confided to her diary that she believed that Kristian, who had come to America from Germany with his parents in 1935, had been tapped by the Nazis to spy on coastal activities in the area.

The barn—the one at the top of the mountain, tilting sideways and abandoned. Good heavens, Abby hadn't ever suspected something like this. It wasn't just a simple affair with the help. Edith had found herself smack-dab in the middle of espionage, with her husband off fighting the war and an enemy spy in her bed.

Torn between loyalty to her country and the demands of her heart, Edith wrote how she couldn't reconcile the Nazi with the man who had been so kind and loving to her and her daughter. Abby frantically flipped through the pages until she came to the entry detailing the night Edith finally confronted him about his allegiance.

Kristian confessed everything: how he was pressured into joining the Nazi party by his parents, how he was trapped spying for a cause he didn't believe in . . . and more importantly how he'd turned double agent for the Americans. Abby's heart broke as she read the smudged lines on the page when Edith described how Kristian made the crucial decision to leave Jewell Cove in order to protect Edith from his double life and took an assignment with the Resistance overseas.

Sailing the Atlantic in wartime was a dangerous proposition, and Edith's journal was filled with both worry over Kristian's welfare and the dangerous job he was about to do. Pages of the diary were filled with her despair. Each day Edith prayed Kristian wouldn't be caught or killed. That one day they would find each other again.

Finally Abby came to one of the last entries in the diary, dated in October of 1943. Edith's elegant handwriting was cramped and excited. Kristian was coming home. Abby remembered the letter she found under the floorboards in the nursery and smiled thinking about how happy Edith seemed in the diary pages, but as she continued reading, the smile slipped from her face. A scarce month later Elijah came home—wounded, battle weary, and with a changeable temper that made him even more unpredictable. *Elijah is home,* Edith wrote. *Nothing will ever be the same.*

Abby found herself wiping away tears as she read about Edith and Kristian's tearful good-bye the night after Elijah's return. Staying and carrying on their affair was too dangerous. No matter what Kristian had done, they loved each other. And if nothing else, Iris had been conceived in love in a world and time filled with hate and intolerance. There was something beautiful about that.

Abby closed the cover carefully and put it on the floor beside her. She'd been through most of the chest now, with just a few items left at the bottom. There was a pair of knitted bootees that were impossibly small, and a pink and white quilt that was the perfect size for a crib, pieced together with tiny stitches. Abby didn't need confirmation to know that it had been Iris's, and she put her hand on it, missing her grandmother terribly. Abby lifted the quilt to get a better look and something fell out and hit the floor.

It was a letter, precisely folded and written on pale

blue stationery. A letter, Abby thought, that seemed particularly hidden and had never been sent. She handled the pages gently, looked at the elegantly looped handwriting she now recognized as Edith's. *Mother and Dad*, it said on the outside.

Abby's fingers shook as she unfolded the pages and began to read.

> *May 8, 1945*
>
> *Dearest Mother and Dad,*
>
> *Please forgive me for saying good-bye this way. If there were any other choice, I wish I could have seen it so I could spare everyone pain. It's so very selfish of me to choose happiness when I know that choice will make others unhappy. So I'm sorry. Sorry I wasn't a better daughter, a stronger woman. Sorry if I've let you down.*
>
> *When I married Elijah I thought I was doing the right thing. It was easy to be dazzled by him—rich and charming and smart, and he catered to my every whim. Even then I sensed the kind of man he was and willfully ignored it. Things changed shortly after our marriage. I tried to put a good face on it publicly, but he wasn't—isn't—a kind husband. I soon felt trapped in an opulent prison. The one blessing that came of our marriage was Marian. I love her so much and her innocence and enthusiasm for everything reminds me of what I used to be like. The way I hope to be again.*
>
> *In Elijah's long absence, I fell in love. His name is Kristian. He is a strong, kind man who makes me laugh. I'd nearly forgotten how, you see. When I am with Kristian, I know everything will be all right somehow. I know having an affair was wrong, but*

*he saved me. He gave me back myself and I find I can't be sorry for that. He also gave me Iris. I suspect Elijah knows Iris is not his daughter, though he has yet to accuse me of anything.*

*Today the war is over. It should be a time for celebrating. Instead Kristian is waiting for us at the barn at the top of the hill, waiting for us to arrive, and then we are all going to be together. We are going to leave Jewell Cove and go far away to become the happy, loving family I always wanted and that I know you wanted for me. I want you to remember the good reasons why I'm leaving—for love and happiness and contentment.*

*I don't have much time, but I hid a keepsake box in the nursery under the floor. There you will find the letters Kristian wrote to me, a lock of his hair, and his father's watch that he gave to me before he left last time. Perhaps you can find it and keep it for me . . . when we meet again.*

*Tomorrow we'll be on a ship to a new life. When that happens, remember, Mother—and Daddy—how much I love you. I will think of you both often, and write when I can and share stories of Marian and Iris's escapades. And maybe one day we can all come back and sit in the rose garden again.*

*Your loving daughter,*
*Edith*

By the time Abby got to the end she was crying. The elegant, curved writing was filled with love and affection for the two girls—and for her parents. Kristian had been waiting in the barn, then. Her vision made sense now—the suitcase with the clothes scattered about, Marian in her little jacket hiding in Edith's skirts. Edith had died on the stairs. And Iris had been sent away to live with Edith's parents, never knowing the truth.

Leaving Marian behind. To live with a man Edith proclaimed was angry and unpredictable and unkind. Maybe, despite the obvious wealth, Iris had been the lucky one after all.

Finding out the truth—solving the mystery—should have made Abby happy. Instead it left her feeling empty and wanting because having the answers changed nothing. In fact, she felt like she was somehow losing her grandmother all over again, in addition to losing a family she hadn't even known.

Abby put on her running shoes and her blue sweat jacket and made the trek back up the mountain to the summit. It was her favorite spot on the property, wild and free. She breathed deeply as she gazed at the view. It was easy here. Her chest felt like it was expanding and she felt taller. Here, she realized, she was in absolute control because it was the one place she felt safe to be herself. She was going to miss it.

The barn stood behind her, dark and dilapidated. She examined it, thinking about Edith and Kristian and all she'd learned. How horrible it must have been to find him there, to discover his terrible secret. How exciting to think of him waiting to whisk her away to a new life. She wondered if the barn held other memories, too. Of secret trysts and whispered promises.

Kristian had been Edith's happiness. Her home was where he was, because Edith had been prepared to uproot her entire existence to be with him. She'd even been willing to leave her family behind. What did that sort of devotion feel like?

A chilly breeze blew at Abby's back and she turned,

startled to see black thunderclouds closing in rapidly. When she'd left the house, fat, puffy clouds had been floating carelessly on a pale sea of blue. She'd known showers were forecast for the afternoon but she hadn't expected them to blow in this soon.

If she ran now, she might make it back to the house before getting soaked, but she doubted it. Already a gray sheet of rain was trailing behind the clouds, obscuring the view beyond. Lightning forked, a searing, jagged jolt touching the ground. Only a few seconds elapsed before it was followed by an earthshaking grumble of thunder. It was coming up the coast fast. There was no way she'd make it home before getting drenched.

The first cold, fat drop hit her face.

She would have to wait it out in the barn.

The splatters came faster as she jogged to the old structure. The door opened with a drawn-out creak, the hinges rusted from years of neglect and the salty moisture of the sea air. She stepped inside, her heart pounding in the darkness. Pinpoints of dim light shot through holes in the roof and walls, illuminating dust motes. Hay had been left here at some point, the scent old and musty.

She jumped when she heard the flap of wings overhead, her breathing coming in short gasps. It was just a swallow, though, dipping and flitting about before settling in its nest on one of the high rafters, waiting out the storm just like her.

She walked farther inside, the sound of the rain muted against the old roof. It was bound to leak so she kept her eyes open for holes and tried to avoid the drips. The pinpricks of light were gone now, leaving the space in dark shadow as the black clouds completely blocked out the sun. The wind howled around the empty spaces and gaps in the building, a mournful cry that Abby felt clear to the soles of her feet.

Something moved, just inside her field of vision on her right. For the space of a second her body froze and she couldn't breathe. She knew instinctively she wasn't alone.

She remembered Art mentioning bears liking the blackberries . . . surely one wouldn't come into the barn, would it? Her body was paralyzed with fear even as her pulse leaped, thrumming so loudly it pounded in her ears. She turned her head to see what was watching her. Poised to run if she had to . . .

It was a who, not a what, that stood in the back corner. She recognized Kristian from the blue eyes and fair hair. He wore a brown traveling suit, very ordinary, much the same quality as Edith's plain blue dress, and a suitcase sat beside him on the floor. They'd been looking to blend in, not stand out, hadn't they?

She shouldn't be surprised to find him here. If she'd seen Edith, why not Kristian, too? Her pulse steadied. She wasn't frightened of him. Instead a sweeping sadness washed over her as she swallowed thickly. It felt like the end of a dream. The death of hope.

"I'm sorry," she said, her voice echoing strangely in the open space. "Edith isn't coming, Kristian."

The light in the barn changed, lighting up like a camera flash. Abby's eyes widened as she stared out the open door. Hail drummed against the barn, hard pellets of ice that bounced off the ground like white marbles. And then there was another blinding light and a resounding crack that filled her ears like a gunshot.

Abby dropped to the floor, covering her head with her hands as splinters of wood fell all around her, the vision of Kristian temporarily forgotten. The noise was deafening now, odd creaking and snapping as everything surrounding her tilted. She scrambled forward on her knees, rushing toward the only open space she could see—the door.

She was nearly there when the weight of the roof shifted in a gust of wind and the walls beneath it trembled from the strain. With one heavy sigh, it all leaned until the wall buckled—and the barn came tumbling down around her.

# CHAPTER 19

Tom had the power shut off as he worked on installing the chandelier. It really should have been a two-man job, considering how heavy the damned thing was. If Abby were here, she could at least help him hold it up while he connected the wiring and then put it in place. But when he'd arrived the house had been eerily silent. And that damned FOR SALE sign had taunted him from the front lawn.

She couldn't be far. Her car was still in the yard and her purse was sitting next to the phone on the hall table. But she was nowhere in the house or garden.

He frowned, cursed as he adjusted the fixture on the makeshift scaffolding he'd concocted from a spare stepladder and a piece of plywood in his truck. She was avoiding him. There was no need. They'd called a truce and he'd meant it.

But she hadn't wasted any time getting that FOR SALE sign up, had she? It had annoyed him from the moment he'd caught sight of it when he'd turned up the lane. For a woman who claimed to care so much about family, who appeared to have a tender heart behind her sharp tongue, she sure found it easy to just pick up and leave.

Tom had his faults, but at least he'd never run away from his problems. Hell, she'd accused him of still being hung up on Erin. Funny thing was, he was pretty sure that he hadn't been in love with her for some time. Guilt was a far more prevalent emotion than grief or love. Guilt for how he'd handled their last meeting. And also a little guilt about moving on. Because he *had* moved on. He was pretty sure he cared a great deal for the aggravating Miss Foster.

Well, little did she know. She might be determined to bail, might not care for the house, but he did. With the money she was paying him for the renovations, he had enough for a down payment. And if he could talk the asking price down a bit, his savings would cover the mortgage for a while.

And he could always sell his cottage. It was small but it was prime waterfront property. It would make someone a good summer home when all was said and done.

He just didn't want her to know it was him buying it until the deal was done.

The light through the windows dimmed and he squinted, focusing on twisting a marrett around the wires. Whether she was avoiding him or not, there was a storm blowing in. He'd felt it earlier, in the uneasy heat of midday, saw it in the way the leaves were flipped over in the restless breeze. It was already clouding over and the wind was coming up, gusting at the windows. As he screwed the mounting plate into place, he scowled. The first rolls of thunder were rumbling along through the valley. If Abby were out there, she'd better be hoofing it home by now, or else she was going to get caught right in the middle of it.

He didn't realize how much the weather had changed until he took down the sheet of plywood and went to put it back in his truck. The sky was ominously black and the cold bite of the wind told him there was a good chance they'd get hammered with hail. Worried now and a bit angry that she was out wandering around, he cupped his hands to his mouth. "Abby!" he called, his voice swallowed up by the wind. "Abby!"

No answer.

Something was wrong. He couldn't explain it, had no proof but the heavy, frightened feeling that was centered in the pit of his stomach. He remembered the sensation far too well to ignore it a second time.

The thunder and lightning grew louder and he scanned the hill behind the house, willing her to appear at any moment. Instead the skies opened up, pouring down sheets of rain. He raced inside, flicked the light switch and remembered that he'd turned off the breaker. There was a brilliant flash followed by a crash of thunder that made the glasswork rattle above his head. When he flicked the breaker and hit the switch, nothing happened.

The rain seemed to ease for a second, but the storm had merely taken a breath. It only paused for a moment before the hail started.

He had to find her. He hadn't passed her on the way up the hill, so she couldn't have gone toward town. That only left one direction. Up. He ran out to the truck and started it, turning on the wipers as he made his way down the lane toward the road. Maybe she was still at the top. The old barn was there. She could have taken shelter. Maybe she was snug as a bug after all. He could always hope. If not, she'd be soaked to the skin by now. The dark feeling persisted. *Or worse,* the little voice inside him said. He wouldn't let himself go there. It was just a storm. She would be wet but all right.

A half-mile up the road he was stopped by the gate. It was secured with a heavy chain and lock—nothing his tools could cut through. He slammed the door and began to jog up the hill. "Abby?" He called her name now and again, holding the hood of his jacket up over his head against the sting of pelting hail.

He could see the barn at the crest of the hill. God, he hoped she was in there. If not, he'd have to take shelter until the storm passed before making his way back down again.

He was only a hundred yards away when the lightning struck. He'd never seen anything like it. The sharp report was like a cannon going off and wood shrapnel flew everywhere as one side of the barn literally exploded in front of his eyes. The heavy weight of the rotted roof was too much for the wounded wall of the barn. It began to tilt, leaning to one side as the support started to crumble.

Then he saw her. Her bright blue hoodie stood out against the gray of the barn and the storm as she crawled toward the doorway. He ran forward, his heart pounding, terrified he wouldn't reach her in time.

The barn came down in a dramatic puff of dust and wood, and he couldn't see the blue hoodie anymore.


Abby coughed as dust rose all around her. Her ears rang and she blinked slowly. For the space of a heartbeat she thought she saw him again. Kristian. Blond hair, blue eyes, sharp cheekbones. And a gentleness and understanding that made her soul ache.

The barn had come down. She understood that much. The rubble was strewn all around her and she seemed to be lying in a pocket of space, surrounded by wood and old curled shingles. She wrapped her hands around herself as goose bumps rose on her arms. It was cold, so cold. She should head back to the house. Something about the thought didn't seem quite right, but she couldn't put her finger on it.

She couldn't seem to make herself move. Maybe if she just closed her eyes and rested for a minute or two. She pictured the FOR SALE sign at the end of the lane. She'd felt an odd sense of loss looking at it today. But what else could she do? She'd done what she'd come to do, hadn't she? She'd found the answers she'd come for. But then it had been more. She'd gotten *invested*. Dead or not, it wasn't about names on paper. Those names had stopped being *relatives* and had become her *family*.

She looked around her. Kristian had been here that long-ago night. How had he felt when Edith and the children hadn't shown up? What had he done? Slipped away quietly or gone looking for them? As the hours had gone by, had he worried? Given up hope? Wondered if she'd changed her mind?

Abby tried to move her legs and winced. Her knees hurt and there was a long scratch down her thigh that was bleeding.

"Help!" she called, then slumped against some broken timbers. No one would hear her up here. No one knew where she was.

No one cared.

And she had no one to blame for that but herself. It was her own fault she kept everyone at arm's length, never letting them close enough to truly be a part of her life. Too scared to let them in only to have them leave again. Except being alone all the time pretty much sucked.

"Abby?"

She must have hit her head, because she would swear she heard Tom's voice calling her name. Tom. Just thinking about him made something warm and tingly flutter in her belly, like little winged butterflies. She cared for him far more than she could ever let on. If she regretted one thing, it was stopping him from making love to her that morning. He would have been patient and gentle and thorough. The kind of lover she needed, and she'd pushed him away.

He was the sort of man who loved deeply and forever, wasn't he? She could have had just a taste of that, to know just once what it was like to be the focus of all that intense devotion. Maybe it wouldn't have been real and it probably wouldn't have lasted, but it would have been enough.

"Abby! Please answer me! Are you in there?"

Okay, so that wasn't just her name she heard, but his voice making demands. Hope spiraled through her heart. "I'm in here!" she called back, pushing herself to a sitting position with a wince. God, she seemed to hurt all over.

There was the sound of boards being moved aside and his panicked voice again. "Abs? Where are you?"

The relief at knowing it was truly him was so great that she started crying. "I'm over here. Be careful. There are boards everywhere and I don't know how stable things are."

"Hang on. I'll be careful. Are you hurt?"

"I don't know. I don't think so."

"Keep talking. I'll be there before you know it."

She got herself together a little. "Tom?"

"Yeah, honey?"

She almost wept at the endearment. "It's so good to hear your voice."

There was a ripping sound and one of the boards closing her off from the entrance was pulled away. She could see his work boots and she started to laugh through her tears. How she loved those damned boots.

He knelt and peered through the gap. "Hang in there. I'm going to move these and get you out, but I have to be careful. I don't want to make the rest come down."

"Like a game of Jenga," she responded. Pain from the gash was starting to radiate up her leg and she winced.

"Exactly."

When he'd created a big enough hole, he held out his hand. "Can you make it over here? I'll pull you out."

She put down her hands to crawl to the opening, but the moment her knees touched the floor she cried out.

"I can't," she answered, breathless with pain that felt like needles sticking through her kneecaps.

"Go on your butt," he suggested calmly, "and slide over. If I can get my hands under your armpits, you'll slip right out."

It took a while but she managed to scoot over to the opening. Tom's hands were sure and strong as he anchored them under her arms and pulled her free. When she was out, he picked her up and gathered her in a strong embrace.

She wrapped her arms around his neck, clinging to his solid, reassuring bulk. "I've never been so glad to hear your voice," she whispered, her voice clogged with tears. "The lightning hit and it felt like the whole thing exploded."

"It did."

"How did you know where to find me?"

He started walking down the hill, away from the ruin of the barn. "Your car and purse were at home. I didn't pass you on the road on the way to the house, so it only made sense that you'd go up."

"For once I am very glad of your common sense and powers of deduction." As much as she enjoyed being cradled in his arms, she felt silly. "Tom, put me down. I can walk."

His eyes skittered away from hers, evading the command. "It's okay, I can carry you."

"But . . ."

"Indulge me, okay? I left the truck by the gate. It's not far." He grinned. "Let me be a knight in shining armor for once."

The hail had passed and now they were being soaked

by a steady rain. Before long Abby could see the truck, and Tom wasted no time going to the passenger side. "Can you open the door?"

She pulled on the handle and he deposited her on the seat, slammed the door again, and jogged around to the other side.

"Out of the rain, at least," she mused, marveling that she could manage to make such a mundane comment when she'd nearly died just minutes earlier. Reality felt very surreal and skewed at the moment.

Tom's gaze pierced her, making her feel strange as he started the truck and cranked on the heater. "Take off your hoodie," he commanded, reaching into the back. He held up an old sweatshirt, a heavy navy thing with the words GONE FISHIN emblazoned on it in gold.

"I'm fine," she insisted.

"You're soaking wet and probably in shock. Take off your shirt or I'll do it for you, Abby."

She fumbled with the zipper and sleeves, the wet material clinging to her skin. Beneath the hoodie her T-shirt was also wet. "That one, too," he said.

"Tom, I . . ."

Sympathy softened his eyes. "It's okay," he said quietly, gentling his tone. He reached for the hem of her shirt and pulled it over her head, easing it down her arms. There was nothing sexual about it, just tender caring. He held out the sweatshirt, making it easier for her to put her arms in the sleeves and pull it over her head. It was enormous on her much smaller frame, but it was soft and warm and smelled of lumber.

He put the truck in gear and turned around, pointing them down the hill again. Abby curled into the sweatshirt, relieved that the heater in the truck was working. She didn't understand why she was so cold.

And then she remembered her leg.

"Your seat!" she exclaimed, looking down. The blood flow had slowed, but there was still a rusty-red streak on the beige upholstery.

But that wasn't the worst. She finally saw her knees and the sight of the raw skin stubbled with splinters sent sickening tingles from her stomach right down the backs of her legs to her toes. This was why he hadn't let her try walking.

"It's not as bad as it looks," he said quietly.

"Are you sure?"

He went right by her driveway and kept on going toward town.

Was it so bad then that he was taking her to the doctor? She bit down on her lip. "My purse and everything is at the house."

"The storm knocked the power out," he explained. "We're going to my place. Even if there's no power there either, I have a generator."

She laughed shortly. "Of course you do."

Now that she'd seen her knees it seemed they started stinging worse. She spent the remainder of the drive with her eyes closed, trying to breathe evenly. But when she closed her eyes, she saw Kristian's frightened face just as the walls started tumbling down. And she heard Tom's voice calling her name and it seemed to make her heart expand and warm all at once.

It was better if she kept her eyes open after all.

"I finally got through the rest of the attic stuff," she said, the idea taking her mind off the pain.

"Find anything interesting?" he asked.

They'd left things in a bad way between them, with a reluctant truce. And yet Abby still trusted him. He'd been with her through this whole journey and it seemed strange, not giving him the whole story. "I found a little chest. It was a pile of Edith's personal things. Makeup, hairbrushes, books . . . her diary."

For a moment Tom looked over at her, his gaze sharp. "A diary, huh?"

"The lock was broken off it. If Elijah did that, he would have been livid after reading it. He was not a nice man, Tom."

"So we gathered."

She took a breath, let it out slowly, trying to ease the stabbing in her knees. "Remember I said I saw a suitcase in my . . . well, let's call it my vision. There was a letter to Edith's parents that she never got to give them. She was planning on leaving him that night. On V-E Day. She was taking the kids and meeting Kristian and leaving. Only she never got the chance."

"Are you serious?" Tom's eyebrows lifted and once again he took his eyes off the road and looked over. "Where were they going to go?"

"That's the thing." She felt odd just speaking about it. The very idea was so fantastic, so surreal. "It seems Kristian wasn't who he seemed."

"What do you mean?"

"I mean he wasn't just the chauffeur. He was put here to do a job. For the Third Reich."

Tom started to laugh. "Okay, are you sure you didn't hit your head? Your imagination is running away with you. Are you saying he was a spy? Here in Jewell Cove?" He laughed again.

"That's exactly what I'm saying. You can read her diary if you want. Edith uncovered a secret meeting in the barn that nearly killed me just now."

The mirth left his face. "Holy shit. You're serious."

"Completely. What is really crazy is that he gave it all up and turned spy for the Americans." She pressed a hand to her heart. "Each time he left it was to protect her, you know? Until the last time when he returned to take her away for good.

"Edith had the courage to choose love, no matter how wrong it might have been." Tom shook his head. "I'm not sure if that's wonderful or selfish."

She shrugged. "I'm not sure there is always a right and a wrong, Tom. Elijah was not the husband he should have been. He'd dishonored their vows long before she met Kristian. He was a tyrant who insisted on having his way in all things." She shuddered. "Their lives shattered that night. She died. The girls were split up, and Edith's parents raised Gram as their own. I wonder if Elijah threatened to reveal Iris's true parentage to the world if they ever tried to make contact with Jewell Cove again. It just doesn't make sense that they would never tell Gram about her sister or mother unless something was holding them back. After what I read, I wouldn't have put it past him."

Abby was pulled from her thoughts, when Tom turned into his gravel driveway. She'd never actually been to his cottage before. It was off the main road in an inlet called Fiddler's Rock, a few miles south of Jewell Cove, not marked by any road signs but known to the locals by the simple landmark. His cottage was nestled in among a stand of trees with glimpses of the water just visible between the branches.

Tom jumped out of the truck and came around to open her door. He eased her down out of the cab and scooped her into his arms, carrying her to the tiny house.

The power was still on, so he flicked on a light and carried her straight through to the small kitchen, pulling out a chair at the drop-leaf table. "Sit here. I'm going for the first-aid kit," he said.

She took a minute to look around. She was sure the table and chairs were handcrafted. The furniture was simple but cozy, and the windows looking over the water were left uncovered so the view remained unimpeded. It was the kind of place that suited him perfectly—sturdy and plain and ruggedly beautiful.

He came back with a basin of water and a kit, which he put on the table. "You hurt anywhere else but your legs?"

She shook her head. "I don't think so. My hoodie covered a lot."

He went to the cupboard and took out a glass, filled it with water and brought it to the table along with a bottle of pain relievers. "Take two of those. I'm guessing you're going to be hurting later."

As she obediently took the pills he cleaned along her cut with a soft cloth. "This isn't deep," he said. "Not enough for stitches. I'm going to bandage it up though, to keep it clean."

It wasn't until he went to work on her knees that she gritted her teeth, inhaling with a hiss.

First he sprayed them with an antiseptic to dull the pain and get rid of any dirt. "I'm sorry, Abs. This probably isn't going to be pleasant."

"Just get them out," she said tightly, bracing herself. Dragging herself to the door as the building fell had left several splinters and scrapes along her knees. As gently as he could, he employed the tweezers in the kit to remove the splinters. One by one he plucked them out, each one leaving a little pocket of relief in its wake. Blood oozed in a thin layer from the raw skin as she breathed through her clenched teeth. It seemed to take forever, but he attended to her carefully, patiently, calmly. Her head was hanging over the back of the chair when he finished with the first knee and she wished it were all over. But there was still one more to go, and by the time he got to the last splinters of wood she was close to crying again.

The tweezers dug into her flesh to grip a particularly deep shard and she bit down on her lip so hard she tasted blood.

She flinched as he dabbed at the torn skin, cleaning out any remaining dirt. "I think I got them all," he said softly. "I'm sorry. I know it hurt."

He put squares of gauze over the cuts and used surgical tape to hold them in place. "They'll sting for a while, but once they scab over you'll be fine."

"Pretty," she breathed.

"You got off lucky," he replied, standing and gathering bits of bandage and tape to put in the garbage.

"I know I did," she answered, finally relaxing her neck. She put her hand on Tom's wrist, halting it from picking up the tweezers. "Lucky that I wasn't killed when the barn came down. And lucky that you were there to pull me out. I can't ever thank you enough, Tom. I was so scared." Her lip wobbled. "Why is it that you are always there when I'm scared?"

He put down the tweezers. "Maybe I'm supposed to be. Have you thought of that?"

His hand stroked along her arm and she shivered. Right now it seemed like too much to think about. Everything felt overwhelming, thoughts crowding on top of other thoughts until they were a big jumbled mess.

"You're still cold. Now that your knees are fixed, let's get you into something warmer."

He'd misread the reason for her shiver, but she didn't mind. He came back with a pair of gray sweatpants and handed them over with a crooked smile. "I'm afraid this is all I have."

She shrugged. "They'll do." The cuffs of her shorts were wet and chafed her thighs. She was already starting to feel stiffness in her arms and back, but she stood and began to unbutton her shorts. "Turn around, okay?"

His dark eyes shone at her for a moment before he smiled. "Yes, ma'am."

He turned around, and stoically holding in any sounds of pain, she managed to shove her shorts down over her ankles, step out of them, and into the sweats. They were very baggy and she had to pull the drawstring in as tight as it would go, but she did feel better. "Okay," she said, gingerly bending to pick up the damp shorts.

"I'll throw them in the dryer with your shirt," he suggested, and disappeared.

When he came back, she had gone to the window and was staring out over the water. He came up behind her and wrapped his arms around her, pulling her back against the hard wall of his chest. "Don't ever scare me like that again," he murmured.

"I didn't mean to. I just wanted to go for a run."

"To avoid the house because you knew I was coming."

She turned, looking up into his face. There was real pain in his features. He truly had been worried about her. And it hurt him to think that she'd rather be caught in a thunderstorm than in the same house with him.

He'd saved her today. Despite their screwed-up relationship, he'd searched for her and pulled her out and doctored her wounds with gentleness.

Abby sighed, resting her forehead on his broad chest. She was in love with him, she finally admitted to herself. And it wasn't just because he'd rescued her but because the very act of it had showed her the kind of man he was. He was the one she went to with her secrets. It didn't matter anymore that his heart belonged to someone else and probably always would. That was completely separate from the demands of *her* heart. And right now hers was telling her that Tom was the most amazing thing to ever happen to her. It was, in that moment, the most thrilling and terrifying realization of her life.

"I wasn't running away from you," she said, reaching up and touching his face. "I just needed to clear my head."

"I don't understand."

"I know. But maybe it's time you do. Can we sit down?"

Her knees ached as she followed him to the sofa. The cushions were deep and thick and she sank into them with a sigh. His cottage wasn't big but it was cozy. She thought she could probably sit here and watch the birds and the ocean for hours.

"This place suits you, you know. Peaceful. A good place to hide away from the world."

"You know me too well." He sat beside her and tucked one foot beneath him so he was half turned in her direction. "And sometimes I feel like I don't know you at all."

"And I feel like you know me better than anyone I've ever met." She smiled a little. "I'm being cryptic, aren't I?"

"A bit."

She looked down at her lap. "You've been very open with me, Tom, far more than I've been with you." She reached over and squeezed his hand. "You told me about Erin, and that couldn't have been easy. I trust you, and that's something very new for me. And more than a bit scary."

Their fingers were still joined and she rubbed her thumb over the warm, rough skin of his hand. Tom had working hands. Caring hands. Strong hands that had pulled her from danger. Hands that had touched her skin and set her on fire. She lifted his hand and pressed his palm to her lips.

"I've never really had what you'd call a stable home life. When my father died, my whole world got turned upside down. My mother ran out on us when I was just a baby, so when she got custody of me, I had no stability. We were always moving around. I didn't make many friends because I knew I wouldn't have them for long. I blended in. I missed my father so much, but Mom didn't want to hear it. She just wanted to have fun and a kid didn't really fit the image she was going for. I tried running away once and social services put me in foster care for a short while before sending me back to my mom. God, she was so angry that I'd drawn any attention to us."

"I'm sorry, Abby, but I don't get—"

She smiled sadly. "Bear with me."

He squeezed her hand. "Okay."

"My mom was killed in an accident when I was fifteen. She was driving drunk and hit a tree, and as much as I thought I hated her, she was still my mother, you know? By then my grandmother was all I had left. I finished high school, stayed close to her for college, but then she died, too. And I was all alone. Then I found out that there was this whole family out there that I never had the chance to know. I felt like my relationship with Gram had been meaningless, because she'd kept so much hidden. I never really knew her, you know? Every person I'd cared about, the people I'd trusted to be there for me . . . suddenly all gone."

"Abs," Tom said, softer now, and he put his arm around her shoulder and pulled her close.

"That was the lowest I'd ever been, losing her," she confessed. "Gram had always told us that her parents died when she was a baby and she had been raised by her grandparents. They were in their seventies and died right before she got pregnant with my dad. And that was that."

She leaned back, away from his embrace. "Don't you see? Coming here, meeting you, all of it, it's just been so confusing. I've never really had a home before. I'm not sure I'd even know what to do with one."

She swallowed, looked out the window. "Everyone I've ever cared about has disappeared," she murmured. "It hurts so much. If I stay here, if I start to care about this place . . . about the people . . . Today, I wasn't avoiding you. I was just trying to get some clarity."

# CHAPTER 20

Tom felt like all the air had been sucked from his lungs. Things that hadn't made sense suddenly clicked into place. Her insecurities and her independence. The way she stood on the fringes, holding herself away from getting too close to anyone. Her need for control.

He closed his eyes. The way she'd melted in his arms, and the way she'd stopped him before he could make love to her. The way he'd yelled at her at the cemetery. Just as he'd started holding bits of himself back after that night at the Rusty Fern, Abby had built walls around herself. Walls that, if he were right, were in danger of being broken down—if he were willing to push.

"I wish you'd told me sooner," he murmured, opening his eyes and looking into her pale face. "I would have been . . ."

"What? More sympathetic? The last thing I want is anyone's pity."

She was so much stronger than she gave herself credit for. "That day in your room. When you asked me to stop . . ."

Why was it he couldn't seem to finish a thought? Even

now, he was afraid of saying the wrong thing. Of revealing too much.

She smiled at him. It wobbled a bit and her cheeks flushed. "You're going to think me terribly innocent now. But the morning with you on my bed . . . I meant it when I said it had been a long time. I've never even—" She broke off and looked away. "Well, it wouldn't have been my first time, but let's just say I've yet to have my mind blown."

What was she saying? That she'd never experienced good sex? A climax? The idea made him instantly hard. He would have made damn sure it was as good for her as for him.

Tom looked at her, dressed in his baggy clothes, her hair loose around her collar, her rain-washed skin glowing in the lamplight. She was a beautiful, confident, scarred woman. He thought briefly about Erin, who had sat on this very sofa and begged him to run away with her. Who had said she couldn't make it without him. Tom had felt guilty that he couldn't love her anymore, couldn't take care of her. Erin had needed him and made no secret of it.

Abby was different. Abby didn't expect anyone to take care of her. She relied on herself. From the first day, she'd gone toe-to-toe with him as he'd put his foot through her porch floor.

She was far more fearless than she realized.

He reached over and touched a finger to her cheek. "You are the strongest woman I've ever known."

She smiled so sweetly his heart ached with it.

"I don't know about that. But it's nice of you to say so."

She deserved so much better than the hand she'd been dealt. A home and security. A man who loved her. Maybe a couple of kids running around. She was kind but firm—she'd be a great mother. And he was torn between wanting to be the one to give those things to her and afraid he couldn't. Time and circumstances had conditioned Tom not to fight. And while she'd opened up to him this afternoon, the whole tone of the conversation felt like a prologue to a new chapter called Moving On.

But that didn't stop the chemistry from fizzing between them. Their gazes clung, and without saying anything more to ruin the moment, they began drifting closer, closer. His gaze dropped to her lips and they parted slightly, anticipating the touch of his mouth on hers—

When the phone rang they both jumped. "It can wait," he said, his voice soft and husky. "Let it ring."

She sat back. "No, answer it. With the storm it might be something important."

He squeezed her hand and got up, going to the kitchen for the handset, disappointed at the interruption. When he returned to the living room moments later, he sat heavily on the sofa. There was a stinging behind his eyes that he couldn't quite blink away.

"What is it?" she asked immediately. "What's happened? It's bad, isn't it?"

He shook his head and gazed into her worried eyes. "That was Jess. It's Sarah. She lost the baby."

Abby's eyes instantly filled. "Oh, God."

"She's in the hospital in Portland. They want to keep her overnight just in case."

"They were so excited," Abby said quietly. "After trying so long, for this to happen . . ."

Sadness settled around them. "The whole family is there," he said. "One thing you have to say for the Collinses. They stick together when the going is rough."

He used to be a part of that circle. Still was, but only to a point. It hurt sometimes, because he was as close to his cousins as if they were his sisters . . . and brother.

"You need to be there. Go."

"What about you?"

"I'm going with you."

She surprised him by standing up. The Abby he'd come to know shied away from anything bordering on personal involvement.

"I'm not sure my being there would be the best thing," he suggested.

"Well, here's a newsflash, Tom. This isn't about you. This is about your cousin. And if Jess didn't think you should be there, she wouldn't have called you." She tugged at his hand. "They are your family. Do you know how lucky you are to have them? Don't you think I'd give anything to have mine again?"

She was right. But, big man that he was, Tom was scared. Of reaching out and of having his hand slapped back again.

"Jess and Sarah are right about one thing. This thing with Josh has gone on too long. Put it aside for this one day and just be there for her."

How could he argue with that? She was absolutely right. There was just one problem.

What were the chances Josh would be on the same page?


Josh paced the hallway, away from Jess and away from the knowing eyes of his mother. Meggie saw too much when she looked at him and being here wasn't easy. Right now he wished he was just about anywhere else.

But Sarah needed the family around her. He'd heard a lot of talk about God's will lately. Well, if this was God's will, it sucked.

And now they were all left outside in the hall, waiting for Mark to come out of Sarah's room, waiting to go hold her hand or kiss her cheek and fumble about with trying to find the right words to say when there weren't any right words at all. Nothing could make this better.

He stopped and looked out the window, staring unseeing into the sunny afternoon. The thunderstorms in Jewell Cove had blown through here earlier, leaving everything scoured and clean, like nature's pressure washer. Pristine and beautiful while inside his guts were churning.

He'd wanted babies. Erin's babies. He'd secretly hoped that she'd retire from the military with him, that she'd get pregnant with their child and opt not to do another tour. They'd talked about it, even. About starting a family and leaving the military life behind them for good.

But she had shipped out one last time. One final chance to do her part, she'd said, before coming back to Hartford. But he'd known all along. It wasn't about duty or patriotism that last time. It had been to put distance between them and the marriage that never quite seemed to work.

After she was gone he'd discovered the receipts for her birth control. She'd been on them for months. The whole time they'd talked about having a baby and lamenting each month when she got her period, she'd been secretly taking them to prevent it.

He knew why she'd done it. It wasn't that she didn't want babies. She didn't want *his* babies. And that hurt most of all.

Jess went by him, focused on something down the corridor, and he turned his head to follow her movement. "You came," he heard her say, and he saw Tom walking toward them.

Josh's fingers tightened into fists.

That woman was with him. Abby Foster, the one who'd inherited the mansion and had so coolly made him feel like an idiot at Sarah's barbecue. She was dressed in a pair of sweatpants and a sweatshirt that fit so loosely on her tiny frame that he knew they were Tom's.

Maybe he should be grateful that Tom had managed to do what Josh, so far, had not. He'd moved on. Instead he just felt angry and jealous.

"How is she, Jess?" Abby's voice reached him, and he had to give her credit. She seemed genuinely concerned.

"About how you'd expect."

"The whole family's here," Tom said, and his gaze slid to Josh.

There was no animosity in the way his cousin looked at him. He simply waited . . . for what? For Josh to say he was sorry? For them to bury the hatchet? Josh knew he hadn't always played fair. At the barbecue Tom had said that Josh won, but he was wrong. Josh had always known exactly where he stood in Erin's heart. And he'd let that fact eat away at him a little each day.

And for what? Erin was gone.

He and Tom had been like brothers growing up. To say that he'd missed that closeness would be an understatement. Seeing Tom on the docks had hurt. It brought back memories of how things used to be along with a knowledge that they could never be the same again.

Since Erin's death, holding on to his resentment had been all that had kept him going sometimes. He couldn't do it anymore. He couldn't live with the poison of it eating up his soul.

He stepped forward, his heart knocking around a little bit as he wasn't used to either backing down or apologizing. But maybe Jess was right. Maybe it was time to put pride aside. For the sake of the family.

"Tom," he said, holding out his hand.

Josh was dimly aware of Jess's mouth dropping open and Abby's eyes widening, but he made sure he kept his gaze solidly on Tom. A muscle ticked in Tom's jaw and then he reached out and clasped Josh's hand, a firm grip that transported Josh far into the past, to a time when they had sworn to always be brothers, not cousins. To stand up for each other, not against. Josh had so many regrets. God, he'd made a lot of mistakes. He didn't quite know how to go about fixing any of them. But as Tom's fingers tightened around his, he felt, for the first time in years, like he wanted to try.

"Thanks for coming," he managed, but his voice sounded all strange and choked.

"It's what family does," Tom answered roughly. "Sticks together. Though it took Abby kicking my sorry ass to make me see it."

Josh released Tom's hand before he embarrassed himself by pulling him into a man-hug. He looked down at Abby. "I owe you an apology," he said. "For the way I acted at Sarah's. I was a jerk. No excuses."

She shook her head. "It's fine. I understand, Josh. And I'm so sorry for your loss."

She could have made it difficult and instead she was being generous. He looked back at Tom. "You'd better hang on to her."

Tom's brown eyes glinted with the touch of humor Josh remembered. "She's too good for me," Tom answered plainly.

"Shit, we all know that," Josh replied, and Tom's answering low chuckle took the tension away.

"Jess?" Meggie's voice came from a few feet away. "Sarah wants to see you."

Jess slid away and Abby excused herself to see if she could get anyone coffee, leaving Tom and Josh standing in the middle of the hallway.

"I suppose we should talk," Tom said. "Seeing as how I don't think you're going to punch me again. At least not today."

"I think the time for that's past." Josh looked over his shoulder, watched as Jess went in the hospital room. "I feel so damned sorry for Sarah. She wanted this baby so much."

"Sarah's the softest heart in the bunch of us," Tom admitted. "It doesn't seem fair."

A few moments of silence hung in the air until Josh decided he might as well get rid of the elephant in the room. "I know now's not the time, but I know why Erin did that last tour, Tom. I only had to see her face when someone mentioned your name to know."

Tom swallowed. "I swear to you, Josh, I didn't mean for that to happen."

"I know that. I did what I could to love her enough, but it was always you. I hated you for it."

Tom came forward and laid a hand on Josh's arm. "We never, ever had an affair. Please believe that."

"Not even when she went to you before her last deployment?"

Josh expected to see guilt on Tom's face. He wasn't prepared for the pain.

"You knew."

"I knew," Josh confirmed. "She told me she was going to Boston to see some girlfriends. I knew it was a lie. When she got back I checked the history in her GPS."

Awkward silence fell. Tom cleared his throat. "She came to see me. She wanted us to be together, permanently, said she'd stay Stateside and—"

"And divorce me." The words were harder to say out loud than he could have imagined.

"What was I supposed to do?" With a sharp exhale, Tom turned away. He ran his hand through his hair. "If I . . . if we . . ." He glanced up at Josh. "If we'd slept together, it would have been betraying you and the promise I made myself to not put myself in the middle of your marriage. I couldn't do it. I'm not proud of how all this shook down but I do have a little bit of self-respect that I try to hold on to. So I said no. And by turning her away . . ." He stared off into space. "I practically sent her on that last deployment. And she never came back."

Tom blamed himself? Josh felt like sitting down. He hadn't seen that one coming.

"I wasn't enough," Josh admitted. "I thought if we started a family, a life in Hartford, that she'd forget about you. But she didn't want that. She made sure there were no babies to tie her to me." Josh sighed heavily. "I found her birth control pills. She didn't want me. I wasn't you, you see."

More silence as they both absorbed the truth.

Loving Erin had cost them both so much. Perhaps too much.

"Things won't be the same," Tom finally said quietly. "I know that. But not beating on each other every time we're in the same room would be a good start."

Josh couldn't help the smile that flickered on his lips. "That's just because I always win."

"You wish," Tom replied, and a bit of the old comfort between them came back.

"So you and Abby," Josh said, warmer this time. "She's plucky."

Tom snorted. "Plucky?"

Josh shrugged. "Well, it's the first time anyone's seen you with a woman in . . . well, never mind. We've covered that. But show up in public wearing your sweats? That kind of says it all, don't you think?"

Tom ran a hand over his face. "Actually, it wasn't like that. It's a long story, too long for today. Anyway, don't get your hopes up. It's complicated, and she's put the house up for sale. I don't think she's hanging around for much longer."

There was the sound of a door opening and closing and the men turned to the double doors that marked the entrance to the ward. Bryce came through and halted as he saw the two of them standing together. A smile spread across his face. "Boys," he said, coming forward. "Looking for a referee?"

Abby handed cups of coffee to Meggie, Tom, and Josh. Another of tea waited for Jess in the cardboard cup holder and she sipped at her own beverage, suddenly exhausted. Her legs were starting to pain as the meds wore off, so she sat down in one of the waiting room chairs to give them some relief. Tom was standing with Josh and Bryce and the three of them were talking. Their faces were somber, but not angry. The three of them made quite a picture—Bryce's and Tom's muscled, dark features against Josh's leaner, lighter coloring.

"That's not a sight I thought I'd see anytime soon," Meggie said, taking a seat beside Abby.

"They put their differences aside for Sarah." Abby looked at Tom's aunt. "How is she?"

Worry clouded Meggie's eyes. "No mother should ever have to bury her babies."

"Or see their children suffer," Abby said quietly.

"Or that. Mine have had their share."

"Erin's death and now Sarah."

Meggie sipped her coffee. "Jess, too. You have them and want to protect them but at some point they have to go out on their own. It's hard to watch the failures. But wonderful to see the victories." She nodded at Josh. "That feels like a victory today. And I get the feeling you had a hand in it. Thank you for that."

Abby shifted in the chair and the armrest knocked against her thigh. She gasped and clenched her teeth but not before Meggie noticed. "Are you okay? Don't take this the wrong way, but you're looking a bit rough. We all sort of assumed that you and Tom had . . . I mean, with the borrowed clothes and everything . . ." Meggie blushed a little, and so did Abby.

"Oh," she replied. She hadn't quite thought about appearances when they'd hopped in the truck. "Um, not like that. I got caught in the storm earlier. My clothes are in Tom's dryer."

"And the leg?" Meggie's gaze penetrated. "Someone doesn't react like that from a little scratch."

"The short version is that the barn at the top of Blackberry Hill is toast. I didn't quite make it out unscathed."

"What?" Meggie leaned forward. "Are you saying that old monstrosity finally came down?"

"With me inside it, I'm afraid."

Meggie's face paled. "My God, girl, what are you doing here?"

Abby smiled, touched by the concern. "It's okay. I was pretty lucky. Tom bandaged me up. There's a cut on my leg, and my knees got chewed up a bit."

"Let's see."

Abby felt ridiculous. "I'm fine, really."

Meggie frowned, her face taking on that motherly "just do as I say" look. Abby rolled up the cuff of Tom's pants and carefully peeled back the gauze over her knee.

"You weren't kidding." Meggie examined the wound.

"There were a lot of splinters," Abby explained. "I'm afraid it's quite tender."

"Of course it is." She sat up. "Josh?"

"Meggie, please . . ."

"Josh is a doctor. He should have a look." She frowned. "Tom should have taken you to him in the first place. Oh, well. At least fences seem mended now."

Josh approached, followed by Tom and Bryce.

"Take a look at Abby, will you, Josh?"

Josh knelt down and examined her knees. "Good Lord. How did you do this?"

She met his alarmed gaze. "Trying to crawl out of a falling building. I didn't quite make it."

He peeled off the remaining gauze and tape. Tom put his hand on her shoulder as she winced at the gentle touch. "She had splinters, but I think I got them all out."

"A falling building, huh?"

"Lightning hit the old Prescott barn," Tom explained.

"And Tom pulled me out," Abby replied, reaching up and squeezing his hand. "Did I actually say thank you yet?"

He squeezed back in return.

Josh frowned. "You're okay otherwise?"

"I think so. There's a small cut on my leg."

"You should have your tetanus updated if you haven't in a while. I'll see to it, okay?"

"Josh, really, I—"

He put his hand on her ankle. "It's the least I can do. Besides, it'll keep me busy. I'll be back in a few minutes."

Meggie gently replaced the bandage, anchoring the tape and rolling down the cuffs of the pants. Abby's eyes stung. Twice today people had tended to her with care. Right now Abby was feeling rather mothered, and it was something she'd missed more than she realized.

Tom went to put his cup in the garbage. "You're really selling the house?" Meggie asked, sounding disappointed.

The question made Abby uncomfortable. She really didn't know anymore. Why did it seem to matter to everyone? "It's awfully big for one person. I didn't know much about my family when I got here, but I've filled in the blanks, which is what I set out to do. There's no reason for me to stay."

Meggie looked at Tom. "Isn't there?"

Josh returned with fresh materials and in no time he had her knees rebandaged and she'd endured a tetanus shot. She felt silly, knowing she was fine while Sarah was the one in the hospital room going through hell. But she let Tom's family baby her just this once. Once she was squared away, Tom offered to go out and pick up some food for everyone. Bryce went with him and Josh went to speak to the doctor.

Jess came out of Sarah's room. "I'm going to take Mark to pick up the kids," Jess said. Her eyes looked tired and slightly red. "Mom, she wondered if you'd go with me and pick up some of her things for the night."

"I'll sit with her for a while," Abby said, rising. "I can't do much, but I can get her something if she needs it."

"Thank you, Abby," Jess said. "I don't want her to be alone."

Abby went into the room, her steps tentative. Sarah was in the bed, covered to her armpits in a white sheet and wearing a hospital johnny shirt. Abby sat on the edge of the bed, struggling not to cry herself. Maybe she'd never lost a baby, but she was no stranger to grief. She took Sarah's hand in hers.

"I am so, so sorry," she said quietly.

Sarah looked up at Abby and tears filled her eyes.

"You don't need to say anything," Abby whispered, knowing that there were times that words just didn't seem to help when a heart was in despair. Sarah put her head back against the pillow and Abby watched, helpless, as a tear squeezed out of Sarah's eye and rolled along her cheek to the pillow.

And then Abby sat there, just holding Sarah's hand as she cried it out, until Sarah's eyelids finally closed and she slid into an emotionally exhausted sleep.

# Chapter 21

"Tom, can I ask your opinion about something?"

Abby stood in the doorway to the kitchen. Tom had come by to replace the door on one of the kitchen cupboards that had come from the manufacturer with a flaw. He was kneeling on the floor holding a screwdriver in his hand, his jeans curved beautifully over his bottom. His T-shirt rode up just a bit, stretched across the muscles of his back.

He was easily the most gorgeous man she'd ever known.

Unfortunately, he was also the most difficult to figure out. Everything had changed since the day of the storm. So many things had been resolved. She'd shared the deepest parts of herself with Tom, and she'd thought they'd grown closer because of it. It was true that Sarah and Mark's tragedy had cast a pall of sadness over the family, but it was tempered by Tom and Josh's tentative reconciliation. Wounds were being healed.

So why did she feel farther removed from Tom instead of closer? Ever since they'd been interrupted on their way to kissing—and that was definitely where they'd been headed—he'd been distant. He'd brought her home from the hospital that night and left her at the door. She'd offered to go to his place to pick up her clothing but he dropped it off one day when she was in town meeting with the lawyer.

That night had given Abby a clarity about herself, her past, and what she wanted from her future . . . or in this case their future. She'd been running away her whole life, afraid of getting hurt, and she was tired of it. Abby wanted a place to call home, a family, friends, Tom. But so far, instead of getting closer, Tom had backed off.

"Fire away," he answered, not looking up from his work.

She stepped inside. "Jewell Cove has a historical society, right?"

The ratcheting screwdriver made grinding noises in the otherwise silent kitchen. He chuckled. "Sure, but you could start up your *own* historical society with what's up in that attic."

"I've already sorted out a lot of things that might be of interest to collectors."

He picked up another screw and set it in place. "Getting their hands on some of the old Foster relics would be a major coup," he confirmed. "I'm surprised the town hasn't asked you about buying the house for a museum."

She ran her hand over the cool granite countertop. He'd done a fabulous job in the kitchen, making it modern and sleek while still maintaining the stately grandeur of the rest of the house. "Oh, I did run into the mayor at Breezes one morning when I first arrived and he might have mentioned it."

The screwdriver stopped turning. Tom finally looked up at her, but she found it impossible to read his expression.

"Has the town put in an offer?"

"Not that I'm aware of. The price tag might be a little hefty."

He looked back down at the cabinet door and opened and shut it a few times, and then fiddled more with the screws.

"Anyway, what I wondered was . . . what do you think of me hosting one last Foster garden party?"

"A garden party? Here?" Tom paused in the middle of his task to look at Abby in surprise.

"I know the yard still needs some work. I thought about asking Art Ellis to come up to show me how the garden used to be. The roses are blooming, but it needs more flowers. Do you know where I should go to buy some annuals to fill in the gaps?"

He sat back on his heels. "Why on earth would you want to hold a garden party when you're selling this place anyway?"

This was the tough part, because she wasn't sure she was ready to lay all her cards on the table yet, to just come out and tell him—and everyone—that the party was her own personal housewarming. She twisted her fingers together. "I think it's a good way to erase the bad . . . I don't know, karma, maybe, of the past. You worked so hard to restore the house and everyone talks about how it used to be in its heyday. Why shouldn't I throw a party? What better way to . . . send it off into the future?"

Except the future wasn't quite what he thought it was. The FOR SALE sign was still up and would remain up— but only for the time being. Tom thought that the party was a last hurrah before she sold, but really, it was a new beginning. For her. And maybe for them . . .

She took a step closer to him. "Think about it. White tents on the back lawn, vases of flowers, ladies in long dresses. We could polish up the good silver and serve tea on that gorgeous Wedgwood china. I counted, Tom. The

Fosters had service for a hundred. Can you imagine? China for one hundred people!"

Tom shut the cupboard door, stood up, and tucked the screwdriver into his back pocket. "So you're what, throwing a going-away party for yourself?"

So much was at stake but she'd never been more determined to succeed. The time for running was past.

"Something like that," she answered, crossing her fingers behind her back. "Anyway, I was wondering if you knew who to contact. I'd like for the historical society to be a part of it."

"Talk to Gloria Henderson. She's the organist at the church. If she can't help you, she'll know who can."

"We've met. Thanks, Tom." She turned toward the door but then spun back. "You'll be sure to come, won't you?"

He raised an eyebrow. "Me? At a garden party? Are you serious?"

For a second Abby felt a flash of panic at the thought that Tom wouldn't be there. She couldn't imagine doing this without him, not when he'd been here every step of the way. It was because of him this was even possible. "But of course you'll be here. You're the reason this place looks like it does. Everyone will want to ask you about the restoration. It's good advertising for your business."

"I'm not dressing up in some silly suit."

She smirked. "Of course not." She tried to picture Tom in an elegant day suit of cream and white and it wouldn't gel. "Just say you'll come and soak up all the compliments on your fine work."

He sighed. "Me coming, is that the favor?"

"Not quite. I was hoping you could tell me where to rent the tents and a good garden center to buy the bedding plants," she nudged again.

"Brian Wilson has a greenhouse out on Oaklawn

Road. I'd go with him rather than some of the bigger garden centers."

"Thanks, Tom."

"Anytime. And there's a place in Rockland where you
can probably rent the tents. I'll text you their info. I know
I've got it at home."

She smiled. "You're a gem, Tom. I appreciate all your
help."

"You're welcome. And you're all set here, so unless
there's something else . . ."

"You want something to drink? I can put on some coffee, or there's iced tea in the fridge."

"I'd better get back. I'm putting together a bid on a new
project."

"Oh."

"I'll be in touch soon, though. See ya, Abby."

He picked up his tools and the old cupboard door and
slid past her, his boots making thumps on the hardwood
floor.

Abby bit down on her lip as she rested against the woodwork of the door frame. She had her work cut out for her,
didn't she?

Art Ellis was more than happy to help with the gardens.
Abby spent several pleasant hours listening to him recall
stories about Marian's time in the house and how she
loved her garden. Petunias, marigolds, pansies, and alys-
sum filled out the flower beds, but Abby also took care
to add some new perennials that would last from year
to year—lilies, phlox, and her personal favorite, cheerful
red bee balm. She knelt in the dirt and Art supervised
nearby. By the time they were done Abby was stiff but
pleased. The garden was alive with color and scent, and
as she put her hands on her lower back and stretched, she

watched a butterfly alight on one of the crimson blossoms.

Help in the form of Gloria Henderson also made things come together. She volunteered her services along with that of the churchwomen to prepare the food for the event if Abby bought the groceries. Together they decided on a very garden party-ish menu of finger sandwiches, petits fours and cookies, punch, and of course, tea.

Jess was enlisted to help with the table decorations, details that Abby left in her capable, creative hands. Tents were rented from Rockland. It was all coming together beautifully.

It was Jess's idea to ask Sarah to help with the invitations. Ever since arriving home from the hospital, Sarah had been withdrawn. It wasn't unexpected but it was increasingly worrisome as the days went by. Jess had somehow acquired a pen-and-ink sketch of Foster House. They scanned it into Sarah's computer, and with the first real energy she'd shown for days, Sarah added the details in an elegant font. Eighty invitations were sent out to local businesses, civic figures, and anyone who'd had a personal connection to the Fosters.

The only thing left was to decide what she was going to wear.

And for that, she needed to make another trip to the attic.


Tom wasn't prepared for the red, white, and blue bunting hanging from the pillars of Foster House. Coming up the drive he could already see the white tents set up in the back, festive and pristine against the blue of the sky. Abby couldn't have better weather if she'd ordered it especially for the day. Tom did a double take as he realized there was a man directing the parking, and that he was dressed in what Tom suspected was the old Foster livery—not a re-creation, but the original, real deal.

How on earth had she come up with that?

There were at least a dozen cars all lined up along the side of the lane, their hoods partially shaded by the row of birch trees. Tom got out, glad for once he had put away his work boots and jeans for something slightly dressier. Maybe he'd had to dig into the back of his closet, but the light blue shirt and charcoal suit pants had seemed far more appropriate. The dress shoes pinched his toes a bit but were livable. He wasn't dressed like some Edwardian dandy, but he figured he'd do all right.

Everything was happening in the backyard, but Tom went to the front door instead. Abby had been right. He should be here because it would be good for business. And since his business had involved the house and not the backyard, he figured he'd better make a showing there first. Besides, he was feeling slightly proprietary about it all today. Abby hadn't changed her mind about selling. Quite the contrary, in fact. Ever since that day at the hospital he'd been waiting for her to take down that blasted sign, but it stayed stubbornly in place, a glaring reminder that her feelings hadn't changed.

She was really going. It was time he accepted the truth and quit waiting. Tom had finally gone into town and put his offer in this morning before the place sold from under his nose.

The door opened before he could raise his hand to knock, and feeling foolish he stepped inside. He felt even more foolish when he saw the man behind the uniform. "Mayor," he said drily.

"Just the butler today, Tom. The historical society is helping out." Luke Pratt winked. "Welcome to Foster House."

Abby had gone all out, hadn't she? As Tom made his way through to the back of the house, he noticed that every inch had been polished until it gleamed. The new drapes she'd ordered had been delivered and hung precisely in place, and the sliding pocket door he'd installed in the kitchen was closed, blocking it from the view of the guests. He stood aside as it slid open and a maid in black and white came out carrying a silver tray.

He'd stepped back in time.

"Tom."

Abby's voice was a welcome distraction from feeling like he'd fallen down a rabbit hole, but when he turned around it felt like all the air had gone out of his lungs.

She looked beautiful. Timeless. Like a picture out of the old Foster photo album only in living, breathing color. "Wow," he managed.

She grinned and spun in a circle. "Do you like it? It's got to be over a hundred years old. When I first discovered it the shirt was a bit yellowed and it smelled like the cedar chest. It dry-cleaned beautifully though, don't you think?"

He swallowed. What he was thinking had little to do with the state of her clothing but with her. The full navy skirt fell in soft folds clear to the floor, and the white blouse was tapered and tucked in all the right places to make her waist look tiny and her breasts . . .

Well. He swallowed again. He'd have to lock that down tight, wouldn't he?

A red, white, and blue sash ran from her shoulder to her hip as well, to celebrate the occasion. "You're looking very festive," he answered. "This is quite the event."

"Come look," she replied, taking his hand and tugging him toward the porch. "The historical society has worked its magic."

What Tom thought was that Abby had been the one to

work magic. She had no idea how much she belonged here. Or that when she went away, they were all going to miss her terribly.

Abby's heart pounded and she forced herself to keep her composure. Tom looked delicious today, out of his customary jeans and into what she'd consider business casual. The way his trousers hugged his hips and the blue shirt spread across the wide expanse of his chest . . .

Time hadn't taken away the attraction, the need for him. It made the stakes today even greater.

She led him through the sunny porch and down the steps to the backyard. Several tents were set up, and beneath their shade were tables with blindingly white cloths. Each table held a bouquet of flowers in patriotic colors. Abby tilted her head up at him, her heart full of gladness that he'd actually come. She'd been afraid he wouldn't. "What do you think? Red roses, white carnations, and blue irises—those for my gram."

His gaze met hers. "It's beautiful, Abby. Your gram would have loved it, I think. But it must have cost you a fortune."

She lifted her shoulders in a noncommittal shrug. "It was worth it. Besides, I wanted it to be an event worthy of the house, you know?"

"Especially if it's the only one you ever have, right?"

She looked away, inexplicably stung by the way he said the words—almost like an accusation. "I should go," she said, some of her enthusiasm dimmed. "More people are arriving and I need to be a good hostess. Excuse me, Tom."

She made her rounds, ensuring the food was circulated, tea was served, and the punch bowl always filled. She never lost sight of Tom, though. The light blue fabric of his shirt emphasized his summer tan, and he'd left the top button undone. She swallowed thickly. She did like the look of an unbuttoned man. But today it wasn't just any man. It was Tom Arseneault and frankly she was terrified that at the end of it he was going to drive away in his truck and never darken her door again.

He'd put an offer in on the house. The Realtor had wasted no time calling her up and giving her the news. He'd hedged when she'd asked the name, but he'd given in eventually.

Tom was so sure that she was leaving that he was going to buy her house himself, just like he'd proposed that very first day. She leaned against the trunk of a tree and looked out over what had been a pasture decades before. The grass grew tall and wild there. He expected her to sell him the house and hit the road as she'd always intended. Go back to her life and her job. Play it safe.

But he was in for a surprise. She'd done a lot of soul-searching since that afternoon at the hospital, surrounded by Tom's family. She wasn't that scared girl any longer. Sure, she'd been a little slow on the uptake, but looking around her house filled with laughter and friends, Abby knew she was right to refuse the offer, take it off the market, and finally make this her permanent home. She laughed a little to herself. When she'd first driven into town, she couldn't wait to get back out again. Now she could admit to herself that she loved Jewell Cove. Abby was finally being honest with herself, and the house wasn't the only reason she had for staying in Jewell Cove. She wanted a life here, and there was no way she was going to sit back and live here, seeing Tom day in and day out, without first fighting for them. She just had to get the courage to actually say something first.

"Penny for your thoughts," a voice said.

Josh stood at her shoulder. "Oh, goodness," she gasped. "You startled me."

He smiled. "Sorry."

"Don't take this the wrong way, but I didn't expect to see you here today. It's not generally a guy thing."

"Sarah made me promise to come with her. She said she would if I would. She needed to get out of the house, so . . ." He let the thought hang.

"What about Mark?"

A cloud darkened Josh's face. "He took the kids somewhere. It's been rough on the whole family. And Mark thought that Sarah needed a break."

"I'm sorry." Abby turned a little and rested her shoulders against the tree. "They'll be okay, though, right?"

Josh's eyes were somber. Abby realized she'd never really seen him smile or laugh. "I hope so," he answered. He lifted his chin at the activity behind them. "This is quite something, you know. Foster House has been quiet for as long as I can remember. The town's going to be talking about how you brought it back to life for a long time. Too bad you're not going to be here to enjoy it."

His gaze was just a little too knowing and Abby made sure she focused her attention on the guests and not him. "Ah, well. A last hurrah for the Fosters, I guess."

"How long are you going to torture him, Abby?"

Her gaze snapped to his before she could think better of it.

"I know what Tom looks like when he's in love," Josh said. "And I know what he looks like when it's killing him and it's right there in his expression today."

She saw Tom standing on the perimeter of the lawn, talking to someone. He had one hand stuck casually in his pocket. "He looks fine to me," she replied coolly, but she probably wasn't fooling Josh any more than she was fooling herself.

"He's not fine. He's waiting."

"Waiting for what?"

Josh sighed. "Waiting for you to choose him. I loved my wife, Abby, but I know why she married me. I was a better prospect than Tom. Erin had money. Or rather, her family had money. There were . . . expectations. Tom never met those expectations. And she put those above her heart and married me. And then regretted it."

"Josh," Abby said quietly. Lord, how it must have hurt his pride knowing that. "I'm sorry."

"Me, too. Turns out both Tom and I were second choice, just in different ways. You have to make him your first choice, Abby. I think especially because there are some similarities between you and Erin."

"Similarities?"

He frowned. "You inherited a family fortune. You don't need him. And Tom is used to being needed."

"I know."

"You do?"

She nodded. "I don't know what Tom's told you about me . . ."

"We've made up. We haven't made it to baring our souls yet."

Abby laughed lightly. "Let's just say I had to get through a bunch of my own stuff first. And I do love him, Josh. I'm just afraid to be the one to take the first step. I've been afraid of . . . well, losing someone else I care about."

They were silent for a few minutes. Then Abby spoke up. "I don't think he wanted me to know, but he put an offer in on the house today. He's so sure I'm going to run."

"Have you given him a reason to believe otherwise?"

"I've been figuring things out."

"God, the two of you make a pair. Stubborn fools."

Josh put his hand on her arm. "Don't wait. Don't let pride or fear stand in your way. Just be honest and tell him how you feel. If it doesn't work out, it doesn't work out. But you have to try."

She knew he was right and it terrified her to bits. "For someone who hated him a few weeks ago, you sure are pleading his case."

Josh let go of her wrist. "No sense in both of us being miserable," he answered, and while Abby was left trying to think of a suitable response, he walked away to join the party.

The afternoon dragged on. Tom drank two cups of punch that was a bit sweet to his taste, tempered it with black tea, and then simply wished for a cold beer. He made a show of eating finger sandwiches and tiny sweets with pastel frosting off antique china, made small talk with Abby's guests, and answered questions about his renovations on the house. He managed to escape Summer Arnold's flirting green eyes and instead spent some time with Sarah, who was smiling just a little too widely for him to be comfortable. And when four o'clock arrived and the crowd started to filter out, he figured he should probably head that way, too. And he might have hurried, except a very long evening seemed to be the only thing waiting for him.

He'd probably spend the evening on his deck eating one of his usual grilled burgers and pondering the significance of the universe.

"You're not leaving already, are you?"

Abby came up behind him, holding her skirts in her hands as she quickened her step. A few strands of hair had come loose from her elaborate hairstyle, the effect softening her face and making her look slightly undone.

Any man who figured a woman had to prance around in next to nothing to be sexy simply hadn't seen Abby Foster buttoned up in her vintage clothes. All it did was make Tom want to reveal what was beneath—button by delicious button.

"Things are starting to wind down," he observed.

"But . . ."

"But what, Abby?"

If she wanted him to stay, he wished she'd just say it. Ever since the day at the hospital she'd been toothachingly sweet, pleasant, and impersonal as hell. He'd had the thought once or twice that she'd simply got her shit together and that the sorry truth was she didn't need him anymore. House fixed, family mystery solved, thanks for your help, bye.

"Will you stay?"

"Why?"

The question put her off balance, he could tell. A strange look passed over her face as she deliberated her answer. After several long seconds, he huffed out a sigh and turned on his heel.

"I know it was you who put a bid on the house," she said.

He paused. "You weren't supposed to know that yet."

"Were you planning on telling me yourself sometime today? Or just keeping it a secret?"

He turned to face her, ignoring the curious stares of the makeshift house staff who were clearing away silver platters and dirty china cups. He kept his voice low but each word was perfectly clear. "What does it matter? You wanted to sell the house and I offered for it. A solution I suggested from the beginning, if you remember."

"Is it really only about the house for you?"

Damn, what was she trying to get him to say? "Can we shelve this for another time? When it's more private?"

"Everyone will be gone soon. No one's coming for the tents until tomorrow. I can send them all home now if you like."

"How very Lady of the Manor of you." The FOR SALE sign at the end of the road was clear. Abby Foster wasn't staying. Why would she want to settle in a little nowhere town like this with a simple contractor who preferred beer and boots over garden parties and champagne?

"And how snobbish of you to point that out." She met his gaze evenly. "I'm not Erin, Tom. I don't care about wealth and status."

Her honest words struck him square in the chest. Not just because she was right but because she knew she was right and she'd used it against him.

"Ouch," he said roughly, turning to go.

"Would you rather I not be honest with you, Tom? We could pretend it doesn't matter but it does. We can pretend that Erin isn't in the picture but it would be pointless because it does matter. And if you're going to walk away from me, you can at least be man enough to tell me why."

He turned back. She had her chin lifted and she stood defiantly in the corridor, but he saw the vulnerability, too. In the softness of her lips, the quick rise and fall of her chest.

He took a step forward. "Me? Walk away from you?" He pointed toward the door. "You're the one with the FOR SALE sign in your front yard."

"And you're the one offering to buy it."

"So?"

They were standing off against each other when one of the kitchen maids entered from the side door. "Excuse me, but we're done in the kitchen, Abby. Do you want us to look after the linens and vases, too?"

Abby finally looked away from Tom and smiled. "No,

I'll do that later, thanks, Cindy. Tell everyone thank you for me, will you?"

Cindy looked from Abby to Tom, and back to Abby again. "We'll just get out of your hair, then," she said quietly. Tom watched her make a retreat with a soft swish of her black skirts. Voices quieted as the last of the ladies exited the house, leaving them alone.

Tom considered joining them. Getting in his truck and driving away. And yet he couldn't make himself do it.

"Don't leave," Abby said quietly. "There are things I need to say. Please. Will you wait while I change out of these things?"

He sighed, knowing he couldn't really say no to her, not when she looked at him the way she was now. "I'll wait."

"Promise?" Her blue eyes were uncertain as they met his. "You won't wait until I'm upstairs and then take off?"

He held her gaze. "I'll wait," he said, and the connection that had been missing for the past days was suddenly there again, tethering them together. He'd been a fool to think they could just walk away from each other easily.

She whirled in a swish of skirts and disappeared up the stairs, jogging down again in record time in jeans and a T-shirt.

"Let's go for a walk. Let's go to the top of the mountain and look down over Jewell Cove and the estate." She reached out and took his hand. "You are the one who took this falling-down mansion and made it beautiful again. You're the one who's been here from the very beginning."

"I can't argue with that," he replied hesitantly. This was already difficult enough without prolonging the torture. And yet time alone with her was a gift he wasn't ready to give back.

They strolled up the road to the gate, the sun soaking

through the cotton of his shirt. As they skirted the barrier, Tom reached over and took her hand, helping her over the rough hump of gravel beside the post. Once they were on the dirt road, he kept her fingers in his.

When they reached the summit they stood for a moment and stared at the rubble of the barn. Then she turned to look up at him and smiled. "Come on. Let me show you my favorite view."

She led him to the outcropping surrounded by grass and wild blackberries, not yet ripe.

Tom sat next to her in the grass. She was so beautiful. So strong . . . and headstrong. That one trait bugged the hell out of him and yet it was one of his favorite things about her. He admired it and yet it left him wondering what he had to offer.

"It's pretty, right?" she asked quietly.

"Gorgeous." But he didn't look down over the town, as she was doing. He simply watched her, the tiny smile that flickered on her lips, the way the light touched her hair. From now on he would always consider this spot theirs; that whatever happened in the next several minutes mattered little. Right now it was he and Abby together, inextricably linked by threads that were beautiful and complicated. Whatever happened in the future, nothing could take this moment away from them. From him.

"Look," she said softly, nodding at the stately house that had once been a neglected mausoleum.

"What am I looking at?" he asked.

"Home," she replied.

# CHAPTER 22

"Home?"

She nodded, nervousness expanding exponentially in her stomach. This was such a big leap of faith. One she felt good about, but one that came with risks to her heart, too.

He reached for her hand and squeezed. "What do you mean, *home*?"

She let out a breath. "I mean, Tom, that I've made a decision. The house on Blackberry Hill is no longer for sale."

"You're staying?"

Something big and awesome expanded in her chest at the hope she heard in his words. It was now or never. "Yes, I'm staying. For good."

"You're saying that you're going to live in that house."

She smiled, the expansive feeling growing, making her certain that this was absolutely the right decision. "I'm going to live in that house," she confirmed. "I'm going to keep it alive and have friends and music and a book club in the library and a rose garden in the summer. I'm going to put down roots, Tom. It's time."

His dark eyes softened. "I'm happy for you," he said, squeezing her fingers. "Disappointed for me, but happy for you."

Tom gazed into her face. God, how she'd fallen for him. Now that she'd made the decision to stay, the next part was even harder. She didn't want this to be the end of them but a new beginning. And yet she was smart enough to know that for that to happen, they had to talk about everything that had been unsaid since that day at the hospital. She knew there was still a chance that this wouldn't work out between them, and the fear tempered the fizzy feeling of celebration.

She looked away for a minute, gathering her thoughts. In the soft, early evening they could see sailboats bobbing on the water below and a white line that marked the long wake of a speedboat in the bay. Puffy white clouds slid across the sky as the sun mellowed into peach and periwinkle. The town was quiet now, but in a few hours everyone would gather at the ball diamond for fireworks. *Home,* she confirmed to herself. She finally had a place to belong.

"You're really sure about staying, Abby? You were so determined to leave this place behind."

"It's time I stop running," she answered simply. "I've been too afraid to settle anywhere, to make any lasting bonds, because I know what it feels like to lose everything. But know what? I found my family—or at least my family's history, the good and the bad." For a brief second she thought about Edith and Kristian. "I think I understand now why Marian wanted it to stay in Foster hands, you know? Even though she knew I technically wasn't a Foster, but a Prescott. The house needs to be with family."

"It's a big commitment. It's a small town. It can get claustrophobic. There's no theater, no hospital, no—"

"It's not like it's far to find all those things. Jewell Cove has lots of other charms." She smiled. "It's not just the house. It's the town. It's the people here. I want to belong somewhere, Tom. I haven't in such a long time. This feels like home for the first time since I was a very little girl."

He was so quiet it made her nervous. "What are you thinking?" she asked, toying with her glass.

He shrugged. "I'm just surprised, I guess."

She chuckled. "Tom Arseneault, you are doing it again. You aren't saying what you really mean. I wish you'd stop that."

"I once said exactly what was on my mind and it didn't go so well. I'm not good at this whole honesty thing. It makes me feel vulnerable. Naked."

"I know that," she replied. "When you first wanted the job of fixing this place. The barbecue at Sarah's. I get it, Tom. But this isn't the Rusty Fern and you can't be like that forever. At some point you have to trust that someone isn't going to turn the truth against you. Can't you trust me by now?"

"You don't need me," he said. His voice sounded oddly tight. "You've already made up your mind. You have your house and this new start in your life. What can I offer you that you don't already have?"

She put her hand along his jaw. "Tom," she murmured softly, "if you don't know that by now . . ."

"Maybe I need to hear you say it," he answered.

Abby had started to lose hope, but now Josh's words came back to her. *He's waiting for you to choose him.* She wasn't sure if Tom really thought he had nothing to offer her or if he thought she wouldn't want what he was offering. He was wrong on both counts.

She sat up and took his hands in hers. "I have this amazing house," she said softly. "I have a bank account with more money than I ever imagined I'd have. I have a new car. I can choose any life I want."

"I know that."

"What if what I want is you?"

Abby looked at his rugged, handsome face and thought back to all the times she got a little too close to someone. Her usual game plan was to pack up and move on. But not anymore. Not when she thought about what she'd be giving up.

"Abby . . ."

There was emotion in the word. And if nothing else, if this never worked out, she would leave here knowing she'd bared her soul and been honest with him right down to the very last thing. She squeezed his fingers. "Erin loved you but she never offered to share your life. She was crazy, Tom. And maybe I shouldn't bring up her name right now but if I don't she'll always be between us and I don't want that. I want to share your life. I want you to share mine."

"I'm a carpenter with a two-bedroom cottage," he pointed out.

"And I couldn't care less if you had two nickels in your pocket. Am I going to have to spell it out for you?" Her throat tightened as she gazed into his eyes. "Here it is, then. I love you. The only thing I want from you is your heart. That's enough for me."

Tears filled her eyes and she tried to blink them away. "You believed me when what was happening here was crazy. You made me laugh and made me angry and kissed me, making me forget all the reasons why I've been afraid to let someone get close. You saved me, not once, but twice. You showed me your compassion, your honor, your loyalty. I'd be crazy to want more from you."

For a long second she thought he was going to reach for her. He held back but she could tell—at least she hoped—that it was costing him. Tom shook his head like he couldn't quite believe her. "You think I did all those things, but you're the one who fixed me, Abby. I knew it the moment that barn came down and I thought I'd really lost you."

She frowned a little. "If that's true, why did you back off? After the hospital, you barely said two words to me."

"You thought that I didn't care?" He put his hands on her arms and squeezed. "It wasn't that at all. God, woman. Every day when I saw that FOR SALE sign, I knew that nothing had changed for you. I hate that damned sign." He glowered down the mountain at the sign that was all but invisible from this vantage.

The little thread of doubt she despised reared its ugly head. She might as well come right out and ask the one burning question she'd wanted to ask since Sarah's barbecue. "Do you still love her?"

Tom's dark gaze delved into hers once more. "I've had some time to do some thinking. And the truth is, Abby, I was holding on to her memory for the wrong reasons. I thought I loved her. I did love her—once. But the last few months . . . they've been far more about guilt than grief. I realized that the day Josh and I talked."

Relief slid through her. She hadn't been sure she could ever measure up to Erin's memory. If Tom had really, truly put Erin's ghost to rest . . .

"Please tell me I'm not hanging out here alone," she whispered. "That this isn't all one-sided."

He pressed his forehead to hers, his broad, strong hand resting against the tiny knot of a bun at the back of her head.

"You're not alone," he murmured, and he pressed his lips to hers.

The kiss was slow, deep, and beautifully long. Abby melted against him. There was no hesitation this time.

This was the man she loved. The first man she'd loved and she wanted him to be the last.

Tom braced himself on a hand and she wrapped her arm around his shoulders, holding on, fighting the gravity that wanted to pull her on to the flat part of the rock and away from the strong breadth of his chest. As the kiss tempered and their mouths parted, he pulled away the slightest bit. "You really mean it, don't you?" he asked.

"Of course I mean it, you silly man." She slid her fingers over his shoulder. "I've been in love with you for a long time. Long before I was ready for it."

"Me, too," he admitted. "I think since the night I brought you home from Jess's and walked you to the door."

"Go on," she chided playfully, running her fingers down his arm. "You said that kiss was a mistake."

He grinned, that teasing, dangerous flash that had captivated her from the beginning and had scared her to death with its potency. "I lied," he said. Then his smile faded and his expression turned serious. "I love you, Abby, and God help me, it scares me to death."

She offered the best reassurance she could at the moment—she leaned forward and kissed him again, deliberately and tenderly. This time when they broke apart their breathing was accelerated and there was a new light in his eyes.

"Stay with me tonight," she invited. "Let's go home, Tom. I want to be with you . . ." Her heart pounded with anticipation and nerves. "I want to *really* be with you. And then I want to wake up with you in the morning in my big four-poster bed and look at you across the table while I have my morning coffee."

Right now Abby wanted Tom with an urgency that far outstripped any lingering hesitation. She reached out and toyed with the button at the top of his shirt. "Love me," she said softly.

He didn't answer, but helped her up off the rock. They held hands as they descended the mountain in the wash of a summer sunset. And yet they didn't hurry, as if they were basking in every single moment of this night, making it last.

When they reached the front door, Tom swept her off her feet, making her stomach flip with excitement.

Then he closed the door with his foot, sheltering them away from the world.

# CHAPTER 23

The first thing Tom noticed on his drive up the lane was that the FOR SALE sign was gone. It gave him a feeling of satisfaction seeing it off the front lawn. The house belonged to Abby. It always had, and he was glad she was keeping it. He'd put in the offer, but he had never quite figured out how he was going to live in it when her memory would be in every room.

She was in town this morning. He knew that because Jess had called yesterday asking her if she wanted to take a candle workshop. She'd be gone until at least noon, giving him lots of time to set up his surprise. He'd finally finished the entertainment unit and had stained it a rich walnut to match the other furniture in the library. It was her favorite room in the house. The room she'd first fallen in love with, the one she spent the most time in.

Rick followed behind in his own truck, here to help move it inside. Tom had hesitated when Rick had offered, but Rick had been adamant. "I'm fine if we use straps," he insisted. "I can still use my arm." Tom couldn't argue. Rick had struggled enough dealing with his disability. Far be it from Tom to tell Rick he couldn't do something, especially when the guy finally seemed to be getting his crap together.

Tom used his key to get inside, and he and Rick shuffled furniture around until the inside corner of the room had sufficient space for the cabinet. Together they wrapped straps around the unit and then eased it through the front door, down the hall, and finessed it around the corner and into the library. It nearly didn't fit through the doorway, but once it made it through they both let out their breath and put it in its place, angled in the corner, before standing back and looking at the piece, wiping sweat off their foreheads.

"It's perfect," Rick said, shaking his head. "I don't know why you do contracting when you do such beautiful furniture work."

Tom shrugged. "It's like a treat. I'm afraid I wouldn't love it as much if I had to do it as a job."

Rick put his good hand in his pocket. "I think I understand that," he said quietly. "Sometimes you need a place to put all the things you don't want anyone else to see."

Tom wondered if Rick was referring to himself, but the only thing he'd seen Rick indulge in was too much drink. Not so much lately, though. Maybe things were turning around for the ex-Marine.

"How's the new job going?" he asked.

"Eh, it's going," Rick said with a shrug. "It gets me out. And I'm still off enough to help now that Mom's doing treatment."

Tom frowned. It was no secret that Roberta Sullivan wasn't doing so well. "Yeah. So what do you think, should we bring in the rest?"

"There's more?

Tom nodded. "It's kind of empty, don't you think? There's a TV in the backseat of my truck, and a DVD player. Enough to get her started until she gets cable hooked up. She might want to shop for speakers and stuff, too."

Rick pierced him with an assessing look. "You're really hung up on this girl, aren't you?"

Tom thought about waking with Abby the morning after the garden party. She'd looked so beautiful, soft and peaceful, as she slept on. He'd known in that moment that today was coming. Nothing had prepared him for the kind of love he'd felt holding her in his arms, making love to her in the folds of the soft duvet. It had knocked him off his feet with its awesomeness. With its *rightness*. There'd been no fear, no holding back. Just giving to each other in ways he hadn't known existed.

"I'm in love with her," Tom admitted.

"I'm glad," Rick answered. "It's time you moved on and let yourself be happy. Your cousin too, though I expect it might take him a little longer."

Together they moved in the television and DVD player and hooked them up. Tom closed the doors on the unit, hiding the screen away. He'd made the doors especially because he knew there would be times that Abby would want to keep the library more formal and less like a living room.

When everything was in place, Rick left with a wave to go to work and Tom was left in the house alone.

It was nearly one o'clock when Abby returned home. Tom was out in the garden, pruning some deadwood from a couple of shrubs, when she came through the porch door. "Here you are! I saw the truck but no sign of you."

He straightened and looked at her. She was so pretty today, in a white peasant shirt and jeans that came to just below her knees. She was wearing the funky sandals again, the beaded ones he remembered from the first day, but in so many ways she looked completely different from the woman he'd met only a few months ago.

The woman before him now was comfortable, relaxed, happy.

Happy. He wanted her to be happy, and nerves bubbled around in his gut. Today was more important than she realized . . .

"The FOR SALE sign's gone."

She nodded, coming out into the garden. "Not much point in having it still up, is there?"

He shook his head. "Did you have a good time at Jess's?"

"Of course. I left my candles there, though, because they were still hot. When I go back she's going to show me how to decorate my candleholders." She held up a paper bag. "I was too full for dessert at the café, so Linda sent me home with a piece of her triple-layer chocolate cake. You want it?"

He really didn't; he was already nervous, but he wasn't ready yet for what was coming next, and the cake was a reasonable procrastination technique. "I skipped lunch, so that'd be great."

They sat on the bench in the garden for a few minutes as he ate his cake with a plastic fork. He was nearly done when Abby put her hand on his arm.

"Tom? Is something wrong? You look worried."

He looked at her and saw a crease between her eyebrows. "Nothing's wrong." He put the fork in the Styrofoam container and shut the lid. "I've just been waiting for you to get home, that's all. I have a surprise for you."

"You do?" The crease disappeared and her eyes lit up.

He wanted to be the cause of that look forever.

"I told you I did when you came back from Halifax, remember?" Her trip to Nova Scotia felt like years ago, instead of weeks. So much had happened since then.

"I'd forgotten all about that!"

"I didn't. But you have to close your eyes and promise me you won't peek."

"I promise." She stood up and promptly closed her eyes. He took her hand, but one look sideways showed she was trying to open one eye just a crack.

"No peeking!" he commanded, feeling the nerves, trying to ignore them and just enjoy the moment. "I mean it, Abby."

Once they were inside he stepped behind her and covered her eyes with his hand. "I don't trust you," he whispered in her ear, taking in the scent of warm vanilla.

She giggled. "You're a smart man, Tom Arseneault."

He hoped so. He nudged her inside the library, turned her to face the cabinet, and slid his fingers away from her eyes.

"Happy housewarming," he said softly.

Her mouth dropped open and her eyes shone as she saw the gleaming wood and antique hardware. "Oh, Tom. This is . . . it's stunning! You made this?"

Relief and pride rushed through his veins. "I did. Is the stain okay? I tried to match it as closely as possible to the existing furniture."

"It's perfect! But you must have started this weeks ago!" She turned to him in astonishment. "How long have you been working on it?"

"Since before Memorial Day," he admitted. "I have a workshop behind the cottage where I tinker."

"Oh, this is much more than tinkering." She went up to the cabinet and opened the doors and gasped again at the TV inside. "Tom, what have you done?"

"I figure now you can get cable and Internet in here. All that's missing is the sofa you've been wanting."

"You starting building this when . . . God, Tom. What if it hadn't worked out?"

He shrugged. "I would have sold it. But it belongs here."

She came over and hugged him, her floral-scented hair

soft against his cheek. "Thank you so much. It's just what this room needed."

"You're welcome."

His heart began hammering in earnest now and his hand went to his pocket, touching the box nestled inside the cotton. "There's more, Abby."

"More?" Her eyebrows rose. He wasn't sure he'd ever seen her eyes so blue. Maybe it was too early. Maybe he should wait . . .

But he didn't want to wait. He didn't want to give her the chance to get away, didn't want to waste any time when he'd already learned that time could be far too short.

Abby looked up at Tom, wondering what more he could possibly surprise her with today. The entertainment center was a huge gift, and it meant even more because he'd made it with his own hands. She was startled to realize that every room in this house had a bit of Tom in it. He was everywhere she turned, and she couldn't ever remember feeling this happy.

He'd become more than a friend. He'd become her lover, and it was thrilling. He'd been gentle and considerate, knowing she needed it. He'd been passionate and giving, and she'd needed that, too. Never in her wildest dreams could she have imagined the completeness she felt in Tom's arms.

The last few days she'd felt like she had simply everything. So the idea of more was quite mind-boggling.

He squeezed her hands, making her look up into his face, so handsome, so serious, and something strange and exhilarating started to wind its way through her body.

"I love you, Abby," he said. "God knows I didn't want to. I was—I am—a bit afraid to. But I love you anyway.

You came in and shook me out of my rut until I didn't know which way was up. You scared me. You made me question everything, even my sanity sometimes."

"I think we both questioned our sanity," she said, an emotional laugh escaping her lips.

He brushed a piece of hair back from her face. "What do you think about a two-bedroom cottage on the ocean?"

A smile blossomed on her lips. "I think it is very cozy and romantic."

He kissed her then, softly, tenderly, reaching in and touching her heart, like touching a match to a candlewick and lighting her from the inside out.

She smiled against his lips. "What about you? How do you feel about a five-bedroom historic mansion?"

He chuckled and she felt the vibration of it where his lips were touching the skin beside her mouth. "I hear the guy who did the repairs has a fairly skilled hand. It should hold up for a year or two." She kissed him once more, cupping his face in her hands. Then she stepped back and took his hands in hers.

"Do you want to know why I was going to sell it?" It was a question that needed no answer so she continued. "I knew long ago that it is the sort of house that needs to be full of life. Parties and friends." She twined her fingers with his. "Husbands and wives and children." With a laugh she remembered that first candle-making session at Jess's. "Do you know what someone said to me once when I wondered what I'd do with a house this size? They told me to marry you and fill it with babies."

"Do you want babies?" he asked.

"I think I do." She nodded. "Though not for a while. I might like to prolong this being-in-love thing for a bit."

He pulled her close. "I'd like babies, too. But I kind of like your strategy. Maybe we can practice while you plan your next garden party. Say this fall? We can be sure to invite the minister."

His tone was light but when he finished speaking the gravity of it sank in. It was a beautiful, wonderful thing.

"Are you saying . . ." She let the sentence hang while her breath caught in her chest. Could this really be happening?

He reached into his pocket and took out a small square box. "Marry me," he said. "Just . . . marry me, Abby."

He opened the box and revealed the most perfect ring she'd ever seen. "Oh, Tom." She reached out and touched a tentative finger to the yellow gold band studded with diamonds. She could tell from the look of it that it was an antique, and an expensive one. "This is beautiful."

"If you say yes, I'll put it on your finger."

Marriage. Love. Children. It seemed so incredibly impossible but incredibly right. She laughed a little, even as tears gathered in her eyes and she waggled her fingers at him. "Yes. Yes, I'll marry you."

He let out such a huge breath that she suddenly realized how nervous he'd been. As he slipped the ring over her knuckle, she said, "Did you really think I'd say no?"

"I hoped you wouldn't," he admitted. "But I was scared to death you might."

She stood on tiptoe and wrapped her arms around him. "I love you. And together we're going to bring happiness back to this house."

She wiggled her finger, admiring the diamond setting. "Where did you ever get this? It's really beautiful. It must be a hundred years old!"

"Closer to a hundred and fifty," he said. "Remember the story about the pirate in our family?"

She nodded.

"The story goes that this ring was part of his treasure during the Civil War, and that he gave it to an abolitionist woman he fell in love with on his travels." He grinned. "Apparently she reformed him from his wicked ways and he gave up privateering to become part of the Underground Railroad. All I absolutely know is that my great-grandfather gave it to my grandfather, who gave it to me. And now I'm giving it to you. Maybe I'm no pirate, but I feel like you saved me anyway."

She looked up at him, wondering how on earth she ever got so lucky as to have him put his foot through her veranda.

# EPILOGUE

Abby reluctantly gave one last turn in front of the mirror, admiring the ivory silk of the dress. It was time to take it off. The waist and bust needed alterations to fit properly but she was in no doubt. This dress, the one she'd first found in the trunk in the attic, was her wedding dress. And in three short months she'd walk down the aisle of the church and say I do to Tom. It seemed like an eternity away—and yet too short a time to plan everything that needed to be done.

After the wedding they would start their life together here and begin filling the house with the love and laughter it finally deserved. It was time to break the pattern of sadness and tragedy and make the lofty house on Blackberry Hill into a home.

She was admiring the dress spread over her duvet while buttoning up her jeans when she heard a car coming up the drive. A quick check at the window told her it was Ian Martin, her lawyer. She frowned. All the business with the house was supposed to be over and done with. She hoped there wasn't any further problem.

Ian tapped the new brass knocker on the door as she

was going down the stairs. She opened the door with a polite smile. "Ian. Did we have an appointment I forgot?"

He smiled. "Not at all. Just one last piece of business from your aunt's estate."

Curiosity mixed with anxiety. She stood back and opened the door all the way. "Come in. Coffee?"

He bent and picked up a banker's box from the spot by his feet. "I can't stay. I have an appointment in an hour. But thanks."

She led the way to the kitchen where they'd have the biggest workspace. "What's in the box?"

"Something your aunt gave me for safekeeping, with firm instructions as to when to give it to you."

"How long have you had . . . whatever is in that box?"

"About eight years."

Ian Martin was barely forty. He would have been a young lawyer in a new town when Marian hired him to look after her will and estate.

He took out a thick envelope first. "This is a letter from Marian. She asked me to deliver it to you, along with this box, once you had decided to stay permanently in Jewell Cove."

"But how could she have known . . ."

"She didn't. If you sold and left town, I was to burn it in the town incinerator and all her secrets with it."

Abby sat down heavily and took the envelope from his hands. Just when she thought she had all the answers . . . Aunt Marian found a way to surprise her again.

The front door slammed again. "Abs? Honey, you in here?"

"In the kitchen," she called out. She was still getting used to the easy, affectionate way they moved within each other's lives. And wondered if the tingly, fluttery feeling would ever go away years from now when he was nearby or said her name. She hoped not.

Tom came through, looking delicious as always, this time wearing cargo shorts and a pair of flip-flops. "Hey, Ian," he greeted, but went right to Abby and dropped a warm kiss on her lips. "What's going on?" he asked.

"Just when we thought we had all the answers," she replied. "Marian is full of surprises."

"My only instruction was to deliver it. Now that I've done that, I'll leave you two alone." Ian shook Tom's hand and smiled at Abby. "Congratulations, by the way."

"Thanks. And Ian—thanks for everything you've done with the estate."

"You're welcome."

When he was gone Abby ripped open the sealed envelope. There was a handwritten letter on embossed stationery. That was all.

Tom pulled up a chair and sat across from her, putting his hands on her knees. "Are you okay to read it?"

She nodded, touching the old paper with her fingertips. "I think so."

Tom's hand tightened on her thigh. "Would you rather be alone?"

She looked up into his eyes. "No, I want you with me. We're partners now. I don't have any secrets."

She unfolded Marian's letter.

*Dear Abigail,*

*I'm sorry you and I never got to meet. By now you've had time to fall in love with the house. I hope you have, anyway. It's a very special place. Not without its secrets, of course. But I've always thought the secrets were part of its charm.*

*You're probably wondering how the family got separated. I wish I had more complete answers for you. I remember my mother only vaguely, but I remember the emptiness I felt when she was suddenly no longer with me. I don't know what truly happened that night, and my father would never speak her name in this house. I remember Iris, too—just a tiny baby in my memory. I always thought maybe Father couldn't bear to look at her and that was why he sent her away. He confessed right before he died that we had different fathers, but if there was ever any evidence of it, it's long gone.*

Abby paused. Looked up at Tom. "She didn't know. About Kristian. About Edith's death. All of it. She must have blocked it from her mind." It also meant that Edith's ghost hadn't revealed herself to her own daughter. Why had she chosen Abby?

Tom squeezed her hand and she turned back to the letter.

*I want you to have this house. It can never make up for the past, but if there is a scrap of Edith—my mother—in you, it is in good hands. By the time it falls to you, I'm afraid it will need some loving care. That is why I directed Ian Martin to deliver this to you after you've decided to stay in Jewell Cove. If you're staying, I know you love this house and this town as much as I did. Treasure it. Be happy in it. It needs happiness.*

*My father was a hard man, and I wish I could say I loved him but if there was any love it was born out of duty and not affection. Before he died he told me how he paid the Prescotts to take Iris and made them promise to never contact us again or else he would ruin our mother's name. I can only assume the scandal was her infidelity.*

*If we had to be separated, at least she was with*

*our family. I do wonder at times if her life didn't
end up being easier than mine. After Father died,
I initiated contact between us. She'd been denied
her family but so had I. Unfortunately, I think some
wounds are just too deep. Iris was determined to
leave this part of her life behind.*

*There has always been speculation about why I
ran a home for unwed mothers. The truth is that I
fell in love once, and with someone utterly unsuit-
able by Father's standards. Father forced me to go
away. The delivery was early, though, and the baby
was stillborn. The complications left me unable to
ever have more children. I made it my mission to
help as many girls as I could—either finding good
homes for their babies or helping them get started
on their own. I never made a cent brokering adop-
tions, though I could have more than once. That's
not what it was about.*

*So now we come to the box. Inside you'll find a
few keepsakes I wanted to pass on especially. I'm
leaving you my pearl earrings, which were the
only jewels I have that were my mother's. There
are some pictures too, and knickknacks that have
sentimental value—including a jewel box that
someone very special made for me many years ago.*

*I wish you love, and happiness, and peace. It's
past time that this house had enough of all three.*

*All my love,*
*Your Aunt Marian*

"She could have told me all this when I inherited the
estate," Abby said, folding up the letter and handing it to
Tom. She was touched by the sincere words and emotion
with which her aunt had written.

Tom skimmed the pages, holding her hand the whole while. "Wow," he said, coming to the end. "Even Marian had her share of secrets."

Abby smiled a little. "We might not have a pirate, but it seems there are lots of bones rattling in the Foster closet."

"Why do you think she sent this to you now?"

Abby sighed and slid over into his lap. She leaned her head on his shoulder for a moment. "I suppose because I'd proven myself. Because I'm staying and I'm in it for the long haul." She smiled and looked into his eyes. How she loved looking into the dark depths of them. It felt like she could see right into his soul, and he into hers.

"You definitely are," he decreed, and he smiled, little crinkles forming at the creases of his eyes.

A movement caught her attention at the threshold of the kitchen. Edith, dressed in the same plain blue dress. But this time her lips held a secretive smile. Abby felt Tom stiffen beside her, and he swallowed thickly as Edith turned and walked away without looking back. It was, Abby realized, good-bye. And with a startling realization, Abby knew that she was going to miss her.

"That was her, wasn't it?" Tom's voice was low and awestruck.

She nodded. "She showed herself to you, too. She must trust you a lot, Tom. I think she was saying good-bye."

"That was . . . that's just . . ."

Abby laughed softly. "I've had longer to get used to it. Take your time."

The banker's box sat on the table while Abby got up to make a pot of tea and sandwiches for lunch. It wasn't until the plates were cleared away and the teacups rinsed that she couldn't hold back her curiosity. With Tom at her side, she carefully opened the lid and began to sort through the contents.

The hand on her shoulder stiffened as Tom reached past her with his opposite hand, taking out a photo that had caught his attention.

"Tom? What is it?" Abby put down the jewel box and leaned over to see what he held in his hand.

The picture was old—maybe twenty or thirty years by the fashions. She recognized Marian, smiling brightly behind a couple and a new baby. "That's the Sullivans," Tom said. "That baby must be Rick. But what was Marian doing there?"

He turned the photo over and his breath came out in a rush. *Last clients of Foster House* was written in blue ink on the back.

"Rick," he said, and dropped the photo back into the box as if it were on fire.